"What the hell a

Conner stepped inside and closed the door.

"Oh, Conner, you startled me. I was hoping Mr. Cuddy could give me the budget for the office party—"

"You were in here alone, with the door closed. Drop the dumb-blonde act, Jillian. I happen to know you're highly intelligent. So I'll repeat myself. What the *hell* are you doing in Cuddy's office?"

"What did *you* come in here for? You didn't even knock."

"I needed something from my office for the meeting. Since I was headed this way, Cuddy asked me if I'd get his...his phone."

Jillian couldn't believe this. Conner was lying, too!

"I don't see his phone," Jillian said casually.

"Guess he didn't forget it after all. Probably put it in the wrong pocket or something."

"Is that the story you're going to stick with?"

He crossed his arms. "Mine's better than yours."

For the span of a few heartbeats they stared at each other, challenging.

A rattling of the office doorknob caused Conner's eyes to widen with apprehension. "Follow my lead." Without warning he wrapped his arms around her and planted his mouth firmly on hers.

Dear Reader,

What was your most humiliating incident in high school? Almost every woman can remember a moment during her vulnerable teen years when she wished the earth would swallow her up, or she could move to a different state and change her name. And was there a boy involved? If you could see him again today, what would you say?

Fortunately, most of us can laugh at those cringe-worthy memories. But Jillian, the heroine of *Hidden Agenda,* isn't ready to laugh. At age fourteen she was humiliated *and* she had her heart broken. Now, just when she gets a chance to prove herself in the eyes of her Project Justice colleagues, she has to work side by side with the boy— now a man—she used to love with all her heart, then vowed to hate forever.

I had a great deal of fun with Jillian. She's made an appearance in all five Project Justice books, and I'm excited to give her her own story. I hope you enjoy her journey.

All best,

Kara Lennox

Hidden Agenda

KARA LENNOX

TORONTO NEW YORK LONDON
AMSTERDAM PARIS SYDNEY HAMBURG
STOCKHOLM ATHENS TOKYO MILAN MADRID
PRAGUE WARSAW BUDAPEST AUCKLAND

Recycling programs
for this product may
not exist in your area.

ISBN-13: 978-0-373-71791-0

HIDDEN AGENDA

www.Harlequin.com

Printed in U.S.A.

ABOUT THE AUTHOR

Kara Lennox has earned her living at various times as an art director, typesetter, textbook editor and reporter. She's worked in a boutique, a health club and an ad agency. She's been an antiques dealer, an artist and even a blackjack dealer. But no work has ever made her happier than writing romance novels. To date, she has written more than sixty books. Kara is a recent transplant to Southern California. When not writing, she indulges in an ever-changing array of hobbies. Her latest passions are bird-watching, long-distance bicycling, vintage jewelry and, by necessity, do-it-yourself home renovation. She loves to hear from readers. You can find her at www.karalennox.com.

Books by Kara Lennox

HARLEQUIN SUPERROMANCE

HARLEQUIN AMERICAN ROMANCE

‡Project Justice
*Blond Justice
**Firehouse 59
***Second Sons

Other titles by this author available in ebook format.

For my best friend in high school and college, Anne O'Connor. We sure had some adventures.

CHAPTER ONE

I'M IN! JILLIAN BAXTER tried not to let the sense of triumph show on her face as the personnel director, Joyce Carrington, droned on about vacation policy and 401(k) plans. Jillian had crossed her first hurdle as a field investigator at Project Justice: she'd been hired by Mayall Lumber. Now she would infiltrate the company and catch a murderer.

"Well, we can go over all this when you officially start," Joyce said breezily. She was a pleasant, matronly sort with a cloud of dark, frizzy hair escaping from numerous barrettes, a blouse with a coffee stain, and a desk piled high with messy stacks of paper itching to be sorted and organized. "We'll make the job offer official as soon as Mr. Blake signs off."

"Mr. Blake?"

"He'll be your direct supervisor," Joyce said. "I'll warn you, he's quite challenging. He's been through four admins this year already. But with your experience, I'm sure you'll have no trouble."

Jillian's experience was mostly fabricated. Daniel Logan, CEO of Project Justice, had put together a résumé that had made her sound like the best administrative assistant in all of Texas, making sure her stellar references would check out.

But Jillian had full confidence in her ability to please this Mr. Blake, whoever he was. He couldn't possibly be any more demanding than Daniel was, and she'd been Daniel's personal assistant for years before transferring to the foundation's investigative arm.

"I'll walk you over to his office." Joyce stood, bumping one of the precariously balanced stacks of paper, which fell to the floor in a flurry of printed reports, invoices, newspaper clippings and employee candidate résumés.

Jillian hopped out of her chair to help clean up the mess. One particular paper caught her eye; it was a memo from the company's public relations office with lots of capital letters and exclamation points.

Under no circumstances should anyone speak with reporter Mark Bowen— That was as much as Jillian could read on the fly.

"Oh, goodness, thank you," Joyce said. "I'm afraid I've gotten behind in my paperwork. Things have been a little crazy around here the last few weeks."

Jillian wasn't surprised. When one of your employees was murdered and found in the trunk of your CEO's car, it probably created all kinds of havoc.

Jillian made no reference to the scandalous situation. "Business is booming, then?" she asked innocently.

"Well, yes, business is good. But that's not… It's just that we've lost some key people recently. Others are retiring, including our acting CEO."

Hamilton Payne. He was the one who had contacted Project Justice, and the only person working here who knew of Jillian's true purpose.

"Your job must be quite demanding," Jillian said sympathetically as she stacked the last of the fallen papers and laid them on the desk. "I hope *you* have a good admin."

"On maternity leave," Joyce said glumly.

"If I have any extra time, I'd be happy to help you out." Jillian wasn't just being generous. Joyce obviously knew the ins and outs of Mayall Lumber—who the key players were, their salaries, their responsibilities. She and her office could be a gold mine of information.

"Trust me, working for Mr. Blake, you won't have much free time. He'll keep you busy."

Jillian hoped this Mr. Blake wouldn't be too ghastly. But no matter how bad he was, she would make it work. She only had to put up with it for a short time, just until she found something to prove Stan Mayall's innocence.

Mr. Blake's office was on the third floor, in the executive wing. Mayall Lumber was a medium-size operation, with two sawmills, one large lumberyard and a posh corporate headquarters overlooking Houston's Buffalo Bayou. They had only one retail outlet, a small place that specialized in exotic woods of the highest quality for furniture and cabinet makers. Most of their business involved selling to the construction trade and small lumber retailers. Daniel had provided tons of information on the company, which Jillian had dutifully memorized. Her knowledge had obviously impressed Joyce.

The personnel director stopped in front of an oak door and tapped softly. "Mr. Blake?"

"It's open," a deep voice called from inside.

Jillian barely had time to register that something about the voice struck a chord of familiarity before Joyce ushered her inside the gorgeous office.

The first thing Jillian noticed was the wood—wood floor, paneling, box beams holding up the ceiling. It was all stained a dark cherry color with beautiful grain. The furniture was made of wood, too. Despite the lack of upholstery, the chairs looked warm and comfortable.

The desk, big as a Humvee, was made of some gleaming, exotic wood with a stripe pattern, reminding her of a crouched jungle beast. The only softness in the whole room was a low-slung 1960s retro sofa.

Finally she raised her gaze to the man behind the desk, her new boss. Every sane thought, every polished word she'd been about to use to introduce herself, melted away like mist in the sun. The giant, egotistical, bastard sun.

Mr. Blake. *Conner* Blake. The boy who had made high school a living hell for her. The boy she had once desperately loved, then hated with all the angst a fourteen-year-old girl could muster.

The cocky, mischievous boy was now a man, but despite the umpteen years since she'd seen him, he was instantly recognizable. A bit taller, a bit broader in the shoulders, hair more sandy than blond, but the beautifully carved planes of his face had grown only more handsome with the passage of time.

"Mr. Blake, I'd like you to meet your new administrative assistant, Jillian Baxter."

He looked at her then, and she figured the jig was up. She would have to slink back to Project Justice with no job, her first undercover operation a bust because she had, in a fit of adolescent revenge, slashed two of her potential boss's tires, an impulsive act that had only escalated her humiliation into high school legend.

But the look on his face reflected not a hint of recognition, only what she surmised was mild irritation at having to deal with the mundane task of welcoming a new assistant.

She held her breath as introductions, handshaking, and small talk ensued, waiting for the inevitable moment when he remembered. But, amazingly, it never came. Conner Blake had once been the center of her world. Apparently Jillian Baxter had been nothing but a tiny, forgettable blip on his radar screen.

He was still so gorgeous. It wasn't fair that the universe would give one man that much sexy charisma. Even as the feelings of humiliation welled up, fresh as a new coat of nail polish, her heart thumped with an irregular tempo from the simple contact of a handshake and the knowledge that he was sizing her up.

What did he think of her, this new acquaintance suddenly thrust into his working life? While he retained a certain essence of his high school face and physique, she looked very different than she had the last time he'd seen her, as a high school freshman. She'd grown five inches and lost twenty pounds, for starters. The chlorine-bleached, frizzy cloud of hair from high school, courtesy of swim team, was now tamed into a sleek bob with expert lowlights.

She'd still been in braces her freshman year. She'd also worn glasses. And then there was…the nose. She'd broken it at a swim meet her senior year, and since she'd needed rhinoplasty anyway, she'd asked the surgeon to transform her nose so it was more in proportion to her face.

If her name didn't ring a bell, Conner probably wouldn't recognize her by her appearance, and that was a very good thing. If she didn't shine during her first undercover assignment, she might never get any respect from her colleagues at Project Justice. She would forever be Daniel's ex-assistant, the one who'd made a fool of herself by falling in love with her boss.

That's all over now. New life, new goals. Jillian Baxter, finally grown up at age twenty-seven, knew what she wanted to do with her life. She wanted to help exonerate those unjustly accused of crimes. And she didn't want a man—any man. The two men she'd given her heart to, devoted every fiber of her being to, had both brushed her aside with not even a flicker of interest.

The wanting hurt, and the rejection hurt, and why should she put herself through that again? Ever?

"So, I'll expect you to be prompt," Conner was saying. "I start my workday at 7:00 a.m., and therefore, so will you."

"Yes, sir, Mr. Blake," she said with all the icy politeness she could muster even as her mind screamed, *7:00 a.m.? Is he crazy?*

Joyce beamed. "Very good, then. Jillian, come with me and we'll get all your paperwork started." She headed out the door, and Jillian offered a nod to her new boss and followed. "Oh, goodness, I haven't even shown you your work space. It's just around the corner from Mr. Blake's office, here. I'm afraid it's a bit of a mess. The previous admin has been gone three weeks and things have piled up."

Jillian took one look at the office and cringed. It would take her hours to shovel this place out. She couldn't stand to work in a disorganized space.

"I should have warned you Mr. Blake starts the workday early," Joyce rattled on. "I hope that's okay."

"It's fine." Jillian wasn't a morning person, but she would do whatever it took to please her new boss, even if she despised him down to his rotten, cruel core.

"I REALLY NEED THAT REPORT ASAP." Hamilton Payne, acting CEO at Mayall Lumber, sank into the wingback chair opposite Conner's desk. At first glance, Hamilton gave the impression of a doddering grandfather, but Conner knew he wielded a keen mind and as director of sales had cultivated a healthy client base and a steady stream of new business for twenty years or more. He was running things while Stan was incarcerated, but he was on the verge of retirement and didn't relish his new leadership role.

"I'm working on it." Conner shuffled through the papers on his desk as if he could actually accomplish something.

"Maybe your new secretary could help." Ham was obviously trying to keep a straight face, but Conner could tell he was about to burst out laughing.

Conner pinched the bridge of his nose and sighed. "You met her?"

"Joyce trotted her around and introduced her. I don't know why she thinks I want to meet every damn secretary she hires."

"She does it for them—so they'll feel important."

The new girl was hot, that was for sure. The moment she'd walked into his office, Conner's brain had short-circuited and he hadn't heard a word Joyce said. He'd been too busy cataloging those mile-long legs, which her short skirt and stiletto heels showed off to perfection.

The rest of her was just as stunning, from her nipped-in waist, her long, elegant neck to her huge, innocent blue eyes.

Innocent, right. A woman built like her was made for sin. She was a distraction he didn't need. Good thing she wouldn't be around long. For some reason, they never were.

"I'll make the report a priority," he said to Ham. "I've just been a little distracted. With Greg gone, I'm shuffling people around, trying to cover all the bases."

Ham lowered his voice. "Have you learned anything

new? About who might have killed him? You and I both know it couldn't have been Stan."

Conner's throat tightened every time he thought about Stan Mayall toughing it out in a jail cell. Stan wasn't just a boss to him. He'd been a mentor, a sounding board and a good friend. For three years Stan had also been Conner's grandfather-in-law, as dear to him as any blood relative could have been. They'd remained close even after Conner's divorce from Chandra.

"Of course he didn't do it. There's no way a jury would convict him." But the case might not even get to a jury, if Stan's health continued to decline. He'd been diagnosed with cancer just a week before his arrest. "It's not right. He should be at home, where Chandra can take care of him."

"I know." Ham shook his head sadly. "I wish there was something we could do."

Conner *was* doing something. He was peering into every nook and cranny of this company, searching for a motive for murder. He'd even found his way into Greg's email account. So far, he'd turned up nothing concrete. But Greg's personal life was a minefield of broken relationships and family feuds. Maybe his mysterious girlfriend, "Mariposa," was involved. Conner knew of her only through the sexy emails she and Greg had sent back and forth. Maybe Greg had dumped her, and she'd hired a killer and told him to make it look like the murder was work-related.

It was a theory, anyway.

"Keep me in the loop." Ham pushed himself to his feet. "I'm supposed to retire in less than a month. I can't put it off any longer—my doctor and my wife have ganged up on me. But I don't want to leave Stan, or the company, in the lurch."

"I swear, Ham, we'll figure it out. The most important thing we can do is to keep the company afloat. So when Stan is exonerated—and I know he will be—he'll have a job to return to."

And Conner could finally get his own life back. He would gladly walk away from this corner office and burn every one of his silk ties.

JILLIAN COULDN'T RESIST announcing her good news as soon as she bounced into the bull pen at Project Justice late that afternoon. "I'm in! Mayall Lumber hired me!"

The only other investigator there was Griffin Benedict, who was on the phone. He looked up with mild irritation, and she realized she could have been overheard by whoever Griffin was talking to. One of the first rules of working for the foundation was discretion.

She slapped a hand over her mouth, then whispered a quick "Sorry." The only other people in the room were two interns, college students with whom she had worked until her recent "promotion" into fieldwork.

They both looked up at her. Bernie, the nicer one, gave her a tepid thumbs-up, but Kendall, who'd never gone out of her way to say anything nice to Jillian, rolled her eyes.

"Come to lord it over us?" Kendall said. "It's not like you were really promoted. It's just that you have secretarial experience." She said the word *secretarial* as if it were nasty. "Soon as this job is finished, you'll be back in the intern ghetto, licking envelopes and making coffee."

"Probably." Jillian tried not to let Kendall's attitude bother her. "But at least I get to work in the field for a while."

"You say 'work in the field' like you're a secret agent

or something." Kendall didn't try to hide her sneer. "Daniel isn't, like, letting you carry a gun or anything, is he?"

"No, of course not." Not yet. But she'd taken a firearms training course and had applied for her license to carry concealed. That was a long way from Daniel letting her do any such thing, but it was a step in the right direction. "I'm gathering intelligence."

Kendall's eyes lit up. "About what?"

Though Jillian wanted to dish, she knew she shouldn't. *Discretion, discretion.* "I can't really talk about it."

Again, Kendall rolled her eyes.

"By the time this assignment is over, you guys will be back at school. So, this is goodbye."

"We'll miss you." Bernie clearly didn't mean it.

Kendall said nothing.

They were both probably glad to see her go. She'd already been working here several months when they'd arrived for their summer internships, so she'd shown them the ropes and tried to bond with them. But neither had warmed up to her. She was only five or six years older than them, but it was enough to cause a small generation gap.

She'd never been very good at making friends. In high school, at the exclusive Shelby Academy, she'd been shy and withdrawn, preferring books and her active fantasy life to interaction with real people. Swim team had been her only extracurricular activity, and she'd never distinguished herself in the sport, though she still loved the water, and all those laps she'd swum had at least slimmed her down.

In college, she'd fared better. With her new nose, bright, even teeth and long, blond hair, she garnered lots of attention from young men, none of whom impressed her because by then, she'd fallen hard for Daniel Logan. Their fathers had worked together, and all through college she'd spent summers at the Logan estate helping out Daniel's mother.

While the guys flocked around her, other women, even her sorority sisters, had held her at arm's length. She'd earned a reputation as snooty when really, she'd just been shy. She still didn't relate well to other women. Some were put off by her trust fund, others by her attractiveness—she was honest enough to admit she'd turned out rather well in that department, given her shaky start. They didn't want her around their husbands and boyfriends.

"Well, see you around." She left the bull pen and went to find the one person she felt pretty sure would be happy for her—aside from Daniel, who sincerely wanted her to find a place in the world where she belonged.

Celeste Boggs, the office manager, was just shutting things down for the day at her station in the lobby—turning off her computer, packing up the magazines and books she liked to read during lulls in activity.

Celeste was somewhere in her seventies. She'd been the first woman patrol officer hired by the Houston Police Department, and despite decades of service had never been promoted to detective. Now she seemed to be rebelling against years in a uniform. Every day she showed up for work in an outfit more outlandish and age-inappropriate than the day before. Today it was a red polka-dot chiffon blouse with a big bow at the neck coupled with a red miniskirt and rhinestone gladiator sandals. Her long, acrylic nails bore decals of neon flowers, and her unruly gray hair was drawn up into a ponytail atop her head, resulting in a cascade of curls. Huge red dangle earrings completed the ensemble.

"Hey, Celeste." Jillian leaned her elbows on the semicircular granite desk, designed to impress visitors. "What happened to the go-go dancer you mugged to get those earrings?"

"Buried in a shallow grave," Celeste said in a stage whisper. "You like?" She gave her head a little shake. "Bought 'em on eBay."

"Very retro cool. They look great on you." Jillian actually admired Celeste's fearless sense of style. The older woman didn't care what anyone thought of her and dressed solely to please herself, and in the process had achieved a sort of thrift-store chic.

"So, spill it," Celeste said. "Did you get the job?"

"I did."

"Good for you." Celeste took her through her complicated high/low-five sequence. "This is your chance to shine. You do realize, don't you, that you're the first female investigator at Project Justice?"

Jillian frowned. "What about Raleigh?" Raleigh Benedict, Griffin's wife, was head of Legal but also managed her own cases. She was one of the most senior staff members.

"Raleigh runs things from a legal perspective," Celeste said. "When it comes to fieldwork, she gets one of the guys to help her."

"Well, I'm not an investigator yet. This is an important case—Daniel himself is coordinating the investigation. I'm just doing a small part."

"Yeah, but you're working undercover. If you do a good job, you have the chance to move into the vacancy Billy left."

Billy Cantu had recently left Project Justice to return

to the work he was truly meant to do, as a police detective. Only in her dreams could Jillian fill his shoes.

She voiced the question she'd been wondering about ever since Kendall's put-down. "Do you think Daniel asked me to do this because of my experience as an admin? I can't envision Griffin or Ford fetching coffee and making copies for some guy in a suit. Maybe I was the only one he could talk into it."

"It doesn't matter how you got the assignment," Celeste said. "The important thing is what you do with it."

True. But it still rankled.

"Daniel's instructions were pretty clear. I'm not supposed to do anything except keep my eyes and ears open and report to him. He told me not to actively investigate."

Celeste made a face. "Good thing you've got a mind of your own." She shouldered her red patent-leather purse, too large to be legal as an airline carry-on, and made her way to the front door with her enormous ring of keys. "You listen to me, and you'll come out of this operation smelling like a rose. The first thing you have to do is make friends with the other support staff—admins, legal assistants. They'll gossip about their bosses, I guarantee it."

"That's a wonderful idea…in theory. But I suck at making new friends." Oddly, though, Celeste seemed to like Jillian. The elderly woman was fierce and gruff with most everyone else, but she treated Jillian like her baby chick.

Celeste dropped her keys into her purse, then paused to look Jillian up and down. "You're too perfect," she said bluntly. "You intimidate other women. They despise you even as they want to be just like you."

Leave it to Celeste to speak the unvarnished truth.

"Don't worry," Celeste soothed. "It's nothing to do with your personality."

Jillian wasn't so sure about that. Last year, when Daniel's eventual wife, Jamie, got sick, some people actually suspected Jillian of poisoning her.

"But you might try looking more...ordinary."

"Ordinary." Jillian wasn't sure what Celeste meant. She felt she *was* ordinary.

"Like you don't have a trust fund, girlfriend."

"Oh."

Celeste shut off the lights and set the security alarm. Phil, the night watchman, would arrive shortly. Celeste had left him a Snickers bar, Jillian noticed. She licked her lips, wondering if Phil would mind...

"Now," Celeste said, snapping Jillian's attention away from the chocolate temptation, "aside from the other secretaries, you need to get to know the janitors, or anybody who cleans or makes repairs. Those people are essentially invisible, but they see and hear much more than you think. Imagine what they could find out just by looking through the trash."

"That's the key? Getting to know people at work?"

"It's the cornerstone of all undercover work, all police work, really. People have to get to know you before they'll trust you. And they have to trust you before they'll tell you their secrets."

"Thanks, Celeste." It sounded like good advice to her, and she could do it without disobeying Daniel's orders to refrain from actively investigating, something he deemed too risky because she didn't have police training.

"Oh, one more thing." Celeste reached into her voluminous bag and drew out a small, black disk about the size of a quarter. "It's a listening bug. Plant it in the office of someone you want to spy on, hide the digital recorder within a hundred feet. It's voice-activated. The recorder has a memory card. You pop it into your computer and listen to the audiofiles. Elevates eavesdropping to a whole new level. Go on, take it."

Jillian hesitated. "What if I get caught eavesdropping? I'd get fired and my cover would be blown."

Celeste lowered her voice. "Daniel said to listen, right? This is listening. You gotta take some chances sometimes. I worked undercover in Vice playing a prostitute. Had to deal with some pretty shady characters. My life depended on keeping my identity and my true purpose a secret. You just have to be smart about it."

Jillian took the bug and the small recorder with murmured thanks and hurriedly tucked it into her own purse. Despite Celeste's confidence, she wouldn't use it—she couldn't take the risk of getting caught. Not only would Mayall Lumber fire her, but so would Daniel.

CHAPTER TWO

JILLIAN ROLLED INTO THE Mayall Lumber parking garage at 6:45 a.m., bleary-eyed but pleased to have missed the worst of the rush hour traffic. That was one benefit of showing up to work at the butt-crack of dawn.

She couldn't think of any others.

No matter how hard she tried, she'd never been a morning person. Years of 6:00-a.m. swim practice, early college classes and working for Daniel—who also had expected her to rise early—hadn't cured her of the tendency to sleep until noon if nothing woke her up.

Still, she was self-disciplined enough to manage to do a good imitation of a lark when called for. She'd driven through Starbucks for a Venti cappuccino and had been sipping on it nonstop during her commute. A healthy dose of caffeine now coursed through her system; at least her eyelids no longer drooped.

She opened the parking garage door with her new magnetic key card and smiled at the security guard seated at a desk just inside the door. The guard's name tag identified her as Letitia, and she wasn't exactly intimidating with her three-inch fingernails and an avalanche of springy curls pointing every which way. But Jillian tried not to judge by appearances.

Letitia looked at her quizzically, and Jillian showed her the badge on a lanyard looped around her neck.

"My first day," she said.

The roly-poly guard looked her over, then decided to smile, revealing a row of crooked but bright white teeth in her round face. "Yeah? What department?"

"I'm an admin in Timber Operations."

"Don't tell me you're reporting to Conner Blake?"

"Yes, that's right."

The smile turned to a dubious frown. "Good luck, sister. You'll need it."

Jillian saw no reason not to start her undercover work on the spot. Letitia could be a good resource, seeing as she knew everyone and saw them coming and going to and from the building. "He couldn't be that bad."

"If you're still here by lunchtime, there'll be a betting pool started. Everyone puts in a dollar and guesses the exact hour you'll quit. I usually pick 10:00 a.m. the second day—so far, I'm up twenty bucks."

"Really." Was Letitia having a joke at Jillian's expense? "What if I stay?"

"You think you're made of pretty strong stuff?"

Jillian thrust out her chin. "Yes, I do. No one could be as bad as my old boss. Imagine the ruthlessness of Attila the Hun combined with the incompetence of Barney Fife." She hoped Daniel never got wind of that description. He wasn't at all incompetent, but he could be ruthless when he wanted something.

Letitia snorted, almost a laugh. "Maybe your old boss was bad, but was he a murderer?"

Jillian's heart thudded so loudly she was sure Letitia could hear it. "Excuse me?"

"I guess you haven't heard about Greg Tynes."

"Oh, the man who was killed. Yes, I did hear something about that." Jillian didn't want to appear terminally ignorant.

Letitia nodded. "He worked in Mr. Blake's department. We all think Mr. Blake did it."

"Why?" Jillian didn't have to fake her horror. She'd known *someone* at Mayall Lumber might be a killer, but she'd never imagined it might be her boss.

"Mr. Blake is mean, that's why."

"Does he have a temper?" She couldn't recall Conner ever losing his temper, but he did have a devilish streak.

"Not a temper. It's more like…a darkness," Letitia said, warming to her topic. "There's a reason that man can't keep an assistant. They always just…" Letitia lowered her voice to a whisper "…disappear."

Dear Lord.

Letitia clapped a hand over her mouth. "Now I've gone and said way more than I should. Never mind me. I'm sure you and Mr. Blake will work out just fine."

"We will." They had to.

As Jillian rode the elevator up to the third floor, she congratulated herself. With a little idle chitchat, she'd laid some groundwork for getting to know Letitia better, *and* she'd picked up some juicy gossip.

But she was also treading on dangerous territory. Her job was to observe and report, not ask questions, not snoop. In fact, Daniel had told her to talk as little as possible, and to keep to the truth as much as she could. She'd memorized a few pertinent facts about her fictionalized work background, and she was not supposed to elaborate.

But how was she going to learn anything important if she didn't talk to people?

Just before stepping out of the elevator, she checked her appearance one more time. Following Celeste's advice, she'd altered her wardrobe to look more like a working girl. She wasn't chairman of the board, she was a secretary. She'd chosen a pair of wheat-colored linen trousers and a blouse in muted earth-tone stripes. Leaving all her good jewelry at home, she'd opted for inexpensive costume pieces.

But she hadn't compromised with the shoes. She loved her high heels; they made her feel tall and invincible.

She was pleased to see she had beat Conner to work. His office was open and dark. Since no one was about—and since she was feeling brave—she fished the small, black disk out of her purse and peeled off the backing to expose the adhesive surface. Checking the hallway to make sure no one was coming, she dashed into Conner's office, slapped the bug under the front ledge of his desk, then dashed out again.

If the grapevine said Conner was guilty, he was the one to target with her spy tricks.

She placed the recording device in the back of her credenza, placing a ream of paper in front of it.

Now, with that task settled, she could start on her own work space. She wandered down the hall until she located someone else who'd braved the early hour, another admin. Her name plate identified her as Iris Hardy.

"Excuse me," Jillian began. "I'm Jillian Baxter, Mr. Blake's new admin. I wonder if you could help me."

Iris, a plain woman with a round face and the sort of dumpy clothes and hair that indicated she'd stopped caring about her image, smiled sadly. "He's done something awful already?"

"Oh, gracious, no," Jillian said, appalled by the other woman's attitude. It was like her colleagues were setting her up for failure. "He's not even in yet. I'm organizing my work space and I need some office supplies. Should I requisition them?"

"Only if there's something special you want," Iris said. "Otherwise, there's a big storeroom right around that corner. It says Supplies on the door, you can't miss it. Help yourself to whatever you need."

"Thanks. Do you want to have lunch later? If you don't already have plans, that is. I might need advice on what's good in the cafeteria, and what's to be avoided."

Jillian had been trying for a note of humor, but it fell flat. Iris frowned.

"Honey, you won't be here long enough for us to become friends. If you want to save yourself a lot of aggravation, quit now." She turned her attention back to her computer.

Jillian wondered if she looked frail. Otherwise, why would everyone assume she couldn't stand up to the rigors of a difficult boss? Conner couldn't be that bad.

Then again, with that cruel streak he'd shown her in high school, maybe he made Simon Legree look like Mother Teresa. And if he really was the killer...

She located the supply closet easily enough and opened the door, nearly colliding with a man on his way out. The slight man with thin, wiry hair and a face like a weasel widened his eyes in surprise when he saw her. It took her a moment, but she recognized his face from the Mayall Lumber Annual Report. This was Isaac Cuddy, the budget director.

"Who the hell are you?" he asked.

"Jillian. Conner Blake's new assistant. Pleased to meet you, Mr. Cuddy." She held out her hand, but he didn't reciprocate. He was carrying a large box overflowing with legal pads, pens, packing tape, staples and packets of coffee. "Oh, sorry, guess your hands are full. Would you like some help carrying?"

"No, thank you," he said tersely. "I've got it."

She held the door open, and he sashayed out.

What an unpleasant little man, she thought. And how odd was it that he was down here fetching his own office supplies? Surely he had an assistant, maybe a whole staff, to handle such mundane tasks.

With a shrug, she returned to gathering up hanging folders, file boxes and trash bags, pens and sticky notes, an extra ream of paper for her printer. She hauled it all back to her office area and dug in.

She'd been hoping the mess of paperwork might offer some insight into what Greg Tynes had been involved in before he died. He'd been an overseas timber buyer, which meant he worked for Conner's department. But beyond spotting his name on a couple of invoices, nothing she found was of interest. Most of these papers, as far as she could tell, ought to be shredded, as they were duplicates of documents already filed in the computer system.

The filing cabinet used by Jillian's predecessor was almost empty. Jillian remedied that, quickly setting up hanging files with neatly printed labels for invoices, contracts, correspondence and market research.

After almost two hours of dedicated organizing, Jillian's desk was clear, with only a small stack of unpaid invoices and another of correspondence, all of which needed input from her new boss before she could take action. When she learned more about her job, she would probably be able to handle more things without bothering Conner. But whether he liked it or not, she would need his help getting settled in.

That thought worried her a bit. The less interaction

she had with Conner Blake, the better. Just because he hadn't recognized her or her name yesterday didn't mean he wouldn't today.

"What the hell?"

Or right now. Jillian's heart swooped as she looked up to find Conner glaring down his aristocratic nose at her.

"Good morning, Mr. Blake." She refrained from pointing out that it was now almost nine o'clock, when he said he'd be here by seven.

"What happened to all the stuff that was here?" he demanded.

"Sorted. Filed."

"I had a system going here. You shouldn't have touched this stuff until you knew what it was and what I wanted done with it."

"I can find anything you need."

"I need a letter from Gustav Komoroski regarding a parcel of 520 hectares in northern Poland."

He was testing her. She rolled her desk chair to the filing cabinet, opened the drawer and was riffling the folders. She plucked out the single sheet of stationery, rolled back to her desk and handed it to him.

He returned it to her with only a cursory glance. "Call him. Ask him to resend the aerial photos to my email, which is—"

"I know your email address." She'd figured that much out. Did he think she was mentally deficient?

"Also explain to him that he'll no longer be working with Greg Tynes, who's left the company. I'll be his contact until we hire a new overseas timber buyer."

Left the company. That was an interesting way to put it.

Jillian picked up her cobalt-blue Montblanc fountain

pen—a birthday gift from Daniel two years ago. As his assistant, she'd always received nice birthday gifts from him. She would miss that.

"Before you do that, though, get me some coffee," Conner said. "Strong as you can make it, two sugars, no cream." With that he turned on his heel, offering Jillian a sigh-worthy view of his hindquarters in a well-tailored pair of khaki pants.

For a few moments she simply stared as unwelcome memories flooded her mind. Conner had been a fixture at her family home for as long as Jillian could remember. He and her older brother, Jeff, had met at summer camp in sixth grade, then attended the same private school from seventh grade through high school. They'd become as close as brothers, their parents had socialized, and Conner had been constantly underfoot.

Jillian had considered him a major annoyance—always raiding their fridge, making noise when she wanted to read, executing killer cannonballs in the pool while she swam laps.

But in eighth grade, her hormones had kicked in, and suddenly her brother's best friend had become infinitely interesting.

By then he'd started to look more man than boy. He was driving, his voice had changed, and the donkey laugh that had so infuriated her had mellowed into a pleasing sound that tickled her nerve endings.

All Conner had to do was walk into a room, and she would turn into a puddle of quivering insecurity. She'd seen the girlfriends he sometimes dragged around with him—long-legged cheerleaders with cleavage and sleek hair and lots of mascara—and seethed with envy.

She'd lived for the day she would outgrow her awkward adolescence. She favored her Danish mother—

everyone said so—and Mona Baxter was beautiful. Jillian just knew that someday, when her teeth were straight and she grew boobs and lost her baby fat, Conner would finally notice her.

By the time she entered high school, Conner had stopped teasing her and ignored her altogether. It had broken her heart when he walked past her in the hall, looking through her as if she were invisible—he was way too cool to talk to a freshman. But she hadn't given up hope. She'd planned their wedding, mentally decorated their future home and named their future children.

Then came that wonderful day. The day he saw her. Looked her up and down, in fact. Smiled that devilish smile of his and said, "Jillybean, I need an assistant for my science fair project. Interested?"

It embarrassed her even now to recall how pathetically grateful she'd been for his attention, how she'd fallen all over herself accepting his proposition and had decided that his use of her hated nickname was actually a term of endearment. Of course, far worse humiliation was soon to come.

Little did she know he'd been sizing her up not in terms of her womanly assets, but because of her overall size and shape—which was, to put it bluntly, short and fat. He'd required a female of certain dimensions for his science fair demonstration, and none of his long-legged bimbo girlfriends had fit the bill.

Jillian shook herself, realizing she'd been staring after empty space for some unknown number of seconds after Conner had disappeared. She absolutely could *not* afford to lose herself in the past, to dwell on long-ago injustices.

She had a few present-day injustices to dwell on.

Like the fact Conner hadn't even apologized for making her come in at seven when it was totally unnecessary. And scolding her like a child for doing what any well-trained assistant should do—get things organized.

Then there was the business of ordering her to bring him coffee. She used to bring Daniel coffee all the time, but it wasn't something he expected or demanded. He'd taken her on as his assistant to make his life easier, and it was her choice to perform the more personal tasks that a lot of admins would balk at.

Then again, she'd viewed her role with Daniel as far more personal than she should have. That was one mistake she wouldn't make again.

If she brought Conner coffee, she would be setting a precedent and earning the disapproval of secretaries everywhere. But if she drew a line in the sand now, he might fire her. She had to keep her eye on the goal: maintain her job at Mayall Lumber. Find out who killed Greg Tynes. Exonerate Stan Mayall of any wrongdoing.

So she'd bring Conner his damn coffee, and she'd do it with a smile. The bastard.

A few minutes later, she tapped on his door, a steaming mug in hand.

"Come in."

She was about to open the door when a tall woman in a tight, stark white dress came striding down the hall. She had an elegant face with a model's bored expression. Her tumble of jet-black hair reached nearly to her waist, and her breasts were one deep breath away from popping out of the low neckline.

Platform white suede boots completed the outfit.

Good Lord. She was beautiful—if you liked silicone, Botox and hair extensions.

The woman tried to brush right past Jillian and into

Conner's office, but Jillian turned and blocked her path. "Can I help you?"

"Who are you?" the woman asked, frowning.

"I'm Jillian, Mr. Blake's assistant."

"Oh. Good luck with that. The first thing you should know is, he's always in for me. I'm Chandra Mayall." She waited a beat for Jillian to recognize the name. "The CEO's granddaughter?" Taking advantage of Jillian's surprise, Chandra took the cup of coffee from her. "I'll deliver this to him. Run along, now."

"CHANDRA. TO WHAT DO I owe the pleasure?" Inside, Conner cringed. His ex-wife showing up in person was never good news.

She handed him a mug of hot coffee. "Just the way you like it."

He took a sip. It was hot, strong and sweet. "You didn't pour this for me." Which meant his new admin had done it. Too bad her job required a bit more than an ability to pour coffee.

Chandra shrugged one elegant shoulder. "Your new girl was about to bring it in. Plucky little thing, and protective. She was guarding your door like a pit bull, almost didn't let me in."

Another point in the woman's favor. "I'm kind of busy. What do you want?"

"I need a new roof. It's going to cost six thousand dollars."

"Really. I thought that house had a new roof put on right before you bought it."

"Hail damage."

"Have you filed an insurance claim?"

"Oh, you know how they are. They give you this

big runaround, and the roof is leaking into the dining room. It has to be fixed now."

"So because you don't want to make a phone call, I'm out six thousand dollars? I don't think so. I'll call the insurance company. Then I want you to get at least two estimates."

"Couldn't you just write the check now, and we'll work out the details later?"

"No. Nice try."

"Our decree says you have to pay for necessary home repairs."

"And I'll write a check directly to the roofer. Now, is there anything else?"

She debated a few moments before leaning on his desk, giving him an eyeful of cleavage. "Conner, I'm desperate. It's my butt."

"Wh— Excuse me?" That got his attention.

"It's fallen. I'm going to Cancun over Christmas, and I tried on my bikini this morning and my butt looks atrocious. It needs a lift."

Conner laughed. "Are you out of your mind? I'm not paying for your plastic surgery. Besides, if you keep going under the knife, you're going to end up looking like a freak."

"Conner. It's not funny."

"No, Chandra. Not a chance."

She seemed to deflate. "It was worth a shot. Guess I'll have to do more Pilates."

He softened his voice. "How's Stan?" Whenever Chandra was sad or worried, she turned to "fixing" herself as her own brand of therapy. She was obviously upset about her grandfather's situation.

"He's terrible, Conner. I'm so afraid. I wish there

was something more we could do. The lawyer thinks no jury will convict him. But his health…"

"I know. He's a tough old bird, though. He'll pull through."

"He better. I'm not ready for him to go."

Chandra might be shallow and self-absorbed, but one thing Conner was sure of—she loved her grandfather. He summoned a smile for her, then stood and walked her to the door. "Your butt looks fine, you know."

She sighed. "How would you know? You don't even look at my butt anymore." She air kissed him. "Ciao, darling." When she opened the door, Ham was standing outside, just about to knock.

"Oh, hi, Chandra. You look stunning, as usual."

"Aren't you a sweetie." She gave him an air kiss, too. "Give my best to Beatrice." Both men watched her strut toward the elevators.

Ham shook his head. "Tell me again why you divorced her?"

Conner laughed. "You know why." They both stepped back into his office.

Ham used to drop into Conner's office almost every morning with a new joke or a funny story about his wife. Conner had enjoyed their conversations. But ever since Ham had taken over Stan's job, he seemed rushed and harried. With two jobs to perform, he had no time for idle chitchat.

He must really need that report. "I'm working on the report today, I swear."

"I didn't come here to harass you. How's the new secretary working out?" Ham asked as he eased himself into his favorite wingback chair. "Is she as useless as she looks?"

"She can pour coffee, at least." Conner took a sip from his mug. It was cooling off. "I don't understand why Joyce keeps pitching these pretty bits of empty-headed fluff at me, expecting things to work out."

This one was worse than all the others put together.

"What was her name again?" Ham asked. "Hilary, Julia…"

"Something like that. Joyce claims this one has impeccable credentials—she was an assistant to some oil company exec. But I could tell with one look she's never worked a hard day in her life."

"You need someone with brains and maturity."

"Or at least one who wears sensible shoes," Conner grumbled.

"Why didn't Joyce promote someone from within the company? At least she would know something about the lumber business."

Conner raised an eyebrow. "Oddly, not a single employee applied for the opening."

Ham laughed. "Whose fault is that? Your reputation has spread far and wide."

"I'm not that bad. I just have a low tolerance for stupidity." He stood and stretched, then walked to the far end of his office to gaze at one of his favorite paintings, a forest scene by a Russian artist. "How does she keep from breaking an ankle, tottering around on those ridiculous shoes?" Those stilettos made her legs look a mile long, but that shouldn't be the aim in a work situation.

It wasn't just her shoes. The suit she'd worn that first day had cost more than his, he was pretty sure. Three years of marriage to Chandra—not to mention growing up with his mother—had taught him to recognize Chanel when he saw it. Then there was the haircut. Hilary-Julia—whatever hadn't gotten that style, or the subtle blond streaks, from a strip mall beauty shop. He pictured her lying back in a fancy salon chair while someone named Marcel shampooed her hair, digging his fingers into the thick, mock-gold strands, her head tipped back, creamy throat exposed….

Good God, where had that come from? He'd been too long without a woman, he supposed, but not many women wanted to spend time with him these days. He was too surly, too impatient.

"Give the girl a chance," Ham said.

"I give her three days. She'll either prove herself completely incompetent, or do something so thoroughly boneheaded that I'll be forced to fire her." He sighed. "I hope this one doesn't cry."

"Of course she'll cry. They all cry. Besides, you're a beast."

"I'd be a lot nicer if I could get out of this damned office once in a while."

"Back to your beloved trees."

"Yeah." God, he missed the trees. At night Conner dreamed about the forest, imagined himself in a hammock slung between two ancient tree trunks, the stillness and utter darkness all around him punctuated only by the periodic chatter or cry of nocturnal creatures. And during the day, he plotted how he would get back there.

"Well, I can help with that," Ham said, coming to stand beside Conner and gaze at the painting. "There's a forest sustainability conference in Jakarta next month. I want you to go."

Obviously Ham expected Conner to be pleased about the junket. But trading in his office for a hotel conference room wasn't high on his priority list.

"I'm not sure I can afford to take time away," Conner said. "This situation with Stan…"

"It's just three days, and it's vital that Mayall Lumber attend. You should also check on Will Nashiki while you're there, see how he's coming along with the job in North Sumatra."

A couple of days in the Sumatran rainforest? Conner could feel a grin spreading across his face. "Why didn't you say that to begin with? Of course I'll go." Maybe, just maybe, things would be more settled by next month and he could stay in the field longer than a weekend. Nashiki would appreciate a chance to go home, spend time with his family. "If you're sure you can spare me."

"It'll be tough, but I'll manage," Ham said, tongue firmly in cheek. He checked his watch and frowned. "Late for another damn meeting. I never realized how many meetings a CEO has to go to." He limped toward the door, leaning heavily on his cane.

The new girl walked in as Ham left. "Good morning, Mr. Payne." She held the door open for him.

Ham gave her a dismissive wave.

"Yes?" Conner asked brusquely as he returned to his desk. His office was Grand Central Station this morning.

"What else would you like me to do? How about if I start organizing in here?"

"No." The single syllable came out more harshly than he intended. "You're not to touch anything on my desk. Please," he added grudgingly. "It might look disorganized to you, but I have my own system."

"Of course," she said agreeably.

"I'm kind of busy here." He shuffled a few papers.

"Are you sure I can't help? I'm good with figures."

"This is a little more complex than keeping your checkbook register up to date." If she even had a checkbook. She probably used plastic for everything, then had the bills delivered to Daddy.

"I'm proficient in all of the most widely used accounting and budgeting software. At my previous job, I assisted an executive in the accounting department of a midsize oil company."

He looked up. "What happened?"

"Sir?" She flashed him a puzzled look.

"Why aren't you working there anymore?"

"Oh. Philosophical differences. As I became more ecologically aware, I realized I could no longer support my employer's policies. I'm a proponent of renewable energy."

A well-rehearsed speech, he guessed, crafted to hide the real reason she'd been canned. Nonetheless, it piqued his interest. She didn't look green to him. The women he knew who were environmental activists tended toward thrift-store clothes, Birkenstocks and no makeup.

He decided to challenge her. "Why a lumber company? We rape the land, too."

"Mayall Lumber has one of the most ecologically responsible reputations in the industry," she promptly replied. "The company is committed to responsible harvesting practices, and it even commits significant resources into saving the old-growth forests that support endangered species, such as the spotted owl and the orangutan. Also, the company has an extensive program for converting waste products into biomass fuel, reducing the world's carbon emissions."

She could have gotten most of that information off the web, but none of his other admins had bothered.

Now he was impressed. He studied her with renewed curiosity. She'd dressed down today, he was relieved to see, though even in casual pants, she appeared quite well put together. The deceptively plain pants were still top quality, probably tailored to fit her long, lean physique. She could easily have walked off the pages of *Vogue*.

"You like orangutans, do you?" he asked.

"I've never met one personally," she admitted.

He gathered up the sea of papers on his desk into one giant pile, picked it up and handed it to her. "See if you can make sense of this. I have to put together a report that shows the dollar amount spent on conservation efforts as a percentage of the gross profits from harvests in the European Union over the past three years."

That ought to keep her busy for a while. And out of his hair. She was one powerful distraction, all long, coltish limbs and svelte curves his palms itched to explore.

"Yes, Mr. Blake."

"And, um, you can call me Conner. We're not that formal around here."

"Very well, Conner."

"And what do you prefer to be called?" He still hadn't remembered her name.

"Jillian is fine. I don't like having my name shortened." She sashayed out of his office, her arms loaded with paper, and suddenly he realized she reminded him of someone…from a long time ago.

JILLIAN HAD TAKEN ADVANTAGE of a few quiet minutes to do an internet search on the forbidden reporter mentioned in the memo she'd seen in Joyce's office. Mark Bowen was easy to find. She'd assumed he would be someone trying to dig up dirt on the murder, or Stan Mayall's arrest. But he wasn't a crime reporter, he was a business writer for some lumber trade magazine. She found a picture of him: in his thirties, kind of a scrawny guy but pleasant looking, in a nerdy sort of way.

He probably had nothing to do with the murder. Jillian debated whether to contact him or not, then decided in this instance she would heed Daniel's orders. She wasn't confident enough to confront a reporter who could write something about her and get her in heaps of trouble.

Besides, her stomach was grumbling. She shouldn't have skipped breakfast.

The small office cafeteria reminded Jillian way too much of the one from her high school. As she pushed her tray along the line and selected a carton of yogurt and an apple, she checked out the tables behind her from the corner of her eye. They all seemed to be occupied by tight groups of people, mostly women. She saw no executive types. They probably went out to one of the many nice restaurants in this neighborhood, or had food delivered.

Her plan was to pay for her food, then boldly set her tray down at a table of women and introduce herself. How else would she get to know more people here?

But in the end, she just couldn't do it. She had too many memories of trying to make friends her freshman year in high school.

That seat's taken.

We don't let losers sit with us.

The pig trough is that way.

Adolescent girls could be particularly cruel, and the cliques at her exclusive private school had been worse than most.

Eventually she'd made friends—swim team girls, mostly. But the popular girls had always ignored her, and after the terrible prank Conner had perpetrated on her, they had actively tormented her. Even the boys had teased her until she cried.

Jillian was about to sit at an empty table when she spotted a familiar face. Letitia sat alone, reading a newspaper. Jillian brought her tray to the other woman's table and set it down.

"Hi, Letitia, okay if I sit here?"

Letitia looked up from her paper without cracking a smile. "You're not very practiced with office politics, are you?"

Truth was, Jillian had no direct experience with office politics. The only place she'd ever worked besides Project Justice was at Daniel's mansion, where her place among the staff as queen bee had been secure. She'd had no need to play games, curry favor or assemble a group of allies. But she'd read enough *Cosmopolitan* articles to understand how it worked.

"Maybe you could help me out with that," she said.

"The first rule is that you sit with your own kind," Letitia said. "You're a top-level support staff. You sit with other executives' assistants. You don't sit with rank-and-file secretaries. And you certainly don't sit with a security guard."

Though stung by the rebuff, Jillian refused to show it. "That's a stupid rule. Anyway, I want to sit with you. You seem like an intelligent and interesting person."

"Oh, sit down. Jeez. Is that all you're gonna eat?" Letitia had the remains of a chicken potpie in front of her. "No wonder you're a size zero."

Oddly, when people said she was too thin—something she heard all the time, although she was a per-

fectly healthy weight—it hurt almost as much as being
called "Jillybean," the nickname she'd endured in childhood. A size four was a long way from a zero but sometimes seemed threatening to certain women of more
generous proportions.

Letitia, however, didn't appear to be malicious with
her observation; she just called it how she saw it. Jillian
set her tray down, claimed a chair and unwrapped her
straw, placing it in her glass of iced tea.

"So, how's your first day going?" Letitia asked.
"Ready to throw in the towel?"

"It's not bad so far. It's hard work, but nothing I
can't handle. Mr. Blake's job is interesting, so I think
mine will be, too."

"Huh. Does he make you bring him coffee?"

"I don't mind." When she got to know him better,
she would request that he not order her around like a
chambermaid. But she had a sneaking suspicion Conner was being a jerk on purpose. He wanted to see how
easily she could be intimidated, how far he could push
her before she either cracked or pushed back.

If a billionaire formerly on death row couldn't intimidate her, Conner certainly couldn't.

"He's got a hot man-booty." Letitia took a sip of her
coffee, then added another packet of sugar. "But I don't
know whether I could put up with him just to enjoy a
little eye candy."

"He's a nice-looking man," Jillian agreed blandly.
What an understatement! "Is he married?"

"No, not anymore." Letitia laughed. "Can you imagine committing yourself to that for life? At least if
you're an employee, you can walk away. No one was
surprised when he got divorced."

Divorced? Jillian had guessed he wasn't married. He

displayed no family photos on his desk, didn't wear a ring and hadn't mentioned a wife or kids. But she hadn't pegged him as divorced, either.

"What happened there?" she asked, going for broke. Why not? Ordinarily she wouldn't engage in idle gossip about her boss, but she was here to gather intelligence, right?

"No one knows. He's tight-lipped when it comes to his personal life. But my guess is, Chandra got tired of sitting at home waiting for him. First he was always traveling, then he was always here, works sixteen-hour days most of the time."

"Chandra Mayall?" That pushy, exotic creature who'd barged into Conner's office that morning was his ex-wife? Of course he would marry someone like that. She'd probably been a cheerleader in high school.

"Yup. The boss's granddaughter—and his sole heir, I might add."

Conner Blake must have looked like a good catch to Chandra. But Jillian agreed that eighty-hour workweeks weren't conducive to a good marriage.

"He's young," Jillian said. "I expect he'll find someone else."

"But not you, I hope," Letitia said. "You wouldn't want to be hooking up with a murderer."

"He's not a murderer," Jillian said firmly, trying not to think too long and hard about how angry he'd become when she'd organized papers without his permission. And how he didn't want her to touch anything on his desk or in his office.

"He's got motive," Letitia said, warming up to her topic. "Greg Tynes was having an affair with Chandra."

"More gossip?"

"This I know for a fact. I saw them together. In the parking garage. Kissing."

This was good stuff! "But Chandra is his ex. Why would he care?"

Letitia gave her a look that told her exactly how naive her assumption was.

She shivered slightly. Was it possible? She could think of little nice to say about the man, but could he possibly be a murderer?

In high school, when his cruel prank was still fresh in her mind, she'd envisioned all sorts of ways she might make Conner Blake pay for his crime. Her revenge fantasies had included such soap-operatic scenarios as transforming herself into a siren, tricking him into falling in love with her, then jilting him at the altar. Or waiting until he was running for congress, then revealing to the press what he had done to her just days before the election.

She'd grown up and realized how outlandish her fantasies had been, how improbable and immature. But never in her wildest imagination had she envisioned sending him up the river.

Now, *that* would be payback—sending Conner to prison. The thought brought her no satisfaction. He might be a despicable fathead, but could she really believe he was capable of taking a human life?

She didn't have to draw conclusions. She only had to report what she found out and Daniel would follow up. Tonight's report would be a juicy one.

CHAPTER THREE

THE NEXT DAY, when Conner returned from lunch, he found a surprise sitting on his desk. Jillian had delivered a report based on the armload of trash he'd shoved at her only yesterday. The papers were sorted into file folders, neatly stacked on his chair, and a printed report—complete with graphs, charts and a spreadsheet—sat in the middle of his desk.

He was torn when it came to having an assistant. On one hand, he needed someone to keep him organized. Paperwork, scheduling, computers, meetings—he wasn't terribly good at any of it. But he hated having assistants underfoot. Give him a nice stand of oak trees and he could read them like a book. He could tell a tree's health just by looking at the color and texture of the bark, the number of branches and how they grew, the gloss of the leaf.

Stick him behind a desk and he was close to useless.

His job performance as director of timber operations was only so-so. This company was only as good as the wood it harvested, and that harvest was only as good as the men and women out in the field finding the stands of trees, evaluating them, negotiating for the purchase and supervising the harvest. From his office he could give his buyers directions, look at photographs and approve purchases or not. But it drove him crazy not to have firsthand knowledge.

And the paperwork—God, how he hated paperwork. All the hoops they had to jump through to keep this certification or that one, proving they adhered to green policies, that they had performed all the correct environmental impact studies. He'd had no idea how hard his predecessor's job was when he'd accepted the promotion.

It was easy to blame Chandra, but deep down, Conner had no one but himself to hold responsible. He was the one who'd been thinking with his privates, rather than his brain and his heart, when he'd agreed to the corner office. He'd have done anything to keep Chandra happy.

In the end, though, his decision to settle down had backfired. Chandra had fallen in love with an adventurer and world traveler who brought home exotic presents—carved teak boxes, silks and Oriental rugs. She'd seen him as a modern-day Indiana Jones.

But she'd grown weary of his constant travel and had begged her grandfather to promote him. Yes, because of Chandra, he had advanced in the company at lightning speed, bringing home ever-larger paychecks.

But an executive who'd traded in his bullwhip for a smart phone didn't interest her any longer. The divorce had been executed with surgical precision. Conner had lost his wife, his home, his dog, his savings, and he'd been left with a job he despised.

He wouldn't be here forever—that was his only consolation. But leaving Stan—a man as dear to him as his own grandfather—in the middle of this hideous controversy over Greg's murder was unthinkable. With treatment, Stan might beat the cancer. But prison would kill him.

Conner simply couldn't abandon the sinking ship.

He'd met with Stan's lawyer, who at Stan's request had allowed him to go over the evidence collected by the police. One anomaly stood out to Conner right away. Stan wasn't strong enough to hoist two hundred pounds of deadweight into a car trunk. That was a point in Stan's favor.

But Conner still had no clue who might have murdered Greg and framed Stan. Any one of the directors, looking to move up, could be responsible. All of them had been interviewed by the police, including Conner. In fact, they'd looked at Conner pretty closely, since he was Greg's immediate boss. But once they'd zeroed in on Stan, they'd abandoned all their other suspects.

Conner forced his attention back to his job, looking over Jillian's report. She'd made a few errors, mostly little details that stemmed from a lack of familiarity with the lumber business rather than outright mistakes. He made some notations, then headed for her desk to return it to her.

Maybe he'd finally found an assistant with half a brain who could get things back on track. Someone to whom he could actually delegate responsibilities.

He found her at her desk, shredding a stack of papers he'd given her permission to dispose of.

"You know, you don't have to do that yourself. Down on the first floor, there's a whole department devoted to managing waste and recycling. You just hand someone the papers and they'll take it from there."

"I prefer to do this myself," she said, sending another stack of pages through the slot and pausing while the blades whined. "That way, I know for sure it was done. In case a question ever comes up. I assume some of these numbers, the bids and such, are confidential."

Today she was wearing a slim black skirt and a

short-sleeved, lime-green sweater that showed him more of her curves than he'd seen on her first day. Her breasts were fuller than he'd thought at first, and her waist was so narrow he could probably span it with his hands. Twenty-four inches, he'd bet money on it. He had a lot of experience sizing up the circumference of trees.

Not that Jillian's body looked anything like a tree trunk.

"Is there anything else you'd like me to work on?"

He snapped back to his senses. He had no business thinking about Jillian's waist, or any other part of her body for that matter.

"Where did you learn to pull together a report like that?" he asked, instead of answering her question.

"I have a business administration degree from Dartmouth," she said. "Is it satisfactory?"

"There are some mistakes," he said gruffly, plopping the report in front of her. "Fix them and print it out again." He turned quickly and walked away before she could see his reaction to her.

Wow. He fell into his office chair and spun it around. Where had that come from? How long had it been since he'd reacted to a woman like that?

No one since Chandra. Chandra, with her traffic-stopping body and long black hair and eyes like cut emeralds, just as sharp, too.

She did nothing for him now, especially since he knew everything about her was fake, from the hair extensions to the augmented breasts to the acrylic nails.

But it wasn't just her physical self that was insincere. She had lied without conscience, without a second thought, to get what she wanted. She'd perfected the fine art of saying exactly what a man wanted to hear, and he'd fallen for it.

No reason to believe Jillian wasn't just the same. She was cut from the same cloth—rich, well educated, groomed to manipulate her way to become a rich man's wife someday.

To be fair, she'd given no indication that she expected him to fill the role of her husband. She'd been nothing if not professional. Even a bit cool.

Which was odd.

Most women responded to him from a…hormonal perspective. The nastier he was to them, the more they tried to win him over. It was the beauty-and-the-beast syndrome. They wanted to tame him.

But not Jillian. She didn't flutter eyelashes, or lean over so he could get an eyeful of her cleavage, or flip her hair or lick her lips. In fact, he suspected she might be sneering at him behind his back.

It shouldn't matter. She appeared to be qualified for her job, and that was the only important thing.

She still seemed familiar to him somehow. Who did she remind him of? If she'd grown up wealthy in Houston, chances were good he'd crossed paths with her at some point a debutante ball, a charity event, even a high school football game. But surely if he'd met her, he'd remember her. Her looks weren't forgettable.

Pushing thoughts of his new assistant out of his mind, he focused on his email. Great, just what he needed, another screwup with harvesting in East Texas. Unfortunately, Greg Tynes was involved. Dissatisfied with Greg's job performance abroad, Conner had brought him closer to home, but he'd continued to make mistakes. Apparently he hadn't understood the protocol and had marked a snag that was a popular owl nesting site. Owls had to be protected not just because they were cute; they were essential to a healthy forest ecosystem.

Conner would have to go there, apologize for the actions of a dead man and smooth some feathers, perhaps literally. But he welcomed any excuse to spend time in the forest, even dealing with disasters.

He had so little time these days. He wondered briefly if he could delegate the trip, then shook his head. Who would he send? Jillian? She might be good with paperwork, but he had his doubts she could manage trees, owls and angry forest rangers.

No, he'd have to go himself. But perhaps he would take Jillian with him. If she was going to stick around for any length of time—and he had to admit, she seemed a good fit for the job—he might as well start teaching her about lumber so she could really be of service to him.

Conner exited his office and strode into Jillian's area, standing above her desk until she looked up. She was in the process of entering the corrections for the report.

"I'll need another twenty minutes for the revised report," she said.

"That's not why I'm here. Were you apprised, when you took this job, that there might be some travel involved?"

"No, actually, I wasn't."

Conner felt a slight sense of relief. She didn't sound happy. If she refused to travel, he could use that as grounds for firing her.

Not that he *wanted* to fire her. Not yet. But having a valid reason when he did send her packing would go a long way toward avoiding a wrongful termination lawsuit. He'd made some of his previous admins very unhappy with his admittedly unreasonable demands and capricious, sudden terminations, but so far none of them had sued.

"On occasion I attend meetings in the field with forestry experts, government pencil-pushers, eco groups, landowners. I need someone to make travel arrangements and keep me organized during the trip. I might need you to pack certain documents, a computer for PowerPoint presentations, and also to take notes during the meeting—make an audio recording, too—and transcribe it later. Is that a problem?"

"No, I don't have a problem with that."

"Good. Set up a meeting tomorrow afternoon in Stirrup Creek. I'll forward the email that has the pertinent information. We'll stay overnight and drive back in the morning. Reserve a Jeep from the company fleet. Do you own a pair of hiking boots?"

"Yes."

"And you're physically fit enough to hike into the woods?"

"Yes."

"Can you operate a digital camera and get decent results?"

"Yes." She looked up expectantly, her gaze direct and slightly challenging. He simply wasn't used to this can-do attitude. No whining? No endless questions about what to wear, what to bring, what they would be doing, where they would eat, what kind of rooms she should reserve?

Just *yes?*

A beautiful woman who said yes. Jillian was dangerous to his libido. Tomorrow, she would show her true colors, he was sure of it. She was probably trying hard to make an extra-good impression, it being her first week and all. But at the first sign of a mosquito she would go ballistic and prove herself inadequate for the job.

"Okay, then." He spun on his loafers and walked away, but Jillian stopped him.

"Conner?"

"Yes?" he asked without turning to look at her. *Here it comes.*

"There's an intercom between our offices. You don't have to keep walking out the door and around the corner. That seems a waste of your valuable time."

He returned to stand in front of her desk again, purposely glowering at her. "You don't like me checking up on you?"

"Is that what you're doing? Afraid you'll catch me watching a movie on my phone or talking to my boyfriend on company time?"

Her gutsy comeback took his breath away, as did her mention of a boyfriend. She acted as if she didn't really need this job. And maybe she didn't. Her paycheck was probably a drop in the bucket compared to her trust fund.

Or maybe it was her sugar daddy who paid for those expensive clothes. "Do you have a boyfriend?"

"I don't see how that information is pertinent to my job," she asked, her tone carefully neutral. No snark. She wanted to please him, but at the same time she wasn't going to take a whole lot of crap from him.

Good for you, Jillian Whatever-Your-Last-Name-Is.

"Some significant others object to an employee's travel schedule. I'd like to know whether I'm causing any domestic discord."

"If there is, I'll deal with it. But thank you for your concern."

"I was checking up on you," he admitted. "It only makes sense that I would keep a close eye on you your first few days."

She thought about that for a moment, then said, "Yes, it does make sense. Thank you for your honesty. I'll make the travel arrangements as soon as I receive the email."

Conner's skin tingled all over as he returned to his office. She definitely turned him on, which was a damned nuisance. What a brilliant move, insisting she accompany him on a business trip when he couldn't spend two minutes in the same room with her before sporting a hard-on.

Way to go, Blake.

"SORRY I'M LATE," JILLIAN said to Celeste, who was waiting for her on the atrium level overlooking the ice skating rink at The Galleria Mall. "The ogre wanted me to type up some notes of his before I went home."

"The ogre?" Celeste heaved her faux-lizard bag onto her shoulder.

"My new pet name for him. It's not enough that he has to terrorize me during work hours. Now he's making me go on a business trip with him."

"Whoa, Nellie, what's that about? He's trying to put the moves on you already?"

Jillian shook her head. "I don't think it's that. He's testing me. Wants to see how much he can abuse me. Apparently that's part of the job description they didn't tell me about—a high tolerance for crap. His former assistants couldn't handle it, but obviously I have to."

"If you want any pointers, just ask me. You have no idea the kind of shenanigans I had to endure early in my career. Hateful stuff. The kind of sexist hazing that would get you thrown in jail nowadays."

"I'm not sure this is sexist." Jillian watched the handful of skaters buzzing around the ice—the little princesses with their flirty skirts, the gangs of boys racing and cutting up. "He's trying to prove he's the alpha, I think."

"The alpha can mate with any female in the pack," Celeste pointed out, which didn't put Jillian at ease. "So what do you need my help with? I'm the shopping queen, but surely you're at least a princess at it yourself. You're the best-dressed person I know besides *moi*."

Jillian tried to take that as a compliment. Today Celeste wore an ankle-length skirt with frogs printed all over it, a fluorescent orange tank top and a denim jacket with the sleeves ripped out. She'd tied her hair up in a hot-pink zebra-stripe scarf. Her dangle earrings were papier-mâché frogs, which at least matched the skirt in theme if not color.

"I need to buy hiking clothes. And boots. And a digital camera."

"Ah, I know just the place."

Celeste dragged her to Cliffs, an upscale sporting goods store, where Jillian purchased two pair of sturdy, canvas pants with lots of pockets, two long-sleeved cotton shirts, thick socks, hiking boots, a wide-brimmed hat, work gloves and a backpack. She also grabbed a handheld GPS, bug repellant, sunscreen, lip balm, a water bottle, granola bars and waterproof matches.

"Matches?" Celeste put her hands on her bony hips. "Oh, come on. Throw in a tent and sleeping bag, and you could hike across the whole country."

"I don't want to be caught unprepared. What about this snakebite kit?"

Celeste just gave her a look.

"Well, there are snakes in the woods." She spotted some machetes hanging on the wall. "Do you think I need one of these, to cut through the brush?"

Celeste walked closer to the display, then tested a machete blade with her thumb. "Sharp. I wonder if this is like the one Leo Simonetti used to cut off his victims' heads. Remember that case?"

"On second thought, maybe it's not a good idea for me to be alone in the woods with an infuriating man and sharp objects." Jillian gathered up her purchases and took her place in the checkout line.

"So, have you made any progress? Finding the real killer, I mean."

"Well…one of the security guards suspects my boss."

Celeste's plucked eyebrows flew up and almost met her hairline. "Your boss? Hot diggity! If he did it, then the evidence must be in his office or his computer, his phone, or his correspondence—he left a trail, they always do. Does he seem…secretive?"

"Yes, actually. He nearly blew a gasket when I cleaned up my own office. He told me he doesn't want me to touch his papers or his computer without his express permission."

"Honey, I think you're on to something." Celeste thought for a moment, then suddenly gasped. "Maybe you already saw the incriminating evidence but don't know enough yet to recognize it. If he suspects you're on to him…maybe he's going to take you into the woods and make you disappear."

Jillian almost regretted confiding in Celeste. "I don't think that's the case," she said.

"Just make sure someone else in the company knows

where you'll be—and who you'll be with. Oh, and I brought you some more gear to help you with your spying."

"I'm not supposed to be spying."

"Do you want to get ahead or not? If you do, you have to take some initiative."

A few minutes later—and with her wallet several hundred dollars lighter—Jillian was seated across from Celeste at a mall café eating a chicken Caesar salad. Celeste, impatient to show off her "gear," started emptying her gargantuan purse. She hauled out a wad of wires and laid it on the table. "To record telephone calls."

"Isn't that illegal?"

Celeste slid her gaze away guiltily. "Okay, how about this?" She pulled out a rather clunky-looking pair of sunglasses. "There's a video camera in the earpiece. Records up to thirty minutes of video on this tiny flash card. You can pop it right into your computer for viewing."

"Celeste, where do you get all this stuff?"

"Mostly The Spy Store. Sometimes I order it from the back of *Soldier of Fortune Magazine*. They have the weird stuff."

"I don't want to record phone calls," Jillian said. "That's wiretapping, and it's a felony." Daniel would have her head if she went against his orders *and* broke the law.

"Even to bring a murderer to justice? Honey, do you want to be stuck filing and making coffee forever? Because that's what happens to women in this field unless they go out on a limb. You have to be smarter, stronger, faster and lots more clever than the men just to break even."

Jillian knew what Celeste had said was at least partly

true, even in this day and age. She considered Daniel enlightened, not particularly sexist, yet Project Justice itself was clothed in an air of macho that favored brawn over brains and subtlety. Even her professors at the junior college where she took her criminal justice classes didn't take her seriously because of her delicate appearance.

"You don't have to tell anyone you made the recordings," Celeste reasoned. "Just let the information you glean point you in the right direction. Make yourself look smart."

Jillian scooped up all of Celeste's toys and stuffed them into her shopping bag. "I'll think about it. And, Celeste...thanks."

Celeste took a big bite of her hamburger and spoke around it. "Us girls gotta stick together."

"Is something wrong, Mr. Blake?" asked Letitia, the security guard, as Conner strolled in through the garage entrance early the next morning.

"Wrong? What do you mean?"

"You're whistling. I've never heard you whistle before." She lowered her voice. "I thought maybe you were trying to signal me that there was some kind of trouble."

Conner shook his head. "No, no trouble. I'm just in a good mood, I guess."

Letitia laughed. "Yeah, right. Have a good day, Mr. Blake."

"You, too, Letitia."

Conner supposed he deserved the guard's derision. Three years working in this building and he'd probably never spared a nice word for her. He was a Grade A grouch. A good mood wasn't a familiar state for him.

But how could he not feel good? In a few hours, he would be in the forest—pine needles crunching underfoot, breeze blowing through the high branches, fresh air washing the Houston smog out of his lungs, birds calling.

A stand of second-growth pine wasn't quite the same as an old-growth forest in Montenegro, or the rain forest in Brazil. There was something special—sacred almost—about a part of the earth that hadn't been touched by human development, and he always felt good knowing that he was protecting those areas from other, less responsible lumber operations that would clear-cut the trees, rather than selectively harvesting mature trees and leaving behind smaller ones for the next generation—and for all the critters who called the forest home.

Sure, his way was more expensive. But landowners and governments who managed public lands were more likely to sell to Mayall because of the care they took.

Conner's musings came to an abrupt halt as he walked down the door to his office and got an eyeful of Dora the Explorer.

Jillian wore pants with enough pockets that she could carry provisions for an army. The camo shirt—what was that, National Guard chic? And those boots—good gravy, they must weigh twenty pounds each. The hat was more appropriate for a survival hike through the desert than a walk in the woods.

He couldn't help himself. He burst out laughing. "What the hell are you supposed to be? Are you auditioning for a role on the next season of *Survivor*?"

The hurt look on Jillian's face immediately sobered him. He hadn't meant to ridicule her.

"I dressed prepared for a hike, as suggested," she said coolly.

He held up a hand. "Sorry. I'm sorry, I shouldn't have laughed, Jilly…Jillian."

Jilly. Jilly. Why had he called her that?

Then it hit him. Jillybean. This situation reminded him viscerally of another time when he'd laughed at a female's expense. Her name was even similar. And that expression of injury on her face—uncannily the same.

Jillian pulled out a compact from her purse and tried to see herself in the tiny mirror. "Surely I don't look that bad."

"No," he said distractedly as he stared at her, studying her features, trying to see something that wasn't there. "You follow directions extremely well and you look…" Adorable. Sexy. How could a woman in camo, covered head to toe, look sexy? "Well prepared. We'll leave in a few minutes, I just want to check my mail." He escaped into his office and shut the door.

What was Jillian's last name? Though the situation had reminded him of something from years ago, this Jillian couldn't possibly be Jill Baxter, his friend Jeff's kid sister. Jill had been short and chubby with a mop of frizzy, green-blond hair, a mouthful of braces, and a long, beaky nose.

Still, Conner rifled through the papers on his desk until he came up with the stack of résumés Joyce had given him to look over, a task he'd never gotten around to, forcing her to make a decision on her own. He flipped through them until he found Jillian's.

Jillian Baxter.

Baxter was a common name—it *couldn't* be the same Jill. But he hadn't seen her since she was fourteen.

That was, what, thirteen years ago? That would make her around twenty-seven now. The age was about right.

Though he and Jeff had been good friends at one time, they'd drifted apart after high school. Their families exchanged Christmas cards, but that was about it. He thought about looking Jeff up on Facebook, seeing if he could reconnect with his old buddy. Or, he could simply sift through Jeff's friends and see if his sister was there, and what she looked like today.

In the end, though, he decided he didn't have time for such a foolish pursuit. There was no possible way the gorgeous woman sitting at her desk just down the hall with the tiny waist and the sleek hair—and the straight, aristocratic, but definitely nonbeaky nose—was Jillybean, the girl he had humiliated in front of teachers, parents and half the student body.

The girl he'd last seen in her underwear, streaking across the football field toward the locker room as fast as her stubby little legs could carry her.

The girl who had vowed to hate his guts for the rest of his days, who had cursed his unborn children and sworn to condemn to hell if she could—according to Jeff, anyway. Conner had been advised not to get within a hundred yards of her if he valued his manhood.

He smiled at the memory; then immediately a tremendous stab of guilt nailed him right in the stomach. The incident had seemed terribly funny at the time, and he'd gotten extracurricular credit for participating in the science fair despite his invention's obvious drawbacks. He'd gained yet another notch of notoriety at his high school—the kind teenage boys thrived on.

But it hadn't been so funny to Jilly. Long after he'd gone off to college, he'd reflected on the incident and realized how mean he'd been to laugh at her expense.

But he hadn't felt bad enough to contact her and apologize.

Had she ever forgiven him? Probably not.

It was a good thing his new admin wasn't the chubby Jillybean from his past, or he might have to think twice about spending time with her in the woods, alone, where there were no witnesses.

CHAPTER FOUR

JILLIAN TRIED NOT TO LOOK AT Conner. Although the four-wheel drive Jeep Cherokee Sport wasn't a small car, it felt small when she was sitting in the front seat with Conner, whose sheer physicality dominated any space he occupied.

Instead, she experimented with her camera, consulting the instruction book, fiddling with the settings.

"Is that a new camera?" Conner asked once he'd navigated out of the worst of the Houston traffic. They were headed for the East Texas piney woods, a trip that would take them about three hours. She wondered why they had to stay overnight—it wasn't that far. But she figured he knew what he was doing.

Celeste had insisted he wanted to get her out of town so he could either murder her or seduce her with no witnesses, but Celeste was prone to drama.

"Yes, I just got it yesterday."

"I thought you said you knew how to use a digital camera."

"I do." The one on her phone, anyway. This one was more complex than she'd thought it would be. She'd snapped a few photos the previous evening just to be sure she had the basics down, but she had much to learn about settings and exposure. "I needed a new camera anyway, and this seemed like a good time to buy one. What will I be taking pictures of?"

"I'm not sure. Apparently the lumbering crew got overzealous and took down some kind of special owl tree."

"Owl tree?"

"A hollow tree that's been a barn owl nesting site for the past ten years."

"Oh, poor owls. So this is a big deal?"

"Since our agreement with the landowner specifically stated that this tree, and the area around it, wouldn't be disturbed, we could get sued. But even without the legal angle, it's still a big deal. Hollow trees aren't that easy to come by. For every cavity, the owls have to compete with other birds, like woodpeckers."

That explained why the back of the Jeep was filled with birdhouses. Apparently Conner planned to offer some alternative housing for the owls whose home had been destroyed, and some for their competitors, as well.

"Are they endangered owls?"

"They're rare in this part of Texas. The state forestry people like owls because the little ones eat insect pests that harm trees, and the larger ones, like barn owls, keep rodents in check. They're an important part of the food chain."

Jillian didn't know anything about owls, but apparently Conner did. He'd always been interested in science, she remembered that about him. His father had been some kind of ecoscientist back before "green" was in. Conner had been smart, too—straight A's. He'd managed to make that look cool.

Even entering the science fair—a notoriously geeky thing to do—had looked good on him.

Jillian stopped, determinedly focusing on the road ahead, the sky, the puffy white clouds. Thinking about that science fair when Conner was sitting inches from her was a dangerous thing to do.

"Your guy didn't destroy a nest, did he? Like, with babies?" Jillian didn't have any pets of her own, but that didn't mean she didn't like animals. She'd doted on Daniel's golden retriever.

"Nesting season is over. But the adult owls were still roosting at the nest site, and they were undoubtedly disturbed."

After a few more minutes Conner turned off the main road, then onto a still smaller road, then finally onto a logging road that was no more than a couple of tire ruts in the red dirt.

Conner was busy driving, skillfully lurching from bump to bump and avoiding the largest of the holes, so Jillian could study him without fear that he would notice. He seemed to change as they left civilization. The deeper they got into the woods, the more relaxed his face became, to the point where he was almost smiling.

She'd seen nothing but anger, impatience and irritation from him at the office; now he seemed to be enjoying himself.

However, his face and body grew tense again as they approached the logging site. This area, scarred by the trucks and saws, wasn't so pretty, littered with the stumps of pine trees.

"What the hell's going on here?" he muttered.

"Is something wrong?"

"Something is very wrong."

Eventually they pulled up behind a huge, flatbed truck half-filled with logs. A U.S. Forest Service truck was parked off to the side. Several men, mostly in work clothes, milled around.

Conner grabbed a folder from the backseat and nearly flew out of the truck.

Ready for anything, Jillian followed, her camera around her neck, a digital recorder in one pocket and a notepad in the other.

One of the workmen, a scruffy-looking redhead with a full beard, was already heading toward Conner, his long stride full of purpose. "Mr. Blake. I didn't know anything about owls, I swear. I was just taking down the trees that were marked."

A second man had come forward, a tall, gaunt man in his sixties in overalls, clutching an unlit pipe in one hand. "He's practically clear-cutting! Our contract states no more than twenty-five percent of the trees were to be cut, and just look at this! It's a good thing I came to check on the progress."

"I only cut the marked trees," Scruffy Redhead said again. "You can check the truck. Every single tree on that truck is marked with blue paint."

Jillian switched on the recorder, then started scribbling notes as fast as she could. This wasn't anything like the civilized meetings she used to deal with at Daniel's estate. It was a good thing she'd developed her own version of shorthand.

"Who did the marking, then?" Pipe Man asked.

"A man named Greg Tynes." Conner's jaw tightened and he all but spit on the ground, so obvious was his contempt. "I personally went over the contract with him and instructed how he was to mark. Obviously he didn't follow directions."

Jillian's heart quickened. So the dead man had been violating the terms of the lumber company's contract with the landowner. Could that be a motive for murder?

"Well, I hope you fired him!" Pipe Man said indignantly. "My forest looks like a wasteland."

"Rest assured, Greg Tynes no longer works for Mayall Lumber," Conner said, giving nothing away. "In fact, he'll never work in the timber business again."

That was one promise Conner could keep.

The young, female forest ranger, who'd been listening intently, finally spoke up. "There's more at stake than just the aesthetics of this woods. Mr. Whatley's land abuts public lands, forming a contiguous forest, the size of which is crucial to—"

"The owls," Conner said.

"Yes. Barn owl populations have been declining over the years. The nest site in question has been monitored by Cornell University for ten years. A camera has been in place for five."

"I get a tax deduction for lettin' 'em do that, you know," Mr. Whatley put in.

"The owls are crucial to our woodland ecosystem," the ranger continued. "They eat—"

Conner put his hand up to stop her impassioned speech. "You don't have to convince me. We've done something wrong here. I want to fix it. I want to make things right. Obviously, Mr. Whatley here will have to be compensated for the excess timber taken from his land. As for the owls—will you show me the nest site?"

Conner retrieved a backpack from the Jeep. Then he, the forest ranger and Jillian began hiking.

"How many acres have been screwed up?" he asked the ranger.

"Between seventeen and twenty." She seemed calmer, now that it appeared Conner wanted to make things right.

He breathed out a sigh. "At least it wasn't the whole seventy-five."

Jillian didn't want to be impressed with the way Conner handled things. She wanted to continue hating him—it was so much easier. But how many men would so easily admit responsibility for a mistake and pledge to make things right, all without anyone making demands or threats?

She well remembered how the suits at Logan Oil, of which Daniel was chairman of the board, consulted teams of lawyers if there was any hint that they might have made a misstep, searching for all possible legal remedies and never admitting to anything until a full investigation had been conducted.

But just like that, Conner had owned the problem.

The hiking wasn't as difficult as Jillian had feared; her two-hundred-dollar boots might have been overkill. But it was warm, given that most of the shade had been cut down, and she was glad she'd bathed in sunscreen and worn a hat and sunglasses.

Not the "special" sunglasses Celeste had provided. Those were bulky and unattractive. But Jillian kept them in her purse, just in case.

Conner had a hat, too, a battered, Indiana Jones–style thing. It made him look quite rakish.

Finally they came upon a huge tree lying on its side. It wasn't pine, like most of the other trees around here, which Conner had said were planted maybe thirty years ago for the express purpose of timber harvesting.

This was something left from an older, slower-growing tree that had probably been here more than a hundred years.

It was dead, that much was clear. Dead, hollow… and marked with blue paint.

"Why the hell would Greg mark this tree?" Conner wondered aloud. "It's no good as lumber."

Poking around a bit more, Conner discovered the owl nest in a hole. A few whitish feathers drifted out on the breeze.

"The female was using that hole as her roost," the ranger said.

Conner took his backpack off and rummaged around in it, producing a pair of binoculars, which he uncapped and used to scan the few trees that remained close by. No one said a word, so Jillian took a few pictures. Her camera lens was naturally drawn to Conner, whose straight back and wide shoulders pivoted this way and that as he searched, presumably for the displaced owl. She'd taken several shots before she realized what she was doing and made herself stop.

What was she going to do next, blow up prints and put them on her bedroom wall? This was Conner Blake, whom she would cheerfully have used for target practice if he ever showed up on the shooting range. Just because he was devastatingly handsome was no reason to stop hating him. After all, he'd been handsome when she'd *started* hating him.

"There," Conner finally said. "She's in that tree right there, third branch from the top on the left."

The ranger had her own pair of binoculars. "I'll be damned, she sure is. How did you spot her? She's camouflaged perfectly with the tree trunk."

"She cracked one eye open just at the right time," Conner replied. "She's watching us."

Jillian squinted at the tree, but she couldn't see anything. "May I borrow your binoculars?" she asked, surprising herself by how much she wanted to see the barn owl.

"Sure." Conner lifted the strap from around his neck and looped it around hers. His fingers brushed her neck, and she gave a delicate shiver.

"You see the tree I mean?" he asked, standing close to her and leaning his head right next to hers. He pointed.

"I think so."

"On the left side, count three branches from the top." His voice was soft, intimate. "A ball of light tan fluff right next to the trunk. She's probably hiding her face under her wing."

"I don't… Omigosh, I see it!" The bird turned its head and opened its eyes, as if it detected Jillian watching it. The round, black eyes shined from a white, heart-shaped face. "She's cute."

"You wouldn't say that if you saw her swallow a whole mouse," Conner said. "Or tear one apart to feed her babies."

"You really didn't have to tell me that." She handed him back the binoculars.

"You can't just put up a nest box and call it good," the ranger said. "Owls are fussy. Although barn owls are more tolerant of humans than most owls, it's very likely she'll go someplace else next year."

Conner seemed not to be listening. He was inspecting the stump, the fallen tree and the surrounding area. At one point he leaned over, and a silver medal of some type, suspended around his neck on a chain, fell out from under his shirt.

When he straightened the chain caught on a branch and the chain broke. The medal landed in the dirt.

"Aw, hell." Impatiently he scooped up the medal and chain and handed them to Jillian. "Can you put that in one of your hundred pockets, please?"

He was making fun of her hiking pants. Well, he could think what he liked—the pants were practical.

The medal was a Saint Christopher. She gave it a brief look before tucking it away. Conner hadn't grown up Catholic. She wondered why he would have such an object.

"We'll put the tree back up," he announced suddenly.

"Beg your pardon?" the ranger said.

"Yeah, it can be done. Get a forklift out here, maybe a winch and a truck and some strong guys. We'll drill holes and sink some dowels into the stump, maybe erect some braces—yeah, it'll work."

"That sounds like an expensive project," Jillian said.

Conner shrugged. "Gotta give Mrs. Owl back her house. And we'll reimburse the university for the equipment that was destroyed, of course."

"Really?" The ranger took off her hat, scratched her head, as if she'd never encountered someone so agreeable.

They hiked back to the road, where Conner informed the landowner that no more timber would be harvested until Conner himself had re-marked the trees to be taken—doing it right, this time. "We'll start in the area that's farthest from the owl nest, and we'll make sure not to disturb that area any more than necessary. And, like I said before, we'll compensate you for the extra trees taken above and beyond what was contracted." He took out his phone, punched a few keys, then showed the screen to Mr. Whatley. "Would that amount be acceptable to you?"

Mr. Whatley tipped his hat back. "I expect so."

"You should have a check in your hands no later than next Friday."

"What about me?" the lumberjack said. "Me and

my crew gonna sit around on our thumbs till the trees are re-marked?"

"You'll be back to work by Monday, and you'll be paid for the downtime."

Everyone nodded, and then they just stood there. They'd come fired up to do battle with Conner, yet that hadn't proved necessary. It was like a pall of anticlimax had fallen on the group.

Conner rubbed his hands together. "If that's everything, then, I've got work to do. I'll use red paint to mark the trees." He addressed the lumberjack. "Tell your team to ignore blue paint, cut red paint."

"Yes, sir, Mr. Blake." He and his men piled into an SUV, so covered in dust it was hard to tell the color, and bounced away.

Mr. Whatley and the ranger each shook Conner's hand, then they departed, as well. Soon it was just Conner, Jillian and the trees.

Conner smiled and took a deep breath.

Jillian was impressed, and damn it, that irritated her. She didn't want to feel anything positive toward her boss. *He used you,* she reminded herself. *He humiliated you. He took advantage of a homely, fourteen-year-old girl ga-ga in love with him when he was old enough to know better.*

A surge of outrage rose anew in her throat, a welcome feeling. She pulled her anger around herself like a comfortable, warm cloak, then schooled her features.

"How long will this job take?" Jillian asked.

"All weekend," he said cheerfully. "I'll get a good portion done, then I'll get someone in to finish the job—one of the veteran guys I can trust."

"Shall I extend your reservation at the motel, then?"

"No, I think I'll just camp out. There's no rain in

the forecast, so I don't really need a tent. I brought everything else."

She felt the first stirrings of alarm. Surely he didn't want her to camp out with him! She did not do camping. Hiking in the woods was already a stretch, though it hadn't turned out as horrible as she'd pictured it.

Wanting to remain professional yet still slightly frosty, she formulated her next question carefully. "What do you want me to do?"

"I'll call in some men and equipment. I need you to meet them at the main road and escort them onto the property, then show them where the owl tree is. Will you be able to find it again by yourself?"

"Yes, I remember."

"Good. Once that's taken care of…how do you feel about hanging birdhouses?"

CONNER HAD ALREADY EMPTIED one can of spray paint and was on to the second. Choosing which trees to harvest was part science, part art and part pure instinct. A healthy forest was one that encompassed many different species of tree as well as different sizes. Young trees, old trees and dead trees all provided habitat for different critters; the aim was to encourage a healthy diversity.

This land had been overharvested the first time around. Fortunately Mr. Whatley, the landowner, had seen fit to replant with a few slow-growing hardwoods in addition to the fast-growing pines. Responsible forestry took patience. You had to plan for thirty, forty, a hundred years into the future.

"Ouch!"

Conner's musings came to an abrupt halt as Jillian's voice punctuated the silence. "You okay?" he called to her. She was forty yards distant from him, on a ladder, hanging a birdhouse.

"Just hammered my thumb," she called back. "No emergency."

Conner had to admit, he was surprised by Jillian every time he turned around.

He'd expected her to congratulate him on the tidy way he'd dealt with the disaster. Problem-solving out in the field was something he was good at. But she'd had nothing to say on the matter.

Then, when he'd told her he wanted her to hang birdhouses, he'd expected a flat-out no. All this tromping around in the woods was nowhere in her job description. But she'd agreed.

He had to wonder…why? Did she need her job this badly? She certainly wasn't behaving like any assistant he'd had in the past. Maybe she simply took pride in her job. Whatever, it was a refreshing change.

The birdhouses had turned out to be unnecessary to solving the owl tree problem. But since he had a carful of them in various sizes, he figured it wouldn't hurt to hang a few to encourage the owls and woodpeckers.

Besides, if he hadn't found a job for her to do, she'd have gone back to the motel, and he had this odd desire to keep her where he could watch her.

Watching her was certainly no hardship. Even in her hiking clothes she was hot. When he'd first shown her how to hang the houses—each kind had to be a specific distance from the ground—he'd gotten an eyeful of canvas pants stretching over her rounded bottom, her soft cotton T-shirt molding to enticingly full breasts…

Probably implants, he told himself.

By the time he'd met Chandra, she'd already gone under the knife three times. After they married, she amused herself with makeovers while he traveled. He'd never known for sure whether he would recognize the woman who greeted him at the airport on his home-coming.

His body didn't seem to care how Jillian had acquired her perfect physical assets. He got hard every time he so much as looked at her. Damned inconvenient as that was, it didn't stop him from watching her, even peering at her through the binoculars as she struggled with the unfamiliar tools.

He was pretty sure she'd never climbed a ladder or hammered a nail in her life, but she didn't complain, just went after the task as best she could.

Conner had made a good start on the job of marking by the time the setting sun told him it was time to quit for the day. He loved that about the outdoors, how the earth itself set the pace. No need for watches or clocks or beeping laptops or cell phones. His didn't get a signal out here, anyway, which was fine with him.

He capped his latest can of red spray paint, put it in his backpack, and went to collect Jillian. He'd take her out for a steak dinner—she deserved it.

He stopped at the base of her ladder just as she was climbing down. "Jillian?"

"Oh!" Startled, she lost her balance and damn near fell into Conner's arms. At the last second she righted herself, and Conner was surprised at how disappointed he was. "Don't sneak up on me like that."

"Sorry." Though it was unnecessary, since she'd been climbing up and down the ladder for a couple of hours, he helped her the rest of the way down with one hand at her elbow, the other at her shoulder. All very innocent and proper, but her soft flesh, even through the cloth of her shirt, felt sexy.

"We're done for the day," he said.

"Okay." She lowered the extension ladder, and Conner couldn't help noticing that almost all of her fingernails were broken. He expected to feel some degree of amusement at her expense. It should have been funny, taking a polished city girl like Jillian and thrusting her into the woods, making her perform what was essentially manual labor.

He'd done it on purpose, he realized. He'd meant to make her uncomfortable, and clearly he had.

But he wasn't amused. He had an uneasy ball in the pit of his stomach. Why would he deliberately want to cause a perfectly nice woman discomfort? Was it because she hadn't once flirted with him? Was his ego smarting?

"If you can carry the ladder," she said, "I can get the tools and the last birdhouse. I can hang it tomorrow."

"It's okay, Jillian, you did great. I mean really—you were great today." Praising a subordinate's work was so rare for him, it actually felt weird. He'd believed his previous admins were just oversensitive, but really, he must be an awful person to work for.

"Thank you."

"I bet you've worked up an appetite. How about a steak dinner with all the trimmings? Stirrup Creek is a tiny town, but I bet there's a good steak house somewhere around here."

"No, thanks. I'd just like to get checked in and spend the evening reading. I checked out some forestry books from the company library."

Conner paused to change his grip on the ladder. She was turning down a steak dinner? To study? What had the world come to? No woman had ever turned him down when he offered a steak dinner.

He was honest enough to know that women found him good-looking. He'd known it since he was fourteen. He'd never had to try with any woman. Even Chandra, Stan Mayall's only grandchild and heir to his considerable wealth, had been the one to come to him, seduce him.

So why didn't Jillian like him?

Yes, he'd been a bit brusque with her at first, but now that he knew she was good at her job, he was being nice to her.

And she was being exactly the same as she'd been from the beginning: professional but chilly.

Listen to him. He should have been nice to her the first day he met her, regardless of her competence. He'd been a jerk to treat her like crap just because she reminded him of his ex-wife and he anticipated her being wrong for the job. She probably saw right through him. She knew she was good, she knew she'd proved her value to him, and now she knew, simply by his change of attitude, how badly he needed her.

He wished he could figure out what her game was.

"So, Jillian," he asked when they were back in the Jeep. "What are your career aspirations? Where do you want to be in five years?"

She looked at him with evident surprise, but she answered the question. "I'd like to be the assistant to a corporate CEO," she answered without hesitation. Her answer was textbook perfect for a job interview. He'd been hoping for something a bit more personal from her. "I hope that working for you will broaden my skills."

"So you see this job working out for you?"

"You're a demanding boss. But your job is interesting, and you have a strong work ethic. I can learn a lot from you."

"You think I have a strong work ethic?"

"It appears so."

"I think you just paid me a compliment."

"Merely stating facts."

"Do you not like me, or are you always this impersonal?" Now, he'd done it. He should have left things alone, quit on a high note.

"I've only been working for you a week. I haven't formed a strong opinion about whether I like you or not. But that's immaterial. Regardless of how I feel about you personally, I intend to be the best assistant I know how to be."

Which told him exactly nothing.

"You'd probably like your medal back." She extracted it from a side pocket and handed it to him.

"Thanks. Help me remember to get it fixed. My ex gave it to me because I used to travel a lot, and Saint Christopher is the patron saint of travelers."

"It means a lot to you, then."

Was that a note of disapproval in her voice? Or jealousy? "Not for the reason you think. I'm not still hung up on Chandra."

He waited for her to press him for the real reason he wore the medal, but she remained silent.

He told her anyway. Maybe if she knew more about him, she would like him. "I'm superstitious. I was on an airplane once in India. There was some very bad weather. The plane was going down. When you think you're going to die, you're apt to do just about anything. I held that medal and I prayed to Saint Christopher, even though I'm not particularly religious. I told him that if I lived, I would always wear the medal.

"The plane was about a hundred feet from the ground when suddenly the pilot pulled it up. We made a rough landing in a field, but nobody died. So I wear the medal."

As if to prove the medal had no sentimental value, he stuck it in the armrest console of the car rather than carefully packing it away.

Jillian had reserved two rooms for them at the Traveler's Rest Inn, which was the only motel in Stirrup Creek, a town that clearly didn't get a lot of tourism. It was trying to make itself appealing, though; the one-block business district had a café, a quilt shop, an antiques store, an old-time drugstore and a scrapbooking shop. The old-fashioned streetlights sported banners advertising Historic Stirrup Creek. But the town's only claim to fame was the world's shortest gold rush.

Turned out the claims of gold dust found in the creek were false.

The motel was a bit shabby, but it was clean.

Conner and Jillian had rooms next door to each other. She fitted her key into the lock and pushed open the door, switching on the light.

"Does it look okay?" Conner asked.

"Yes, it seems fine. If there's nothing else, I'll see you in the morning. What time would you like to get started?"

"Let's meet at eight o'clock for breakfast at the café. Then you can drop me off at the work site, and drive on back to Houston. Your time would be better spent, um, organizing my office."

She couldn't have faked the delighted expression that swept across her face. He'd never met anyone who loved sorting papers quite as much as Jillian did. But she quickly squelched it. "I'm happy to do that for you.

Getting organized will make both of our jobs easier. But how will you get back home?"

"Don't worry about me, I'll manage." He would borrow a vehicle from one of the loggers and get it back to him somehow.

"All right, then. Good night." She started to close the door in his face.

"Wait, Jillian…"

"Yes?"

"Nothing." He shook his head, trying to clear the cobwebs. "Nothing. Sleep well."

CHAPTER FIVE

THAT WAS WEIRD. WHAT had Conner been about to say? Maybe he had second thoughts about letting her loose unsupervised in his man cave of an office.

Oh, surely if he had something to hide, he wouldn't even think of giving her access to his office.

Jillian threw the dead bolt on her motel room door, then stripped off her sweaty, filthy clothes and headed straight for the shower.

Every muscle in her body screamed from the unaccustomed exercise. She worked out religiously at her health club, took Pilates classes and yoga, but apparently none of that rendered a body fit for climbing ladders and nailing birdhouses to the trunks of trees.

As she stood under the tiny showerhead, letting the hot water soak into her skin, she again wondered what Conner had been about to say to her.

If he'd found anything about her work lacking, she'd have popped him one. They should give her a special award, Admin of the Year or something, for putting up with his antics.

He obviously was still trying to find her limits, push her until she screamed, "Stop! No more!" But she wasn't going to give him the satisfaction. Staying employed at Mayall Lumber meant too much to her.

Although it wasn't even eight o'clock, Jillian put on her nightgown, a Victoria's Secret silk number. She had no idea why she'd packed such fancy pj's. It wasn't as though anyone but her would see them. But she had to admit it was nice to slip into something so decadently feminine after a day of wielding man-tools in the woods.

Now that her phone had a signal again, she saw that she had two messages, one from Daniel and one from Celeste. Daniel normally didn't call her unless it was something important, and she didn't blame him. Although his wife, Jamie, had always been nice to her, she wouldn't be human if she didn't want Jillian as far removed from her husband as possible.

Jillian sat on the bed, unwrapped a granola bar and munched on it while she listened to the messages. Her heart warmed as she realized both Daniel and Celeste were worried about her.

She returned Daniel's call first. "Jillian. You okay?" He sounded so concerned she almost laughed.

"Of course I'm okay. What's wrong?"

"It's just that Celeste seemed to think you'd gone off into the woods with a serial killer. Then when you didn't answer your phone all day…"

Jillian laughed. "I'm touched she was worried enough to drag you into it, but I'm fine. My new boss had a problem to deal with on a job site and he insisted I come with him."

"Your new boss is a murder suspect."

"Excuse me? I mean, I've heard some gossip, but it sounded like wild speculation to me."

"Yeah, well, I'm working angles on this end. It seems Greg Tynes took over the job Conner had before he was promoted. He and Conner never saw eye to eye, and Stan says Conner was going to fire him."

"For good reason. You should see what he did to this

forest. Clear-cut it, when he was supposed to be taking only select, mature trees."

"But he and Conner could have argued. Things could have gotten out of hand…then Conner got scared, hid the body—"

"In the trunk of his boss's car?"

"To get back at his ex-wife. Stan is her grandfather."

"No way he killed Greg." Jillian said. "And, no, I have no hard evidence of Conner's innocence. It's just my opinion."

"I don't have any concrete evidence of his guilt," Daniel countered. "It's just a theory I'm working on. But you need to be extremely careful around Conner Blake."

"Don't worry, I am." Careful in more ways than one. Today, he'd made it so easy to admire him. And admiring him was only one small step away from liking him.

She could not afford that luxury. Even if she took away the hideous history they shared, she couldn't allow herself even the smallest spark of warmth.

Jillian knew herself. Though she could be blindingly efficient, deep down she was a romantic with a tendency to develop crushes, for lack of a better word. For her, familiarity bred affection, not contempt.

So what if Conner wanted to make an owl happy? So what if he got a goofy smile on his face when he looked at an old tree? He was the enemy. *The enemy.*

She called Celeste back, too, and reassured the older woman that she hadn't been fitted with cement shoes and dropped into a lake. She filled in Celeste on the day's activities.

"Let me get this straight. You hung birdhouses all afternoon."

"Well, I was terribly slow at it. I can count on one

hand the number of times I've used a hammer. My manicure is a lost cause, I'm afraid."

"Your words say it was bad, but your tone of voice says you enjoyed it."

"Me? No. It was torture. Hell on earth." Okay, maybe it hadn't been that bad. She'd never been much of a nature girl, but she did pride herself on her ability to learn new things quickly and adapt to whatever circumstances she found herself in.

The worst part had been forcing herself to stop watching Conner as he did his tree marking thing. Once, she'd paused her own work for ten whole minutes while she watched how Conner strode through the forest, using some secret criteria to select trees for harvest while leaving others. It wasn't random, she was sure, not given the way he would sometimes stare at a tree, feel its bark and leaves, or whip out a tape measure and check the circumference of the trunk.

He was fascinating. *Jerk. Bastard.*

"Did you say something?"

Had she spoken aloud? Oops. "Just cursing a splinter."

"Did you plant the bug yet?"

"In his office. My first day on the job."

She still wasn't sure she could make herself listen to his private conversations. But she would have to get over her squeamishness if she wanted to be an investigator.

"Good girl," Celeste said. "You be careful."

"If he was going to do away with me on this trip, he's had plenty of chances. No witnesses except an owl."

"Call me when you get back to civilization. And make sure you throw the dead bolt on your motel room door."

BREAKFAST WITH CONNER had felt a little awkward. In Jillian's mind, breakfast was the most intimate meal because it was the meal you shared when you spent the night with someone.

She ate her usual yogurt and fruit while Conner tucked into a huge plate of bacon, eggs and pancakes. He also ordered a ham sandwich to go, so he could take a lunch break later.

"Are you sure that's all you want to eat?" he asked.

"Yes, I'm sure."

"No wonder you're so tiny."

She wasn't sure he'd meant it as a compliment, but she took it as one. Losing weight in high school had been torture. But after "the incident," she kept picturing what she must have looked like, running across the football field in nothing but her control-top granny panties, clutching at shreds of the wet, melted dress, dodging the sprinklers someone—probably Conner— had turned on.

She still remembered how her belly fat had jiggled with every step.

Wearing a bathing suit for swim team had been embarrassing enough, but at least the one-piece spandex had contained and covered her, and she'd been either in the water or wrapped in a towel most of the time. Plus, nobody except swimmers' parents showed up for the meets.

Her half-naked bolt for the locker room had been so, so much worse. That very day she'd vowed to lose the chubby rolls of fat that had plagued her since sixth grade, when an unfortunate addiction to frozen Snickers bars and TV combined with puberty had caused her to pile on some serious pounds.

"I haven't always been a size four." She had no idea

what would make her bring up the past. It was dangerous. Except that she still couldn't believe he didn't recognize her or at least make the connection with her name.

"Really."

"I, um, gained weight in college. The freshman fifteen." Daniel had told her to stick to the truth, but she couldn't tell him she'd been a chubby kid. It might get him to thinking.

"I would never have guessed. How did you lose the weight? Lap band?"

"No," she scoffed. More like lap *swimming*, but she couldn't tell him that, either. "The old-fashioned way, diet and exercise. My apartment building has its own work-out room." And a lap pool. "I still have a tendency to gain weight if I'm not careful."

The pool was one reason Jillian had decided to move into the downtown building Daniel owned when she'd left employment at his estate. She'd given up a certain level of luxury, including easy access to an Olympic-size pool and healthy meals prepared by Daniel's chef. She'd learned to prepare her own meals. But swimming was something she had to have.

"You must be very disciplined."

Jillian quickly changed the subject. It was foolish of her to give him hints about her former weight problem, even if the details weren't accurate. She was lucky he had such a bad memory.

Even if he figured out she was Jillybean, maybe he wouldn't fire her. A couple of punctured tires and some idle threats from when she was a teenager…big deal. Surely he could overlook her childish acts of revenge now that she'd proved herself a useful assistant.

But if she expected him to let go of the past, that

meant she had to, as well. And she wasn't prepared to do that. Maybe Conner Blake wasn't the Antichrist, but she still thought he ought to suffer for what he did to her.

Or at least feel terrible about it and apologize.

That was the worst thing about what he'd done to her. He'd expressed no remorse and he'd never apologized. He should have sent her two dozen roses and a box of chocolates so she could at least have the satisfaction of throwing it all in the trash.

Her biggest fear, she realized, was that if he remembered the incident, he still wouldn't own up to what he'd done. That he still wouldn't feel badly for humiliating a vulnerable young girl who thought she was in love with him. That he'd still think it was the funniest prank he'd ever pulled.

That cruel Conner Blake didn't jibe with the one she was getting to know, the one who honored his obligations, cherished the trees and cared about whether an owl had a place to raise her babies.

She wasn't ready to know which one was the real Conner Blake.

It was almost a relief to drop Conner and his survival gear at the job site, wish him luck and head back to civilization, though perversely, she missed his presence in the seat beside her. She was more alive when she was around him. Her body tingled, her stomach quivered about every ten seconds or so, and every muscle was tense with vigilance, lest she say or do something that might give away one of her many secrets.

She arrived back at Mayall Lumber around lunchtime. As she waited for the light to turn that would allow her to pull into the parking garage, she spotted a familiar face—a man standing on the sidewalk outside the garage, casually sipping an iced coffee drink. An employee enjoying his lunch break?

Then she placed him. It was Mark Bowen, the reporter. He'd situated himself where he could spot any Mayall employee exiting the side door on foot.

What was he trying to find out about the company?

She didn't think too hard about what she did next. When the light turned green, instead of pulling into the garage, she pulled up to the curb and rolled down the Jeep's window.

"Mark Bowen?"

He whipped off his sunglasses and approached her car. "Yeah, that's me."

"Get in."

He didn't question her motives but followed orders. "What's the deal?"

She sped off before anyone spotted her talking to the forbidden reporter. Although, come to think of it, the memo had been circulated before she started working at Mayall, so technically she shouldn't have known she wasn't supposed to talk to him.

"I'm a new hire at Mayall. I'm just curious why every employee has been forbidden from talking to you."

"So that's why everybody's ignoring me like I'm something they scraped off their shoe." Then he lowered his voice to a conspiratorial whisper, even though there was no one to overhear them. "Do you know something?"

"I don't know. I guess that depends on what you want to find out about."

"You honestly don't know?"

She didn't want to appear completely stupid. "I

thought at first it might be about the murder. But you're not a crime reporter. You write business stories."

"True. And I'm not interested in the murder per se—I'll leave that to the boys and girls at the *Chronicle*. But I would like to know what Greg Tynes was involved with before he was killed. He'd called me and set up an appointment. Said there was something going on at Mayall Lumber that was so bad, so scandalous, it would put them out of business."

"But he never got the chance to tell you," Jillian concluded.

"Right. Frankly, I'd sort of written him off as a disgruntled employee, not a genuine whistle-blower. Mayall Lumber has one of the cleanest reputations in the whole industry, and Greg was kind of…I don't know how to say it. I hate speaking ill of the dead, but he was kind of a self-important jerk."

"But now you think he really was on to something."

"Yeah. We'd set up a meeting, but he didn't show. Then I found out his body had been found in Stan Mayall's car, and I thought, maybe he'd stumbled on to something bad enough that the company CEO was willing to kill for it."

Jillian tamped down the urge to declare Stan Mayall was innocent, that he'd been framed. That was information she shouldn't logically be privy to as a newly hired clerical worker.

Instead, she played like she was merely curious. "You could be right."

"The fact I'm being stonewalled just adds fuel to the fire," Bowen said. "I don't suppose you have any idea what sort of hanky-panky your new employer is involved in, do you?"

She shook her head. "I just started this week—still trying to figure out how the computer works."

"What department are you in?"

"I'm an administrative assistant to one of the directors. Conner Blake."

Bowen's eyes lit up. "Seriously? Greg worked in your department!"

"He did?" She acted all wide-eyed and innocent. "No one talks about it."

"You're in a prime position to find out what Greg knew."

"I'm just a secretary, really. I'm sure no one would tell me anything."

"Are you kidding? Secretaries know everything." He pulled a card case from his pocket, extracted a business card and handed it to her. "If you find out anything, maybe you could give me a call. I'll keep your name out of it."

"Well, sure…if someone is doing something wrong, I wouldn't want to just turn a blind eye. But I also really need this job."

"Honey, if you help me break this story, and you end up losing your job because the company closes its doors, I'll help you find work. I know tons of personnel directors in all kinds of companies."

She tried not to bristle at being called "honey." "That's very nice of you. But don't expect much. Mostly what I do is really boring."

"Keep your eyes and ears open. You never know what your boss might let slip."

"Okay, I will." But she sure as hell wouldn't reveal anything to a reporter. "And if you find anything out, maybe you could tell me. Just between us. I'd just like to know if I'm working for a company that's doing something illegal. I don't want to be any part of that."

"Sure thing."

She doubted he was any more sincere than she was, but that was okay. She now actually had information to report to Daniel. Other than her revelation about the affair between Chandra and Greg, her daily reports had been on the dull side.

So, Greg Tynes had uncovered something dreadfully illegal that would shut down the company. If that was true, it did nothing to exonerate Stan Mayall. In fact, it gave him a stronger motive for the murder.

She couldn't help that.

What if Stan really was guilty? Jillian had only Daniel's word that the man, an old friend of his father's, was innocent. And much as she wanted to trust Daniel's instincts, his own chef had turned out to be a murderer, so Daniel wasn't infallible.

No, she had to believe Daniel was right. Stan Mayall wasn't stupid enough to kill someone and leave the body in his own car. It was an obvious frame job.

Jillian dropped the reporter off two blocks from the office—she didn't want to risk anyone seeing her fraternizing with the press. She headed straight for the cafeteria and grabbed herself a tuna sandwich and an apple, intending to dive right into Conner's office, a task she actually relished. But Letitia caught her eye and waved for her to come sit at her table.

"You're still here!" Letitia observed with something akin to awe.

"I told you Mr. Blake couldn't scare me off."

"When I didn't spot you all day yesterday, I thought for sure I'd seen the last of you."

"So who stands a chance of winning the pool so far?"

"Well, if you quit today, Iris wins."

Jillian wrinkled her nose. She didn't like Iris, the admin who'd given her such a cold reception her first day. "Iris won't win. Mr. Blake's out of the office all day today, so he couldn't possibly drive me to quit until Monday," she said with a grin.

"If you last until next Wednesday, I win. But if you make it until Friday, Ellen from Purchasing and Juan from Public Relations split the pot."

"Who guessed I'd be here the longest?" Jillian wanted to know.

Letitia consulted a list she'd put in her pocket. "Oh. That would be Mr. Blake himself. Normally the directors don't get involved in our little games, but he got wind of this one somehow."

"And how long does he think I'll last?" Jillian found herself actually holding her breath, curious to know what he really thought of his new admin.

"He gave you three whole weeks."

"Well, that's some vote of confidence," she muttered.

"It's longer than any of the other ones have lasted," Letitia said, doing her best to give Conner's guess a positive spin.

She'd last three weeks and more, even if it killed her.

Jillian wolfed down her sandwich, bade Letitia goodbye and headed upstairs to Conner's office, feeling less exuberant about cleaning up his desk than she had a few minutes ago. She set her things down in her own cubbyhole, locked her purse in her desk drawer, then used the key Conner had given her to unlock his office door.

"Oh! Excuse me—" Jillian's heart skipped a beat

in surprise as she walked in on Isaac Cuddy. What was he doing rummaging around on Conner's desk? He'd flashed a decidedly guilty look before masking the emotion.

"I thought Conner would be out until Monday."

"He is, but he sent me back early."

"Why doesn't that surprise me?" Cuddy said with a nasty tone.

Jillian stiffened her backbone and put a frost in her tone. "Can I help you with something?"

"I don't know how anyone could find anything in this pigsty Blake calls a desk. I'm looking for an invoice for some European boxwood that was felled last month. I can't do budget forecasts without accurate numbers. I tried calling Blake, but he's not answering."

Sounded like a reasonable excuse for Cuddy to be looking for something, but why had he locked the door? Did it lock automatically?

"I think I remember seeing something about that recently. If you give me a few minutes, perhaps I can find it for you." She opened the door wider, an obvious invitation for him to leave the rummaging to her.

"It's essential I have concrete numbers. Mr. Payne is waiting on those forecasts."

"Yes, Mr. Cuddy. I'll make it a priority. If I can't find it today, I'll get word to him."

Although he did head for the door, he narrowed his eyes and treated her to an up-and-down assessment that gave her the creeps. "How come you're still here?"

"I beg your pardon?"

"Just curious who you slept with to get…or keep… this job."

Jillian's temper flared, and she felt the urge to tear Cuddy a new one. No one spoke to her like that! But for her to lose her cool was exactly what he wanted. He was trying to find some way to get her fired. For whatever reason, he didn't want her around. Was it because, twice now, she'd caught him doing something furtive?

So she dug deep and found her composure. "Mr. Cuddy. That comment was highly inappropriate and grounds for sexual harassment. I suggest in the future you keep such comments to yourself."

He rolled his eyes and sauntered out of the office. "Yes, ma'am."

Jillian turned on Conner's computer and checked his email, which was now part of her job. She *had* seen correspondence about the European boxwood. Luckily for her, she had a near photographic memory, and within five minutes she found the letter and the attached invoice. She forwarded it to Cuddy along with a terse note: "This, Mr. Cuddy, is why I'm still here."

What was that guy up to? Her first thought was that he was stealing office supplies, but then she wondered if his actions might indicate something more sinister. Could he be a spy for a competing lumber company? Was that the secret Greg Tynes had died for?

Cuddy would certainly be at the top of her list of suspects.

After organizing the visible surfaces, she moved on to the desk drawers. The first one she opened held a jumble of supplies. Liquid Paper? Who used that anymore? The bottle was all dried out anyway, so she tossed it, along with several obsolete or nonworking tools.

"Hello, what's this?" She extracted a string of plastic packets containing condoms in the most lurid colors imaginable. Might this have something to do with the assistants who didn't stay very long? Did he nail them, then fire them?

Ugh, she didn't want to think why he had condoms at the office. She stuffed them to the back of the drawer and tried to forget she saw them.

She'd had enough organizing for one day, anyway. Maybe this would be a good time to retrieve whatever recordings her listening device had caught. She could see if Isaac Cuddy's ugly remarks had been preserved; it would be nice to have evidence of his harassing accusation should their conflict escalate.

Jillian retrieved the recording device from her credenza and extracted the flash memory card. Celeste had explained that it was simple enough to listen to the recordings. Just pop the memory card into her computer, put on her headphones, and open each audio file. Since the device was voice-activated, each conversation would be in a separate file.

The first conversation was between Conner and his ex-wife. She'd been trying to weasel money out of him…for a butt lift? Good Lord, Chandra couldn't be older than her early thirties. Jillian felt a little sorry for her; a woman that dependent on her youth and beauty was in for a boatload of disappointment someday.

At least Conner didn't fall for her story about a leaky roof.

Jillian squirmed in her chair when the talk got more personal. She shouldn't be listening to such an intimate conversation. She *really* didn't want to know what Conner thought of his ex-wife's butt.

Iris walked by, and Jillian quickly put her hands on the computer keyboard and pretended to be typing from a Dictaphone. But her fellow admin didn't even look her way. Jillian was invisible.

She didn't like being invisible; it reminded her way too much of high school.

Jillian was relieved when Chandra departed. But the audio file continued with a conversation between Conner and Hamilton Payne.

"How's the new secretary working out?" Payne asked. *"Is she as useless as she looks?"*

Jillian gasped, stung by his dismissive tone. He'd been so warm when he'd welcomed her to the company. In fact, he'd reminded her of Kermit the Frog. She should know by now not to trust what was on the surface.

But what Conner said next was like a slap in the face. *"...what I don't understand is why Joyce keeps pitching these pretty bits of empty-headed fluff at me, expecting things to work out."*

Empty-headed fluff? That's what he thought of her?

"What was her name? Hilary, Julia..." Payne again.

"Something like that..." God, Conner hadn't bothered to even learn his own admin's name. *"I could tell with one look she's never worked a hard day in her life."*

Payne replied, *"You need someone with brains and maturity."*

Neither of which they thought Jillian possessed, apparently. She hadn't felt this edge of humiliation since...since...well, since the last time she'd been the butt of a terrible joke, streaking across a football field in nothing but a pair of panties.

Conner was speaking again. *"...I just have a low tolerance for stupidity."*

Her eyes blurring with tears, she longed to close the offensive audio file. But she had a job to do. She gritted her teeth and kept listening. But then the file cut off on its own; it sounded as if Conner and Mr. Payne had walked away from Conner's desk.

CHAPTER SIX

As CONNER ARRIVED AT the office early on Monday morning, he felt better than he had in months. Spending a long weekend camping out, just him and the trees, had done much to restore his spirits.

Spending a few hours with his new assistant hadn't hurt anything, either. His body's involuntary physical response to her had reminded him that he was a man, one who'd been in a bitter, post-divorce funk for two years, and that was too long.

He stopped at Jillian's workstation on the way to his office. She'd arrived before him, as she had every day last week, and was already hard at work behind her computer.

"Good morning, Jillian," he said cheerfully.

Her gaze flickered up at him. "Good morning. I just put the coffee on, it'll be a few minutes."

"Ah...don't worry about the coffee. I'll get my own." On her first day he'd ordered her to bring him coffee, and she'd done so every day they'd been in the office since. But that was when he'd thought she wouldn't be around long. He needed to treat her as a professional, rather than a lackey.

"Okay," she said. But there was something a little off about her instant agreement. And her stony expression. If he didn't know better, he'd think she was furious with him. But he'd done nothing to her. Not recently.

"Are you okay?" he couldn't help asking.

"Yes, I'm fine. Did you finish the job in Stirrup Creek?"

"All done. And I have something to show you." He could have emailed her the photos, but he wanted to see her reaction. She'd loaned him her digital camera so he could take pictures of his snag resurrection project. But it was the images he'd captured yesterday that he thought she might like. He called up the first picture onto the camera's screen and handed it to her.

"What's this?"

"It's the female owl. She's checking out her renovated nest site."

"So, she stuck around?" Jillian couldn't completely disguise her interest in the owl, though she was obviously trying to.

"She watched us all day Friday as we worked to get that snag upright. She stayed away Saturday, but yesterday she came back at dawn, circled the tree a couple of times, then went inside the hollow and went to sleep."

Jillian cycled through the four photos he'd taken of the barn owl. At the last photo of the owl roosting, she grinned for all of half a second before again turning to stone. "Mission accomplished." She handed the camera back to him.

"No, you keep it. I was wondering if you could write up a little article about restoring the owl tree. It doesn't have to be perfect, someone in publicity will jazz it up. But it might make a nice human interest story for one of the industry magazines."

"Yes, I can do that. If you'll provide me with the basic facts of the engineering part—how many dowels, how long, the equipment used and so forth—I'll edit the pictures and do the rest."

"Excellent." God, how he loved the way this woman said yes. "Are you sure everything is okay?"

"Of course I'm sure."

Then why did he feel like something was missing? Or like they'd gone backward somehow? In Stirrup Creek, he'd felt her softening toward him. Well, a tiny bit, anyway. Working together toward a common goal had created the first tenuous strands of a bond, which he'd hoped to build on. She'd smiled at him a few times, he'd complimented her hard work, they'd shared a meal.

Now, it felt like she was shutting him out.

When he entered his office, he shouldn't have been shocked to see how neat and organized everything was…but that didn't stop him from clamping his hand over his mouth. Wow. He'd never seen his office looking so good. Jillian had found some stacking trays and lined them up on his credenza, labeled them neatly, and sorted all of his papers into it. She'd left one large stack on his desk of papers she thought could be disposed of, but she wanted his approval. He flicked through the whole stack in fifteen minutes. Most of it went right into the shred bin.

Even if he couldn't find something, he felt confident all he had to do was ask Jillian and she would know exactly where it was.

He'd had some misgivings about giving her his email password and telling her to deal with correspondence, but he discovered she'd handled that just as efficiently. Many routine matters she'd been able to do herself; a few others she'd written responses, but left them in the draft folder for him to tinker with or send as he saw appropriate.

She had just saved him so much time. She could probably run this whole damn company if she wanted to.

He strode back out of his office and stood in front of her desk, silently admiring the way her newly manicured nails flew over the keyboard.

After a few moments she looked up. "Yes, Conner?"

"My office looks good."

"I hope you'll find it easier to work there, too."

"I'm sure I will."

Ham chose that moment to stroll by. "Good morning, Conner. And...Jillian, right?"

Conner hid a smile. He knew damn well what her name was.

"Yes, Mr. Payne." She smiled at him, but the smile lacked warmth.

"How are things working out?"

"Just fine, thank you for asking."

"More than fine," Conner added, wanting Ham to know they'd misjudged her. "Jillian is incredibly organized. You should see my desk."

"Is that so? Do you think you could spare her for a bit? I have a special project she might be ideally suited to."

Was Ham trying to steal his assistant? If so, what could he do about it? He wanted to say, "No, I need her!" Instead he managed a weak smile. "What kind of project?"

"Planning the company party."

Conner recoiled. That was an awful job. Normally Stan's assistant did all the planning, but when Stan was arrested, she'd been so upset she took an extended leave, and no one wanted to step into her shoes.

"I'd love to," Jillian said before he could warn her not to. "I'm a very good party planner." Somehow, she didn't make that sound like bragging; she was just stating facts.

"Great!" Ham rubbed his hands together. "Every year, Mayall Lumber has a birthday party in late September. We've been doing it for almost a hundred years."

Jillian started taking notes in a steno pad. "Is it appropriate to have a party?" she asked. "Given the current circumstances."

"Not only appropriate, but essential," Ham said. "We have to keep the employees' morale up."

"Okay. Is there a particular caterer you use, or a certain venue? How many people do you expect? Do you invite clients or is it strictly employees? Are families included?"

"You know who can help you with this?" Ham said. "Isaac Cuddy's wife, Ariel. She's always heavily involved with the party. You'll like her."

"I'll give her a call," Jillian said coolly. "But I don't want to neglect tasks I'm doing for Conner."

Conner was grateful for that small crumb. He didn't want to give her up to other people's tasks and agendas; he liked having her at his beck and call. He liked knowing she was right around the corner, ready and willing to do his bidding.

Not like most women, that was for sure.

"Are you sure you're okay with this?" Conner couldn't help asking after Ham had walked away.

"If Mr. Payne wants me to plan the party, then I'll do it. It's perfectly fine."

"Okay." He shrugged and retreated to his office.

It had been a long time since he'd worried about making someone happy. When he and Chandra had first married, after a whirlwind courtship and a crazy-fast but extravagant wedding, he'd devoted almost all of his energy to trying to make her happy. She wanted

a house in the suburbs, they'd buy a house in the suburbs. She resented his frequent business trips, so he
acquiesced when Stan moved him into a desk job, then
the director's job.

Conner had dressed to please her. Cut his hair the
way she liked. Yet nothing he did seemed to make her
happy. The more he tried, the more dissatisfied she'd
become.

His interest in keeping Jillian happy, or at least not
driving her away, wasn't the same, he argued to himself. Doing whatever it took to keep her as his assistant
was merely a sound business decision.

Then why did he feel his heart lift every time she
even thought about smiling? And why was he so preoc-
cupied at night, fantasizing about how he could make
her happy in more ways than one?

He shook his head. Time to get back to work. He
checked his email and opened one from the manager
of a sawmill in Tuscaloosa, Mississippi, Bob Bellaire,
a man whose name Conner had found in Greg's list
of email contacts. Conner had written to every one of
those contacts, hoping to find someone who could tell
him what Greg had been up to.

"All I know is, your man promised me a load of
Grade A pine at a heckuva deal, then it never showed
up."

Conner forwarded the email to Ham, who was di-
rector of sales in addition to his temporary CEO duties.
"Is this one of our customers?" he asked Ham. "Or was
Greg freelancing?"

Three minutes after he hit the send button, Conner's
phone rang. It was Ham. "I'm glad you called this to
my attention," he said. "Bellaire is one of our newer

customers. His order got lost in the confusion. I'll take care of him."

Conner was disappointed; he'd thought he'd found an anomaly, but it was just an oversight. He opened another email, from a Brazilian landowner. Conner had been checking up on Greg's international jobs to see if he'd overharvested anywhere else. The original email had been in Portuguese; his computer had translated it to English, so it was a bit rough, but one sentence made perfect sense: "I already gave this information to your inspector Bowen. I suggest you contact him."

Inspector Bowen? Was he one of the guys from the International Forest Stewardship Council, the watchdog of world timber harvesting? If so, Greg's irresponsible actions may have landed the company into a heap of trouble.

He sent the email to a translator he knew so he could actually understand what the Brazilian man had tried to tell him.

"ALL RIGHT, THEN, SEE YOU tomorrow." Jillian hung up the phone, looking forward to her shopping expedition with Ariel Cuddy. She knew she shouldn't be so excited about planning the company party. She had a business degree from Dartmouth, and she was an aspiring Project Justice investigator.

But Ham had told her, confidentially, that he thought the party planning would give her a chance to mix and mingle with all of the employees, get to know them, maybe pick up some useful information.

That made it okay, she decided. Besides, she *loved* planning parties. It had been one of her primary duties as Daniel's assistant. He was constantly entertaining, whether hosting an intimate dinner, meeting with the executive board of Logan Oil or throwing a huge bash for hundreds of people.

Jillian had always been at the center of it—creating a theme, working with the chef on the menu, buying or commissioning decorations, making each guest feel special and welcome.

As a party guest, she sometimes felt awkward or out of place, not knowing who to talk to—or who might want to talk to her. Shades of high school. But as a hostess, she had a role to fill, duties to attend to. She was always busy, her hands never idle.

Plus, the company party gave her an excuse to put some distance between herself and Conner.

It had taken every ounce of control she'd possessed this morning not to fling her outrage at him. *Empty-headed fluff! Let me just show you how much damage a piece of fluff can do.*

Likewise, she'd also resisted the childish urge to reply to emails he'd receive with strings of obscenities, the online version of slashing his tires.

But she was better than that. She wasn't the same insecure girl she'd been a dozen years ago. She knew her worth—on her good days, anyway. She was a valued employee of Project Justice with an important job to do. It didn't matter what Conner thought of her. As soon as she found a way to prove Stan Mayall's innocence, she would walk out of this damn office without a backward glance and leave Conner high and dry without giving notice, without training a new assistant.

Let him find out just how much work his supposedly brainless fluff did around here.

Planning a party would give her something else to focus on, extracting information from her fellow employees as well as the executives' wives, who were traditionally included in the party planning. Maybe Jillian could gain their trust, be brought into their inner circle, and get them to dish what terrible, illicit activities were going on.

Ariel couldn't have been nicer. She'd expressed surprise and pleasure that the annual party—which had been held every year since 1923, without fail—wouldn't fall by the wayside in light of Stan Mayall's unfortunate incarceration. She'd sounded honored that Jillian sought her knowledge and opinions.

Jillian had already researched what had been done during previous years' parties. The company had thrown everything from grand costume balls to weekend beach retreats in good years, to simple luncheons and potluck dinners in years when budgets were smaller.

Jillian didn't yet know what her budget would be, but even if it was generous, she thought something simple and homespun would be appropriate this year. She was jotting down some ideas when Conner came out of his office.

She steeled herself to maintain her pleasant, professional facade when all she really wanted to do was smack him.

"I'm headed to the board meeting. Wish me luck."

"What do you need luck for?"

"I'm going to have to confess about the money I spent in Stirrup Creek. I didn't get prior approval. If I can't get it squeezed into the budget somewhere, it'll come out of my paycheck."

"Good luck then," she said, but then added, "I'm sure they'll understand. What you did wasn't only good for the client and the environment, it was good for the company."

"Sometimes the board can get very focused on the bottom line. Plus, the original problem falls into my lap. I was Greg's boss, therefore his mistakes are mine."

"They'll get it," she assured him. She hadn't intended to offer him encouragement. But she had a terrible time staying angry at him when she remembered how he'd handled the problem in East Texas.

Her mother had told her that eavesdropping often led to hearing things you rather wished you hadn't. Now she'd discovered firsthand how true that was. People say awful things behind your back that they would never say to your face.

Just imagine if he heard some of the things I've said about him! Even worse, the things she'd thought.

Come to think of it, he did hear a few choice words she'd had for him back in high school. She'd made sure Jeff told Conner exactly what she thought of him.

She actually grinned, recalling the string of epithets she'd spent hours cobbling together, then making Jeff repeat it word for word to his rat-bastard friend.

The grin shocked her. It wasn't funny. Nothing was funny about the pain of a fourteen-year-old girl whose spirit had been crushed.

She wasn't fourteen anymore. She was a dedicated professional intent on becoming a Project Justice investigator. Emotions, negative or positive, had nothing to do with the job at hand. She needed to forget about what happened in high school.

That thought shocked her, too.

She had more important things to do than wage psychological battle within herself. The directors were at a board meeting; that meant they were out of the way, and she could do a little snooping. She knew exactly which executive she would start with, too: Isaac Cuddy.

A guy who stole office supplies might be guilty of something grander, she reasoned. Plus, she just couldn't stand the guy. He'd been rude as hell to her.

She had the perfect excuse for snooping, too, in the unlikely event she got caught. Ariel Cuddy had said her husband, the budget director, would know the amount of money allocated to the party. If anyone happened to see her in or near Isaac Cuddy's office, she could claim she'd gone looking for that elusive number.

Iris, Cuddy's admin, was gone for the day. Her computer was turned off, her printer covered, her lights darkened.

Jillian tapped on Isaac's door. Nothing. She tried the knob, but it was locked.

However, she wasn't willing to give up. She'd seen Iris locking a bunch of keys in her desk drawer. Desks were pretty easy to jimmy; she'd gotten very good at breaking into her dad's desk as a kid, to retrieve the *Breath of Fire* CD he hid from her and Jeff when he thought they needed a break from video games.

Iris's old birchwood desk, though beautifully maintained, had a lock a monkey could defeat. Jillian had it open in seconds, and there were the keys.

Her heart thumping, she quickly found the key to Isaac's office door and slid it into the lock. It snicked open.

She paused, trying to decide whether she was doing the right thing. Daniel would say no. But it was Celeste's voice in her head that screamed the loudest, *Do it! Take the initiative. No one is going to give anything to you, you have to take it.*

What the hell, she was good at talking her way into and out of situations. She opened the door.

Isaac Cuddy's office was tidy, as you might expect

an accountant's office to be, but he had nice furniture, even more spectacular then Conner's. She'd grown up around expensive furnishings, and she'd be willing to bet the desk was genuine Regency period, made in England.

She began her search at Isaac's desk, not quite sure what she was looking for. She saw some papers related to 401(k) retirement funds. Curious what the top brass might be investing for the future, she couldn't resist looking.

Was Isaac robbing the pension fund? That sort of criminal activity was all the rage these days. But she didn't see anything that sent up a red flag.

She was a little surprised by how small the projected pensions were. Then again, she'd been spoiled, working for Daniel, who offered salaries and benefits well above the norm.

What else might indicate criminal activity—a second set of books, large stashes of cash?

A couple of boxes shoved under a table in the corner caught her eye, mostly because the rest of the office was so neat. One contained a high-end labeling machine; the other, a heavy-duty paper cutter. What would Isaac be doing with those? The machines were equipment a clerical person would use; she couldn't imagine the budget director labeling his own files or cutting up paper.

He's stealing them. It made sense that a thief might take pieces of equipment that were shared from department to department by clerical workers who came and went. If someone realized the stuff was missing, a recently departed secretary could be blamed, or everyone could just assume it would turn up.

She doubted Greg Tynes died to hide this secret. He

wouldn't know anything about office supplies, and that wasn't the sort of story a reporter like Mark Bowen would care anything about. It was a little bit juicy that a company director was a petty thief, but hardly something that would bring down the whole corporation.

She lifted up Isaac's mouse pad; people still hid their passwords there despite security warnings. She found no secretly cached slips of paper. But when she flipped it all the way over, she found a list of words and phrases written in ballpoint ink on the rubberized surface. She quickly committed them to memory.

Jillian's stomach tightened, telling her she'd been in here long enough. She was about to tiptoe out when the door burst open without warning.

Her heart stopped beating, and for a moment she thought she was going to pass out from sheer terror. Conner Blake stood in the doorway, looking like Thor himself ready to hurl thunderbolts at her.

He stepped inside and closed the door. "What the hell are you doing in here?"

"Oh, Conner, you startled me. I was hoping Mr. Cuddy could give me the budget for the office party. I talked to Ariel, she's really nice. She said her husband would know—"

"You were in here alone, with the door closed. Drop the dumb-blonde act, Jillian. You might be able to fool some people, but I happen to know you're highly intelligent. So I'll repeat myself. What the *hell* are you doing in Cuddy's office?"

Since her original cover story hadn't worked at all, Jillian went on the offensive. "What did *you* come in here for? You didn't even knock."

"I needed something from my office for the meeting. Since I was headed this way, Cuddy asked me if I'd get his…his phone."

Jillian couldn't believe this. Conner was lying, too! He had no more business in here than she did. Cuddy would have known his office door was locked.

"I don't see his phone," Jillian said casually.

"Guess he didn't forget it after all. Probably he put it in the wrong pocket or something."

"Is that the story you're going to stick with?"

He crossed his arms. "Mine's better than yours."

For the span of a few heartbeats they stared at each other, challenging.

A rattling of the office doorknob roused both of them out of the trance. Conner's eyes widened with apprehension. "Follow my lead." Without warning he wrapped his arms around her and planted his mouth firmly on hers.

CHAPTER SEVEN

JILLIAN FORGOT TO BE AFRAID. She forgot why she'd been in Cuddy's office in the first place. In fact, she forgot where she was and almost who she was.

Nothing existed except what she and Conner created together with that steamy kiss.

His mouth was firm, but gentle, too. With one arm he pulled her so close she could feel every contour of his body against hers; his other hand supported the back of her head so he could deepen the kiss, tunneling his fingers through her hair.

Jillian thought her heart was going to beat right out of her chest. Her blood ran suddenly hot and her hands and feet went numb.

Conner Blake was kissing her.

Every adolescent fantasy she had so ruthlessly squelched years ago now burst from the dark lockbox in her mind. She wanted to laugh and cry at the same time. She wanted to push him away and slap him even as she wanted to feel his tongue in her mouth, his hands on her breasts.

She inhaled sharply, taking in the clean, tangy scent of his skin.

For the second time in as many minutes, the door burst open. "What the hell is going on in here?"

Conner broke the kiss and gently pushed Jillian away

from him. "Isaac. What are you doing here? I thought the meeting would go on awhile longer."

"Obviously." Isaac Cuddy was the picture of outrage. "What are you doing in my office? I mean, I know what you're doing, but..."

"We're sorry, Mr. Cuddy," Jillian said. "But the sofa in Conner's office is hard as a rock."

"Your sofa is a lot more comfortable," Conner agreed. Had he actually winked at her, just now?

Cuddy opened his door wide and stood to the side. He aimed a particularly disturbing leer at Jillian. "I knew I was right about you. Now get out! And do *not* come into my office again without an invitation."

"Yes, sir, Mr. Cuddy," Jillian said, scurrying for the door. Conner whispered something hurriedly to Cuddy, then joined her in the escape, placing a proprietary hand around her waist as they made their way to Conner's office.

Conner closed and locked the door. "That was close."

Jillian couldn't have spoken just then if her life depended on it. She was still reeling from the kiss, not to mention getting caught snooping not just once, but twice.

She was dizzy. Wobbling to the nearest chair, she fell into it and put her face in her hands. She was falling apart—she had to get hold of herself. How was she going to resume any sort of normal behavior after what had just happened?

"You okay, Jillybean?" Conner asked solicitously.

Oh, no, she was not okay, and she didn't think she could tolerate Conner being kind to—

Suddenly her thoughts sharpened. "What did you just call me?"

"Oh, um...Jillybean. A high school friend had a sister named Jilly and I used to call her that because she was about the size and shape of…" Now he was staring at her, saying nothing as a dawning horror crept over his face.

He came closer, making her feel like a squirming butterfly pinned to a board. But she couldn't escape his penetrating gaze, couldn't make herself move.

He'd called her Jillybean, but clearly he hadn't known. Not until this moment.

"You're her." Then a big grin split his face. "Jillybean, it is you! I haven't seen you since…since… Oh, crap." His smile slid away.

"Since your stupid paper dress melted right off my body in front of hundreds of people!" All at once she had no trouble thinking what to do. *Oh, crap,* indeed. She slapped him hard enough to loosen a filling or two.

Her hand stung, but nothing had ever felt as good as that slap. Conner recoiled, his own hand going to the side of his face as if he couldn't believe what she'd just done.

She almost couldn't believe it, either. Holy cow, she'd just assaulted her boss. The jig was up. She'd blown it, and now she'd have to go crawling back to Daniel and admit that her stupid temper had gotten her fired.

That was assuming Daniel didn't have to bail her out of jail.

She waited, trying to control her crazy gasping and machine-gun heartbeat. When he said nothing, she went on the offensive. "If you're going to fire me, I wish you'd get on with it."

"Fire you?" He shook his head. "Oh, no, I don't think so. I just risked my job to *keep* you from getting fired.

But I also practically molested you. If getting slapped is the only consequence, I'll consider myself lucky."

He thought she'd slapped him because of the kiss? The man was utterly clueless. That was no garden-variety slap; that was a blow born of thirteen years of outrage, simmering on a back burner. It was a strike in the name of all awkward teenagers everywhere who'd been laughed at, embarrassed, humiliated and worst of all, dismissed.

Obviously the kiss meant nothing to him. Her world had turned itself inside out, but to him it had been a means to an end, nothing more.

Still, she could salvage her own situation, if she pulled her mind out of the vortex it had flown into.

"Why would you risk your own neck to save mine?" she asked.

He raised one eyebrow. "You don't know?"

Again her foolish heart skipped a few beats. Until he answered.

"You're a very good assistant. I can't risk losing you."

Daniel used to tell her all the time how valuable she was to him, how he couldn't get by without her, and she had cherished every morsel of praise he'd thrown her way, hoping it would lead to something more.

She'd learned her lesson about that. Drawing on all of her reserve, she resumed her mantle of cool efficiency. "I'm glad to be helpful."

"Now, you want to tell me the real reason you were in Cuddy's office?"

"He's stealing office supplies." Brilliant! She should have thought of this before. "I've twice seen him exiting the supply closet with an armload of stuff he clearly didn't need to perform his job, but I wanted to be sure.

He's got a label maker and a paper cutter stashed in there. I bet he's selling them on eBay."

Conner didn't react the way she'd hoped. "Isaac Cuddy is pulling six figures. Why would he risk his job to earn a few bucks with pilfered office supplies?"

"Because he can? I don't know. Some thieves steal for the thrill of getting away with something, or screwing the company they work for."

Conner still looked bewildered. "Why do you care if he's stealing? It doesn't affect you."

"Because he's a creep who's a threat to my job," she said hotly. "When I arrived back at the office on Friday, I found him in here rummaging around in the papers on your desk."

Conner's eyes narrowed. "You should have told me."

"He made some extremely suggestive comments and I threatened him with sexual harassment charges—"

"He did *what?*"

"He implied that I had gotten or kept my job through sexual favors. His suspicions are now confirmed, thanks to you."

"That rat bastard."

"I thought if I had something on him, I could protect myself."

"I'll protect you," he said in his best white knight voice. "You don't want to cross Isaac Cuddy. The guy is ruthless. He'll grind you under his heel. If he says 'boo' to you, I want you to tell me. Don't go taking matters into your own hands."

"I will." Feeling as if one more moment in Conner's presence was going to make her heart explode, she tried to escape, but he blocked her path.

"You really are Jilly Baxter? Yes, yes, I can see it

now. The eyes are the same. I remember those pretty blue eyes."

She narrowed those eyes at him. "You never noticed anything about me. Other than I was the right shape for your paper dress, which would have fit well on a barrel."

"I did so notice you. But something's different—"

Jillian barked out a laugh. "Everything's different."

He snapped his fingers. "Your nose."

"I broke my nose on a diving board, and this is how it came out after the plastic surgeon got done with it, okay?"

"That's right, you were a really good swimmer."

"I wasn't good. I never won any medals at the swim meets. I just liked it."

"I seem to remember a race we had in your pool. Diving for pennies in the deep end. You almost beat me!"

"I was good at holding my breath," she said modestly.

"Do you still swim?"

"I swim laps for exercise. Now may I get back to—"

"How's Jeff doing? Last I heard he was working for some software company. Bet he's married with a bunch of kids."

"He designs games. Doing very well. Still single."

"And your parents?"

"They're doing great. And yours?" Years of proper etiquette pounded into her brain prompted her to ask.

"Both fine. Dad was awarded a big prize last year for his work on biofuels. Mom's still active with the Red Cross and that Labrador retriever rescue group."

Jillian actually smiled. "I remember all those dogs she had. Her foster children."

"Hey, we should get our families together. Maybe over the—"

"No, that's just not possible."

"Why not?"

"Are you crazy? My father would shoot you on sight. You publicly humiliated his little girl, and he has a memory like an elephant. Now, if we're done with Old Home Week, can I please get back to work?"

"Sure, of course."

Conner let her go, hoping she didn't see his own roiling emotions. Maybe bringing up the past wasn't the best way to get on Jillian's good side. He'd felt a simple desire to connect through good times they'd shared as kids. But Jillian obviously didn't want to be reminded of those times.

Just how miserable had he made her, that even her dad had wanted revenge?

Hell, he had to get his mind off her. His quest to prove Stan's innocence should be occupying his full attention.

During his off-hours he'd been talking to Greg Tynes's family, friends, enemies and ex-girlfriends. None of them had struck him as a likely suspect, but his grieving sister had told him that Greg was scared. He'd seen something, or knew something, that was bad enough to get him killed. And it involved his work.

That wasn't much to go on, but Stan had given him keys to every door in the building and told him to do whatever was necessary to find out who had killed Greg Tynes. Now, if Conner could just figure out who in the company had dealings with Greg, he'd know where to focus his attention. That was why Conner had wanted to search Cuddy's office. The guy was a weasel. It was easy to picture him involved in something bad, and threatening Greg. Maybe even killing him.

Conner supposed he had Jillian to thank that he hadn't gotten caught snooping.

He touched his fingers to his lips as he remembered the kiss. What a surprise *that* had been. He'd hoped Jillian would play along, but he'd never expected her to respond to his touch. Prickly, cold Jillian was a white-hot inferno beneath her icy exterior, just waiting for a man's touch to breathe life into the fire.

She hadn't been faking it, either. He'd seen her nipples harden to small peaks underneath her thin sweater. He'd seen her pupils dilate with desire, felt her skin heat and her breathing accelerate. Maybe those physiological reactions had been from fear of getting caught, rather than desire, but he didn't think so.

All this time, had she felt the same sexual pull as he had? If so, she'd hidden it pretty well, but the cat was out of the bag now.

He still had a hard time believing this beautiful, slender, graceful creature was his old buddy Jeff's kid sister. He'd always thought of her as a clever little thing, quick with a smart comeback. He'd known she had a crush on him, too—at least until the science fair. If someone had told him then that he would someday want to make love to her, he'd have labeled them crazy.

He let himself fantasize about taking her to his bed for all of about ten seconds before reality fell on his head. She was his admin. If he slept with her, he'd be no better than Cuddy. All this company needed was a sexual harassment lawsuit.

He couldn't afford to get distracted by a woman, any woman, no matter how provocative. He'd made a reservation today for a flight to Jakarta. The trip was only six weeks away. By then, he intended to have cleared Stan's name, discovered Greg's murderer, and recruited someone to replace him as Director of Timber Operations. The rain forest called to him.

JILLIAN HAD NEVER BEEN to Celeste's house before. They'd met a few times outside of work, but they'd always gone to some public place close to the office.

She was pleased and grateful Celeste had taken such an interest in her and her career. Most people accepted Celeste for what was on the surface—the outrageous clothes, the rough-as-burlap attitude and a certain lack of flexibility in upholding what she saw as her responsibilities.

But Jillian had seen a side to Celeste few others had, a soft center beneath that jawbreaker exterior. Daniel had hired her for a reason other than to scare visitors. She'd been a very good cop, he'd told Jillian; an expert with weapons, a keen judge of character, and a vast repository of knowledge about Houston in general and its police department in particular.

Maybe because Jillian respected her for her role as a trailblazer for women in law enforcement, Celeste had let down her guard in front of Jillian, allowing her to see snippets of the woman she'd once been, before she'd adopted her crotchety-senior facade.

Her home was remarkably ordinary, given how eccentric Celeste appeared otherwise. It was a tract house in the suburb of Alief; Celeste had bought it thirty years ago, when the subdivision was brand-new.

"The yard was nothing but dirt and spindly little twig trees," she explained as she showed Jillian around. Now the house was shaded by gorgeous, mature trees, the lawn a carpet of cool St. Augustine grass. Cheerful petunias lined the driveway while lush azaleas clustered around the front porch.

Inside, the decor was eclectic, an odd mix of antiques and contemporary of no particular style, but it seemed to work. Each room was painted a different color—olive-green in the entryway, dark gold in the living room, vibrant red in the kitchen. The fireplace mantel was crowded with photographs, primarily of Celeste's great-nephew, whom Jillian had met at a party that summer at Daniel's house.

It all looked so normal that Jillian wondered if the eccentric persona Celeste projected at work was her own private joke, and in her home life she was totally normal.

In the backyard, she had her vegetable garden. Though it was late in the year, her tomato vines were still producing. "Be sure to take a few tomatoes home with you," Celeste said.

"Love to." Jillian wasn't much of a cook, but she did like salads. "I really appreciate the invitation to dinner. Working undercover is a lot more complicated than I ever guessed. I could use some advice."

"I'll help if I can." Celeste poured them each a generous goblet of white wine; they sat in the shade on the patio while their dinner finished baking. "If you spot any rabbits going near my squash, let me know. This is the time of day they come out."

Jillian realized her friend had an enormous handgun—a Glock, just like the one Jillian had been practicing with on the shooting range last weekend—lying on the glass-top table next to her chair.

"You don't actually kill the rabbits, do you?" she asked with some alarm.

"No, they don't taste very good. I just scare the stuffing out of them."

Jillian wondered if Celeste had shot and eaten a rabbit in the past, or whether she'd just *heard* they tasted bad. But she didn't ask.

"I really had no idea you were so domestic, Celeste," she said. "A sweet house in the suburbs, a garden, and you cook well, judging from the smells coming from the kitchen."

"Just because I'm a career girl doesn't mean I don't want a nice home and a hot meal at the end of a long day. When you risk your life every day, a safe haven is important."

"Did you ever regret choosing career over, you know, husband, kids, that sort of thing?"

"What makes you think I chose one over the other?"

Jillian realized she'd made a conversational misstep. "I'm sorry. I didn't realize you'd ever— It's just that you never mention— I just assumed you decided to devote yourself a hundred percent to law enforcement."

"I was never married. But that doesn't mean I chose my career over marriage. I always thought I would do both." Her eyes misted over, and she seemed to be far in the past. "In the 1960s, some careers were opening up to women, but men still expected you to quit working when you got married. I always made it clear I intended to keep my job. That didn't fly with…some men."

"Any man in particular?"

Celeste flashed a sly smile. "I thought we were here to talk about you."

"I'm interested in how you managed your role as a woman in law enforcement. I could learn so much from you."

"You don't want to take the route I did," Celeste

said firmly. "Honestly, you don't." There seemed to be a world of hurt in her advice. Jillian wanted to know more, but Celeste had closed the door.

Celeste topped off her wine. "So what's going on with your case? Have you discovered anything juicy?"

"So far I've managed to uncover an office-supply thief and overhear some rather unpleasant comments about myself."

"How are you getting along with your boss?"

"Horribly! I don't know how I can stand another minute working for him, but I know I have to. The only good thing is that Hamilton Payne, the CEO, arranged it so I could plan the company party. That way I have an excuse for talking to everybody and being all over the building."

"At least party planning is something you're good at." Celeste clamped a hand over her mouth. "Oh, that came out wrong. You're good at many things."

"In all honesty, I'm looking forward to planning the party. I'll be working with some of the executives' wives, and I'm hoping they'll drop some good gossip. I'll be spending less time with Conner, too." She ought to feel good about that, but she was a little bit sad that Conner hadn't fought harder to keep her working exclusively for him.

"Oh, dear." Celeste suddenly looked so horrified, Jillian was worried she was having a heart attack or something.

"Oh, dear, what?"

"You've fallen for him, haven't you?"

"The ogre? No! He's a horrible, sexist beast who only treats me with the barest hint of civility because he's realized how much he needs me. I hate him!"

Celeste just shook her head. "Exactly as I thought."

Jillian followed her inside. "No, really, Celeste. Just because I had a little thing for Daniel doesn't mean I'll make a habit of falling for every guy I work for. Conner Blake is a jerk."

She realized she was babbling, protesting way too much. Celeste had seen through Jillian instantly. How much did she give away? She'd always thought herself adept at hiding her feelings. Either Celeste was extraordinarily perceptive, or Jillian wasn't as good as she thought she was.

"I'm only going to say this once," Celeste said. "If you make a fool of yourself over your boss, no one will ever take you seriously."

"I know that. I know." Thank goodness she hadn't confessed the kiss to Celeste, who would go nuts.

In the kitchen, Celeste opened the oven and peered at the casserole dish there. "I think these are done."

"It smells terrific." Jillian was glad to move on to a new topic of conversation. "Is it chicken?"

"No, frog legs. I went frog gigging last night at the golf course. Got some nice fat ones."

Jillian's stomach turned a somersault. So much for thinking Celeste lived a normal home life.

JILLIAN FOUND IT DIFFICULT to believe Ariel Cuddy was married to such a schmuck. For one thing, Ariel was about fifteen years younger than Isaac.

And she was beautiful—not trophy-wife beautiful, more like the wholesome girl next door. She and Isaac had been married eight years, they had a six-year-old son, and by all counts Ariel was deliriously happy with him.

Either she didn't know about her husband's crimes, or she chose to turn a blind eye to his faults.

"I just love planning a party," Ariel enthused as they wandered the aisles of the local Savers Party Outlet with their lists in hand. At the party outlet, you didn't have to bother with pushing a cart around. You just scanned the bar code of anything you wanted, paid for it, and the store would deliver it at the time and place you wanted. "Especially with someone who knows how to spend money. Of course it's terrible about Stan being in jail, but honestly, his wife is such a penny-pincher. She'll drive to ten stores just to save three cents on paper plates."

"We do have to stay within budget," Jillian reminded Ariel. She'd finally gotten the budget from Isaac, and the spending limit had shocked her. But Isaac had hemmed and hawed about the recession and cutbacks, plus the losses he anticipated due to their CEO being in prison, and she'd immediately backed off, grateful she'd been given any budget at all.

It was only a fraction of the money she'd spent on Daniel's parties, but she wasn't planning on ice sculptures or a fireworks display. She and Ariel had decided on an old-fashioned potluck picnic. For a venue, they'd chosen the company's original mill site, which was now a historical park a couple of hours' drive from the office. Buses would ferry the employees and their families.

The company would provide various barbecued meats as well as drinks. Joyce's husband had volunteered to scare up several propane grills and organize the grilling. There would be games like lawn bowling and croquet, kite-flying, pony rides and face-painting for the kids, and gift cards for prizes.

"One year, Stan donated a car as a prize," Ariel re-marked as she scanned some festive paper tablecloths. "Those were the days."

"Times are leaner right now," Jillian said. "But really, this party should be about standing together. Strengthening relationships. Being grateful for the things we do have."

"Of course. But you forgot getting drunk." They'd just cruised into the liquor section. "I've discovered that partygoers will forgive you anything so long as the liquor flows."

"Good point. We'll need a bartender."

"My brother will do it," Ariel said. "He's good and he works cheap." She made a note to call him. "Oh, I just thought of something. We need to send a special invitation to Chandra. Could we maybe spring for a limo?"

"She's Conner's ex-wife," Jillian pointed out. "Won't it be a bit awkward, having her there?"

"Awkward or not, we have to include her. I hate thinking about this, but at some point, perhaps in the not-too-distant future, Chandra will *own* Mayall Lumber."

Jillian skidded to a stop. "What? Really?"

"Stan owns fifty-one percent of the company. Chandra is his only heir—her father, Stan's only child, died years ago."

"Does she know anything about running a company?"

"Doubtful. And knowing her, she won't do something smart, like hiring Isaac to run the company for her. She'll either name herself CEO, pay herself an exorbitant salary and run the company into the ground, or she'll put it on the auction block. Either way...let's just say, this is probably the last company party."

Why hadn't Jillian seen it before? Chandra was the perfect suspect. She had a helluva motive for getting rid of her grandfather. Jillian already knew Chandra was hurting for money, that she couldn't come up with the cash for her desired butt lift. Maybe her whole reason for getting involved in a clandestine affair with Greg was to kill him and frame Stan.

Also…very interesting that Isaac thought *he* should be named CEO. Maybe he and Chandra were in cahoots. He helps her frame Stan for murder, and in return she names him CEO. *Someone* had to hoist that heavy dead body into Stan's trunk.

Better than that modest pension Isaac would otherwise get.

Jillian couldn't wait to tell Daniel of her new insight.

"I don't know about a limo," Jillian said, "but we can certainly spring for a nice car and driver to pick her up and bring her to the picnic."

"Whatever you do, remember she might be the one who has to approve your next raise. Oh, and Conner probably won't come anyway. He avoids stuff like that since the divorce."

They went a little wild in the liquor department, but the prices were shockingly low, not like what Daniel spent on his Crown Royal, Grey Goose and Dom Pérignon.

Next they headed into the cleaning-supply section. "We'll need garbage bags," Ariel said. "Oh, and I need to pick up a few things for myself. I'll pay for them separately, if that's okay."

"Sure, no problem."

They scanned a box of heavy-duty garbage bags, then Ariel scanned four large bottles of bleach.

What the hell did she need that much bleach for? Was she running a laundry business on the side?

Or…bleach could be used to clean up blood. Jillian had learned that in her crime scene investigation class. Greg Tynes had been killed at some unknown location and dumped in Stan's trunk. Maybe the location was the Cuddy home?

Jillian pulled her head out of party mode. This was her prime chance to pump Ariel for gossip; she'd already opened up about Stan's wife being a penny-pincher and Chandra being Stan's heir.

"So you really think Chandra will take over the company?"

"If she does, and Isaac isn't named CEO, he's taking early retirement. Thank goodness he's saved up a healthy nest egg. I don't know how he does it on his salary."

He rips off the company, that's how. Jillian wondered just how big of a nest egg. Could Isaac retire on the proceeds from pilfered pens and pads of paper?

Jillian had been playing around with the list of passwords she'd seen in Isaac's office. She hadn't found an eBay store, but she'd hacked into his bank account. He had thousands of dollars transferring from somewhere into a separate checking account every month. Maybe it was from perfectly legal investments…or maybe the money was coming from his illicit sales.

After paying for their purchases and scheduling delivery, Ariel drove them back to her house, where Jillian had left her car. The Cuddy home was an ostentatious McMansion in a gated subdivision, exactly the sort of place an upwardly mobile executive and his family should live.

"Do you mind if I come in to get a drink of water before I head home?" Jillian asked innocently.

"Water? Honey, it's legally cocktail hour. Why don't you wait out rush hour here and we'll have some wine on the patio? After all that shopping, my feet could use a dip in the Jacuzzi."

"What a lovely idea, thanks." It would give her the perfect chance to snoop, maybe find a large bloodstain. She hated to think of Ariel, who seemed very sweet, as taking part in a murder cover-up, but she had a lot to protect.

"And you can tell me what it's like to work for that delicious Conner Blake. Don't get me wrong, I love Isaac, but Conner wakes up my kitty, if you know what I mean."

Great. Had Isaac told his wife about finding Conner and Jillian kissing in his office? Was her new friend hinting around for details?

Ten minutes later, they were seated on the edge of the Cuddys' opulent hot tub, chilled glasses of wine in hand, their feet being treated to a massage of bubbles.

"So, dish," Ariel said. "What's he like? Has he gotten you in the sack yet?"

Jillian pretended coyness, but she was sure her face was turning bright red. "Of course not. He's my boss, I can't sleep with him."

"Come on, Isaac saw you two kissing."

"We...we did, but that's as far as it went. My career is very important to me. I can't jeopardize it."

"A career is nice, but this—" she spread her arms to encompass her patio, her yard, her home "—this is heaven. I worked in the accounting department at Mayall before Isaac scooped me up. I loved the work—I even kept working for a while, until I had Benjamin. Now I wouldn't go back to my calculator for anything."

Jillian had to admit, her womb had tingled just a bit when Ariel's little boy had rushed to greet his mom upon her arrival home from shopping, hugging her, then jabbering about his day at school, showing her his drawing from art class, then waving shyly at Jillian before rushing away.

"I want marriage and family someday," Jillian said, meaning it. "But I really, really want a career. I want to make a difference in the world."

"And when you lay eyes on that red, squalling bundle in the hospital, you realize you have your chance to make a difference. You have eighteen years to raise that tiny human being into a responsible adult. Could there be anything more exciting, more challenging, more important?"

Jillian couldn't help but be moved by Ariel's passion as a mother. "When you put it that way... I'm not keeping you from family time, am I?"

"No, please, no. Plenty of time later to be wife and mommy. Isaac is playing squash—he won't be home for hours."

Squash—right. Jillian pulled her feet out of the hot tub. At least Isaac wouldn't come home and find her here. "Can you point me toward the bathroom?"

"Sure. Just off the kitchen, down the hallway by the fridge."

Perfect. Jillian entered the home through the patio French doors, but she didn't use the bathroom. Instead she made a whirlwind search of the downstairs, peering under furniture, lifting up one end of an Oriental rug, sticking her head into one doorway after another.

Nothing.

Her kamikaze pathway led her eventually to the three-car garage. Ariel's Jaguar occupied one stall; a second one, where Isaac undoubtedly parked, was empty. The third stall was stacked floor to ceiling with boxes, all covered with blue tarps and bungee cords.

She had a few more seconds before her trip to the bathroom would seem ridiculously long; she dashed across the garage and peeked under the tarp.

Computers. Printers. Scanners. Desk chairs, lamps, rugs. She'd found the mother lode of stolen office supplies.

Just then the automatic garage door opened. *Oh, no!* Panicking, Jillian dashed toward the door into the house. She slammed it behind her just as Isaac's car entered.

Had he seen her?

She scurried back to the patio door, then slowed to a leisurely walk, hoping her breathing didn't give her away. "I think Isaac's home," she announced casually. "And I better get home, too. Laundry calls."

Ariel jumped to her feet. "Oh, he's early." For half a second, she looked disappointed. Then she composed herself. "It was so much fun shopping with you, hon. We'll get the rest of the spouses together next week and we can organize all the tasks."

"Absolutely."

She did her best to hustle Jillian out the front door, but they didn't make it before Isaac strolled into the living room and spotted her.

Jillian steeled herself for his reaction.

He smiled and embraced Ariel, giving her a big smooch on the cheek. "Hello, my love. Hope I didn't interrupt your meeting, but John strained his shoulder and we quit early. Jillian—nice to see you."

"H-hello, Mr. Cuddy."

"Please, we're not at work. You can call me Isaac."

Obviously he didn't want to be his usual nasty self in front of his wife.

"Okay...Isaac. Sorry, but I have to run."

Ariel gave her a warm hug. "I'll call you. Maybe we can do lunch later in the week."

"Sure. Bye, now."

Jillian's heart didn't resume a normal pace until she was through the neighborhood gates. That was way too close for comfort. But she could tell Conner what she'd found—enough evidence to get Cuddy fired and maybe jailed.

And she would tear apart a family in the process and lose her new friend.

CHAPTER EIGHT

"WHOA, WHOA, SLOW DOWN. You went to Isaac Cuddy's house?"

Jillian had come to Conner first thing that morning, babbling about a cache of stolen goods in Isaac Cuddy's garage.

Jillian took a deep breath, making her breasts rise and fall beneath her tailored purple blouse. "Ariel and I were working on the party. She invited me in for a drink. I was looking for the bathroom and I ended up in the garage, and there was all this stuff, hardly even hidden at all."

"I can't go accusing a man of theft because he has some computers in his garage. I have an old computer or two in my garage, doesn't mean I stole them."

"This was brand-new merchandise," Jillian said. "Chairs, lamps, rugs all still wrapped in plastic. I think he's purchasing items through his department, then having it delivered to his home. Who would know? Who double-checks that kind of thing? He's the budget director, and Stan, his only boss, is in prison."

"Hamilton Payne is his boss. I'm sure there are accounting checks and balances—"

"Mr. Payne is overworked and in over his head," Jillian said, though how she would know that was a mystery. "Also, Isaac is planning to retire if...if Mr. Mayall doesn't return. Ariel said they have a big nest egg, a lot bigger than she thought he could save given his salary."

Conner pinched the bridge of his nose. "Oh, boy."

"Maybe you could talk to security? They could look into it. Go over the books. Do an inventory. The man is robbing the company blind. The company's future is already in jeopardy because of Mr. Mayall's...situation. If the company's financial health is undermined, too—"

"I'll take care of it."

That was it? "So I'm supposed to go back to my desk and do my job? Next thing I know, you'll be patting me on the head and giving me a cookie."

"Jillian, you're a new hire, and you're a clerical worker. You have no authority, you haven't built any trust. If you rub people the wrong way, you'll get fired. It's as simple as that."

The look of hurt and defeat on her face squeezed his heart, an organ he'd thought safely encased in stone.

"Why do you care?" he asked, genuinely wanting to know. "Even if what you say is true—"

"*If?* You don't believe me."

"I didn't say that. I'm sure you saw something—"

"I have a nearly perfect photographic memory. I know what I saw."

"Would you please let me finish?"

She looked down at her pink, pointy-toed pumps. "Yes, sir."

Her wardrobe had been gradually morphing from workplace-casual to high fashion, but rather than seeing it as a sign of weakness, Conner was starting to appreciate her flare. Her legs looked amazing in those heels and a short, sassy skirt, the hem of which flipped up enticingly every time she turned.

He forced himself to catch and meet her gaze. "Even

if your theory about Cuddy's activities are accurate, it's not going to bring the company down. A few thousand dollars won't make or break us."

"It's many thousands. And you want to turn a blind eye?"

He very much wanted to. Facing off against Isaac Cuddy was one headache he didn't need. But Jillian was right; he had a duty to stop office pilfering, if that was what Cuddy was up to.

She wasn't stupid. He had to acknowledge the truth of what she'd just reported—Isaac Cuddy was a thief.

"I'll speak to George LeMaster. He handles security. And you need to steer clear of Cuddy. We might be equal on the organizational chart, but he has a ton more clout than me in this company. He, Stan and Hamilton go way back. If it comes down to a showdown, I won't be able to protect you."

She nodded.

"Now, then, what specifically do you know about accounting software?"

"I have a good working knowledge of Peachtree, which is what the company uses."

"IT just upgraded and I'm lost."

"I haven't seen the upgrade. Give me an hour to acquaint myself, and then I'll help you."

Help him? He could see it now, the two of them side by side, peering at the computer screen, her scent teasing his nose, her graceful hands playing the keyboard like a delicate musical instrument, all the while his insides getting tied up in knots.

He never should have kissed her. It had seemed like the most expedient way to get them out of trouble, but now he had the memory of it to taunt him.

Lately he'd had this fantasy that, when he was ready to leave his director's job and go back into the field, he'd take her with him. She had such a quick intellect, plus the physical stamina and curiosity to match him. He would love to show her mahogany forests in Palau, stands of Ceylon ebony trees in Sri Lanka, teak forests of India, coconut palm plantations in Fiji.

He would teach her about the forest. Together they would witness eagles soaring, the Northern Lights, salmon spawning. And they would make love—on the banks of the Euphrates, under the stars in Tunisia, in a tent in Morocco, within the cocoon of the forest canopy on the Amazon.

Would that be before or after Mr. Baxter shot him?

It was a stupid fantasy, given their history, and not even the sort of purely sexual daydream a normal, red-blooded man engaged in. He'd developed some sort of *feelings* for Jillian, and that scared the hell out of him.

Normally, Conner was an intelligent sort of human being. The only other time he'd let emotions cloud his judgment was when he'd been with Chandra. For three years he'd allowed his hormones to rule his life, spending way too many hours of the day figuring out how to win her, how to please her, how to be the perfect husband.

He'd wrecked his own life because of her, taken a job he despised and practically bankrupted himself getting out of the marriage.

No, working side by side with Jillian, the school-mistress of accounting software, would be another co-lossal mistake.

"I was hoping I could just shove my whole budget at you. I've made a mess of it."

"Of course you can. That's what I'm here for."

Did the woman ever say no? She was so turning him on, just standing there doing nothing.

He went to his desk and opened the bottom drawer, where he'd stuffed everything related to his expenditures. Jillian obviously hadn't gotten to organizing that drawer yet; she'd been focusing on the more visible chaos. He pointed to the inside of the drawer.

"That's what I've been using for an accounting system."

"Oh, Conner. Do you print out every email you receive? The idea of email, you know, is so that you don't have to shuffle papers. You set up folders, use filters to sort incoming emails so you can always find—"

"So *you* can always find them."

She sighed again, but she couldn't help smiling, apparently relishing the task of turning his chaos into order. "I'll go get a file box."

She didn't seem as angry with him. Nothing further had been said about the science fair incident, so maybe she was true to her word and wanted to put it behind them. He hoped so. It surely hadn't been his shining moment.

He supposed he should go talk to George. Jillian might trust him to take care of the matter of Isaac's thievery…for now. But if she didn't see some action, she would take matters into her own hands.

Her moral compass, while inconvenient, was yet something else to admire about her. If only she had a few flaws—an annoying laugh or a lazy streak—he would find it easier to dislike her. As it was, he just depended on her more and more.

He couldn't imagine how he'd survived without her.

It felt good for Jillian to dive into Conner's gargantuan pile of papers. Whenever she was in the midst of organizing, she could put troubling thoughts out of her mind for at least a while. She enjoyed learning the ins and outs of a new computer program, typing numbers into blanks, figuring out which categories Conner's expenses should be filed under.

She was very lucky she still had this job. But either Conner didn't remember she'd slashed his tires or he didn't know. He saw their past quite differently than she did—through rose-colored glasses. Get their families together? What was he thinking?

She was relieved, though, that he now knew she was Jillybean, and nothing disastrous had come of it.

As she tamed the pile of papers, it occurred to Jillian—and it was a horrible thought, but she couldn't suppress it once she acknowledged it—that Conner was not very good at his job. As a director, he was supposed to be managing resources—people, time, money. But as she analyzed the various documents he'd provided, she realized the timber buyers who reported to him were sometimes overworked, sometimes idle and not terribly happy with their jobs or their boss.

And he hadn't taken any steps to replace Greg Tynes; meanwhile he was behind schedule with negotiating deals for multiple desirable stands of timber.

He had overspent in some areas of the budget, like travel, and underspent for others.

She felt certain his intentions were good. But he'd become overwhelmed in red tape.

What it boiled down to was, he wasn't suited to a management position—especially if he treated the men who worked out in the field as disrespectfully as he treated his office assistants.

He needed to be out in the field himself. In Stirrup Creek, when he'd been faced with a logistical problem, he'd performed brilliantly. And he'd dealt with the people end of things quite well. He'd seemed to draw energy and wisdom straight from the forest; she could almost see the stress melting out of his body as he breathed in the fresh air and gazed upon his beloved trees.

His beloved trees.

That was how Hamilton Payne had described them. It was a shame to take a man like Conner Blake and pen him up inside four walls. It was like corralling a wild mustang.

Had he loved nature that much as a kid? She did seem to recall that he'd loved being outdoors, even in summer. When Jeff had been content to sit inside with the air-conditioning and watch TV, Conner had wanted to ride bikes or build something.

As she worked on his department's travel expenses, she came across something that stopped her cold. It was an airline ticket to Jakarta. In Conner's name. Scheduled for November.

Why was he going there?

So far as she could tell, Conner's job didn't involve much travel. The trip to Stirrup Creek had been an exception, to solve an urgent problem.

Had something gone terribly wrong somewhere in Indonesia, so that he had to go there himself? She hadn't heard a whisper of a problem. Surely she would have gotten wind of trouble—an email, a phone message. But the last communication she'd seen from the buyer responsible for that part of the world had been just a few days ago, and he'd reported his current job was on schedule and everything was good.

Was Conner perhaps going to Jakarta for a vacation? If so, would he put it on the company credit card?

Another, insidious thought occurred to her. Was Conner preparing to flee? Had the stresses of this job become so bad that he had plans to leave the country, disappear? Once in Indonesia, it would be easy for him to get to any number of destinations where a new identity could be purchased.

Jillian chided herself for thinking such a terrible thing about Conner. Lots of men didn't like their jobs and they didn't intentionally disappear.

Unless they were suspected of a murder.

She'd tried not to give credence to the rumor she'd heard that first day. As frustrated as she'd been with her new boss, she'd never seriously believed he could be guilty of taking a human life—even when Daniel had named Conner as a possible suspect. Yes, he could be brusque, even rude, and yes, he had been cruel to her in high school. It was a big leap from there to murder.

Toward the end of the day, Conner stopped by her desk to provide her with a few more stray pieces of paper related to the budget and to check if she had any questions.

"I do have a question," she said. "Have you taken any steps to replace Greg Tynes?"

"Oh, um, Joyce placed some ads and collected a stack of résumés, but I haven't had a chance to go through them."

Was there something slightly evasive about the way he'd answered that question? Or was she being hyper-suspicious?

"Would you like me to do that?"

"Jillian, you are an amazing person, but you've only been here a week. I doubt even you could have learned enough about the timber business in that short time to know what constitutes desirable qualifications for a timber buyer."

"Well, when you cut some good candidates from the applicants, I'd be happy to set up the interviews. We've got several landowners waiting for us to make a decision, and some options that are expiring at the end of this month."

"I'll see what I can do. It's after five o'clock, you know."

"Is it?"

"You don't have to stick around past quitting time just because I'm still here."

"Oh? I thought your policy was, if you were here, I had to be here."

"C'mon, you know I was just being a hard-ass on purpose."

"Yes, I suppose I did figure that out. You were seeing how hard you could push me. Pretty hard, as it turns out."

"You took all the crap I could throw at you and you came back for more," he said with a laugh. "Why is that, Jillybean?"

Her face grew warm at his use of her nickname. "Please don't call me that." She wasn't sure why she hated hearing it from him so much. She let other people call her that—family members, at least, and it didn't bother her.

"Sorry. I'll try to remember. But I am curious." He propped one hip on the edge of her desk, looming over her. "I can't understand why you would want or need such a menial job. Your parents are some of the richest people in Houston. You went to an elite high school, and Dartmouth isn't a college you go to if you can't cut the competition. I assume you got good grades because you were smart."

He knew that about her? She always assumed he hadn't noticed anything about her—except perhaps her less than ideal proportions.

"You could," he continued, "have become anything you wanted to be—a doctor, a lawyer. You got a business degree, but you work as a secretary."

"There's no shame in clerical work," she said. "I'm good at it. I enjoy it. And I prefer the term *administrative* or *executive assistant*."

"Yeah. But it still doesn't add up."

Suddenly there didn't seem to be enough air. Had he figured out her game? Had he figured out she was working for someone else?

"You must have recognized me long before I knew who you were, yet you didn't say anything. Why is that?"

"Are you kidding? I didn't want you to remember me from high school. Jeff Baxter's goofy kid sister—you would never have hired her! She's a joke, and nothing like the person I am today."

"You're still the same person," he argued. "You can change the outer trappings, but the inner Jillybean is still there."

Jillian was so rattled, she switched off her computer without saving the file she was working on. Why was he torturing her like this? Why couldn't he just drop it, as she obviously wished him to?

She opened the bottom drawer of her desk and retrieved her purse. She wouldn't sit still for this.

"If what you say is true, that must mean you're still a sadistic little prick who gets his kicks from torturing teenage girls."

Any sign of humor fled from his face. "Excuse me?"

"You heard me. What you did to me was cruel. Heartless. Unforgivable." To her horror, tears sprang into her eyes. My God, she had to get out of there fast! She scooted around the desk and headed for the elevator. And when she realized Conner was following her, she headed for the stairs instead.

"Jillian. Wait."

"Good *night,* Mr. Blake."

CONNER LET HER GO. THE LAST thing he'd meant to do was make her cry. He'd be very, very lucky if he still had an admin come tomorrow morning.

He'd never intended for the conversation to take such a bizarre twist. He'd merely been trying to find a way past the cool barrier she'd erected against him. He'd thought that by teasing her a bit—like he did when they were kids—she might soften.

Boy, had he gotten that wrong.

Cruel. Heartless. Unforgivable.

What he remembered of the infamous science fair was hilarious. A melting dress, seminudity on the football field, teachers and parents in shock. Of course she'd been embarrassed, and he'd suffered a small twinge of guilt—later.

Apparently she and her whole family remembered the incident in radically different terms.

He would straighten it out with her. He would apologize, send flowers, whatever it took. But right now, he had another gut-wrenching task to attend to.

He'd talked to George LeMaster about Isaac Cuddy's office theft—without mentioning Jillian's name, or how he came to know about the cache in Cuddy's garage.

It turned out LeMaster already knew, or suspected,

someone was stealing from the company. The thefts weren't inconsequential, either. They amounted to tens of thousands of dollars over the course of more than a year.

LeMaster had narrowed down the suspects to a few key people who had access. Cuddy was one of them.

Together, Conner and LeMaster went to Hamilton Payne.

Poor Ham. The guy just wanted to get through the next few months so he could retire. He hadn't asked to be named acting CEO, but he'd been the logical choice as Stan's right-hand man.

Now, in addition to the accusations leveled against Stan, another director was about to be revealed as a criminal.

The three men had decided to go to Cuddy's house together. They would confront him and ask to see what was in his garage. If he cooperated, there would be no criminal charges, he would simply be asked to resign. It wasn't ideal, but it was better than dragging Mayall Lumber through the mud yet again.

There wasn't much discussion in the car on the way to Cuddy's house. Conner had a knot in his stomach the size of a bowling ball. He wanted to be anywhere but here in this hornets' nest.

He wanted to be in the forest, where the worst thing he might face was a real hornets' nest. Bugs. Skunks. Snakes. Those were things he understood.

People, not so much.

Cuddy's wife, Ariel, answered the door with a big smile. "Well, hi, fellas, what brings you here? Come on in. Isaac," she called over her shoulder as she ushered them into the cavernous, marble-tiled foyer of their home, "you have company."

Conner imagined that when Isaac saw them—the three of them, showing up without warning and looking somber—he would know the jig was up. But he greeted them with a smile as well, though slightly more bewildered than his wife.

"Hey, guys. What's going on?" Suddenly the smile fell away. "Oh, God. It's Stan. What's happened?"

"Stan's fine, as far as we know," Hamilton said. "Isaac, I don't know how to approach this except to just blurt it out. Can we look in your garage?"

"What? Why?"

"I think you know why," George said.

"No." He laughed a little nervously. "Scratching my head here. But if you want to look in my garage, be my guest."

Conner's mouth went dry as paper. Why had Cuddy agreed so easily?

Cuddy led them through a gracious living room, into a kitchen that looked like a magazine layout and down a hallway to the garage. He opened the door and let them file into the three-car garage.

He flipped on the light.

Two cars. A Jet Ski on a trailer. A lawnmower. A couple of transparent plastic storage containers labeled Christmas, which clearly contained ornaments and tinsel.

No office equipment. No blue tarp. Nothing remotely suspicious.

Conner's head spun. He didn't believe for one instant that Jillian had made up her story. Or that she'd been mistaken, that she'd seen something innocent and misinterpreted it.

"Now are you going to tell me what's going on?" Cuddy demanded.

"Someone in the company is stealing large quantities of office supplies and a source identified you as a suspect," George said baldly. "I thought the simplest way to deal with the matter was to check. Obviously I was misinformed. I apologize."

"Wait a minute. You accuse me of being a thief, and then you just say, 'oops, sorry'? Hamilton, did you actually think I could—Ariel, honey, don't cry. It's all right, I didn't do anything wrong."

Isaac put his arms around Ariel, who had her face in her hands, weeping silently.

"I don't know what to think," Hamilton said sadly. "The whole world has gone crazy."

"You'll have my resignation in the morning," Cuddy said coldly. "I'm not working for a company that doesn't trust me."

"Don't make this worse than it already is," Hamilton said. "We had to check it out. It was the quickest, easiest way to clear you."

"Who accused me?" Cuddy asked. "I have a right to know."

George answered him wearily. "The information was given to me in confidence. Just let it drop. Gentlemen, let's go before this gets any more unpleasant."

No one said anything in the car for a good five minutes. Finally Conner had to break the silence. "Someone could have tipped him off," he ventured. "That garage was superclean, like it had been swept. And that lawnmower? Please. If Cuddy mows his own lawn, I'm dating Sarah Palin."

"So you think he put it there…like a prop?" George asked.

"Exactly. If he'd left that third garage bay completely empty, it would have looked odd."

"Maybe so," George said, "but there's nothing more I can do without hard evidence. We'll be lucky if Cuddy doesn't slap us with a lawsuit. I need to know, Conner—who told you Cuddy was a thief?"

"I promised this person could remain anonymous." He couldn't tell them it was Jillian. She'd trusted him to handle the problem. Cuddy might guess she'd ratted him out, but he couldn't know for sure. "If there are repercussions, I'll take responsibility."

CHAPTER NINE

IT FELT STRANGE, DRIVING up to the gates of the Logan estate and having to ask the security guy for admittance. For so many years she'd come and gone from here at will. But though Daniel had never confiscated her opener, it no longer worked. He changed the code at least once a month.

"Jillian, how nice to hear your voice," said Brandon, one of the security guards. "Come on in. I'll tell Daniel you're here. Does he know you're coming?"

"Yes, I phoned him a few minutes ago." She knew better than to show up at Daniel's home unannounced. He didn't like surprises, and she still had to tread lightly here. She and Jamie, his wife, hadn't started out on the best of terms. In fact, Jillian had tried to convince Daniel that Jamie was a gold digger.

Jamie had been nothing but cordial, and had made a point of telling Jillian she was welcome in their home. But it still felt slightly awkward.

Daniel himself met her at the door. "Jillian. Is something wrong?"

"I don't know what to do," she blurted out. "I think I've screwed everything up."

"It can't be that bad," he said in a cajoling voice. "Come on in, let's talk. You're probably hungry—I'll have Cora make you a plate."

"No, really, I couldn't eat a thing." She wouldn't be able to swallow past the lump in her throat.

He picked up a phone in the foyer and ordered food anyway. Then he ushered her through the living room and into the sunroom, a gorgeous glassed-in porch with Spanish tile, potted palms and comfy furnishings. It was a room Daniel had always liked, often taking meals here when the weather outside wasn't comfortable.

They sat at a warm antique oak table, and Manuel was there taking drink orders. Jillian stuck with water. As upset as she was, she didn't want to add alcohol to the mix.

"So tell me what's going on," Daniel said in a coaxing voice.

"First off, there's something I should have told you right away. Conner Blake is someone I knew in high school. He and Jeff were friends. We have a, um, a past."

Daniel's eyebrows flew up.

"No, no, not that kind of past. He pulled a terrible prank on me. I won't bore you with the details, but the end result was, I ran nearly naked across the football field in front of hundreds of people—friends, family, teachers—"

Daniel's jaw dropped. "I remember that. I mean, I wasn't there, I was in college at the time, but my mother told me."

Jillian's and Daniel's parents had been friends; that was how she'd first gotten hired to work at the estate.

Daniel firmed his lips, and she realized he was trying not to laugh.

"Daniel Logan, don't you dare laugh!"

"Aw, c'mon, Jillian, it was kind of funny."

"Not to me it wasn't. I had a huge crush on Conner, and he humiliated me."

"Sorry." He cleared his throat. "I won't laugh. Conner Blake was involved?"

"Totally responsible. But here's the really awful part. He didn't recognize me when I went to work there. Even when he heard my name. So I figured it was cool to keep working for him. Nothing ever happened between us, of course. He was Big Man On Campus, and I was…well, you remember what I was like."

"But then he did remember?"

She nodded. "He had the gall to make light of the prank. We had a big fight. I walked out."

"You quit? After all the work we did to get you in there?"

"I didn't quit. But I don't think I can go back there. I can't face him. And it's not like I was doing much good. The only thing I've done is rat out an office supply thief."

"Don't underestimate your contributions. You provide me with small bits of information, I combine them with other small bits, and it adds up. Don't you worry, I'm having Isaac Cuddy thoroughly checked out."

She suspected Daniel was humoring her, but she appreciated it. "I haven't typed out today's report, but I have a new theory. Did you know Stan's granddaughter, Chandra, is his sole heir? And she's hurting for money."

"Is she? How do you know that?"

She wasn't ready to admit to her eavesdropping. "Gossip."

Daniel made a quick note. "I'll take another look at her. This is good information, Jillian. Why would you want to quit?"

"Because Conner is on to me. Since he knows my

background now, he thinks it odd that I choose to do secretarial work when I had all these advantages—money, education, social standing, blah blah blah."

Daniel took a sip of his wine and thought for a few moments. "Did you defend your choice?"

"I told him I enjoyed the work because I was good at it."

Daniel thought some more. "Maybe I should pull you out. It could be dangerous for you if Conner figures out who you really work for."

"You still think Conner might be responsible? Honestly, Conner couldn't kill anyone."

"Are you sure? Sometimes we're blind to the people closest to us—the people we have feelings for."

"I don't have feelings for Conner!" She realized the denial had come too quickly, too emphatically.

"I think maybe you do."

She sighed, exasperated, and took a sip of water to buy herself some time. "Okay, I feel a lot of things where Conner Blake is concerned. Anger being at the top of the list. But I can't deny my childhood crush has gotten all mixed up in this thing, and I don't know if what I feel is real or new, or just some remnant left over from adolescent hormones. All I know is, I feel miserable."

"Undercover work isn't always fun. That's why I pay my people the big bucks."

He wasn't kidding about that. Her intern's salary, already generous, had doubled the second she'd started working at Mayall Lumber.

"I'm not sure I can face him again. I'm not sure he still wants me working for him, after what I said to him today." *Cruel. Heartless. Unforgivable.*

"Why don't you give it a try?" Daniel suggested.

"It might take weeks or months to get someone else placed inside the company. Stan can't afford that kind of time investment."

At the mention of Stan, Jillian sat up straighter. Maybe she was in an uncomfortable situation, but Stan Mayall was incarcerated and dying of cancer.

There were worse things than a little embarrassment.

"Daniel, I knew you'd know the right thing to do. Of course I'll go back. I'll even apologize, and I'll try to make it work. But I wish…I wish I was helping you more."

"You're doing fine. Undercover operations take time."

"Isn't there something proactive I could do? I mean, I'm planning the company's annual party. It seems so frivolous."

"You're getting to know people. They're talking to you. Sooner or later, something you hear will send us in the right direction."

She nodded. "Okay. But, Daniel, it's not Conner. Really. Sometimes I feel like I could strangle him with my bare hands, but I don't see a motive."

"You told me Greg wasn't a very good employee. That he and Conner had exchanged some snipey emails. And that Conner was planning to fire him. What if he did fire him? And Greg didn't take it well, maybe attacked Conner in a rage. Conner fought back, accidentally killed the man, got scared…"

"But then why frame Stan?"

"His ex-wife's grandfather? Could be some friction there we don't even know about."

Jillian couldn't even bear to think about the scenario Daniel had just described. "My instincts tell me he couldn't do it."

"You've been a field investigator a little over a week. That means you're entitled to instincts—but you can't trust them yet."

That seemed fair. It also made Jillian feel about two inches high. She had a long, long way to go before anyone trusted her. And maybe Daniel was right not to put his faith in her. She'd made rather a mess of things on her first assignment.

"All right."

"I'm just saying, be careful, okay? Don't put yourself in a vulnerable situation. I haven't ruled out Conner as a suspect."

IT WAS ALL JILLIAN COULD do to get herself out of bed the next morning and shower. She dressed with care, choosing a very feminine two-piece, maroon knit ensemble that hugged her curves like a catsuit. The top fastened with a bold zipper down the front, and the skirt was short. She finished out the look with her favorite pair of dark pink, faux-lizard stilettos only a shade tamer than something Celeste would wear. If she was going to lose her job, she'd go out with a bang.

She arrived earlier than normal, even. She figured if she was at her desk, hard at work by the time Conner arrived, it would be harder for him to dislodge her.

"Morning, Jillian." Letitia treated Jillian to an evil grin that could mean only one thing: gossip. "Did you hear the big news?"

"I can't have heard anything since I just got here," Jillian reminded her friend. Well, sort of a friend. They'd eaten several lunches together, and Letitia loved to dish. She only hoped today's steaming plate of gossip had nothing to do with her and Conner having a big fight yesterday.

Letitia looked around to make sure no one else was around to hear. "Isaac Cuddy resigned."

Jillian didn't have to fake her surprise. "Really."

"Apparently Mr. Payne and your boss accused him of stealing from the company. Went to his house, searched his garage."

"Is it true?" Jillian asked, as if this was complete news to her. "Was he stealing?"

"Apparently not. They didn't find anything. But Cuddy was so mad he quit."

Jillian grew light-headed as all of her blood drained from her head to her heart, which had jumped into a double-time rhythm.

They didn't find anything.

How was that possible?

Unless…unless she hadn't gotten away clean when she was snooping. She'd thought she'd made it out of the garage and into the hallway, closing the door before Isaac saw her. But what if she'd been wrong? What if he'd heard the door slam, or seen just one foot or the hem of her dress disappearing through the door?

She'd falsely accused a company director of theft—at least that's what Conner and Mr. Payne must have thought. Why had she even been allowed into the building? Was Isaac filing a defamation of character lawsuit against her as they spoke?

"Jillian, are you okay?" Letitia asked, her round face wreathed with concern. "You look all pale and wobbly."

"Um, I skipped breakfast."

"You shouldn't skip breakfast." Letitia tutted as she reached into her desk drawer. "Here, eat this. And don't tell anyone where I keep my stash."

Jillian started to decline the offer, until she saw the familiar Snickers wrapper. "Thanks." She ripped open the wrapper and took a big bite of the candy bar, letting the chocolate, caramel and peanuts soothe her.

It took every ounce of her willpower not to turn tail and run back to her nice, safe job as an intern. But she'd told Daniel she would show up for work today—she couldn't chicken out now.

Why, oh, why had she tattled on Isaac Cuddy like a vindictive schoolgirl? Because she'd once again let her emotions get involved. Never mind that the theft probably had nothing to do with the murder. Isaac had insulted her, leered at her, and she was getting back at him.

When was she going to learn to keep her emotions in check?

She was still trembling by the time she got off the elevator on the third floor. The hallway was empty. No firing squad awaited her.

Conner's office door was closed, but she could see light coming out from under it. Damn. She hadn't beaten him to work after all.

When she arrived at her desk, she skidded to a stop. Surprises just kept piling one on top of another. A huge basket of flowers sat in the middle of her blotter.

She'd understand it if someone sent her a letter bomb. But flowers?

She found the card and opened it, and her trembling began anew. Conner. Conner had sent her flowers. No explanation, he'd just signed his name.

Conner Blake had sent her flowers! Even as she acknowledged how ludicrous the gesture was, her girlish heart warmed because one of her teenage fantasies had just come true. If she could stomp on her stupid adolescent self, banish her to a closet, she would. But just like Conner had said yesterday, that fat, awkward teenager was still part of her, desperate for crumbs of attention from the object of her undying devotion.

She debated for all of ten seconds before she knew what she had to do. She strode around the corner to Conner's door and tapped softly.

"Conner?"

"Come in, Jillian."

Her hand was slick with sweat as she turned the knob and entered his office.

Conner wasn't sitting behind his desk, where she could usually find him, but on the sofa with one ankle propped on the opposite knee, an iPad in his lap.

He was playing solitaire, a most uncharacteristic thing for Conner to do. He might not be the most effective executive she'd ever encountered, but not for lack of work. He never goofed off.

"What's the deal with the flowers?" she asked point-blank.

He put the tablet aside and stood up. "Jillian. Close the door. Come sit down. Please," he added.

After closing and locking the door—she didn't want to take the chance someone would walk in on the discussion they were about to have—she strode across the polished wood floor and chose a chair a safe distance from him.

He reclaimed his seat, but his eyes never left her. "The flowers are to go with an apology. Long overdue, apparently. Jillian, I am so sorry I talked you into wearing the paper dress. But as God is my witness, I didn't know it would melt."

"You expect me to believe that?"

"I entered the science fair trying to shore up my extracurriculars so I could get into a good college. I wouldn't have deliberately sabotaged the whole thing."

"Hmph." His apology was too little, too late. "Am I supposed to think you didn't turn the sprinklers on, either?"

"I was standing right there. How could I have turned on the sprinklers?"

"I assumed you had an accomplice."

"No. I had nothing to do with the sprinklers."

"This sounds a whole lot like a bunch of excuses, rather than an apology."

"I just wanted you to understand. I didn't mean to hurt you. I knew you were mad at me—Jeff made that pretty clear. But I had no idea how distraught and embarrassed you were. I am sorry. I take full responsibility for everything that happened."

She studied her manicure. After imagining his apology a hundred different ways, the actual event felt somewhat anticlimactic. "You don't even know the worst part of it, do you? It's not the prank itself."

"No?"

She folded her hands in her lap and met his gaze. "You laughed at me. You could have thrown a tablecloth over me or made sure I found some clothes in the locker room, or at least shown a tiny bit of remorse for making me the butt of a very bad joke, no pun intended. But you stood there laughing like a donkey, laughing so hard you were clutching your stomach.

"I was *naked,* or nearly so, in front of *everybody*." She could feel the tears building in the back of her throat. God, no, she was not going to cry again.

"I'm sorry," he said again. "I was a teenage boy. Teenage boys are horrible people—self-centered, egotistical, obnoxious. If I could go back and undo what I did, I would."

She took a deep breath. He did seem sincere. As

she'd reminded herself many times lately, it had all happened a long time ago and she should be over it by now anyway.

Could she forgive him? She toyed with the idea of how that would feel. It was like a weight had lifted. How much had her angry grudge cost her? Whether he deserved forgiveness or not, she was going to give it to him. For her own sake.

"All right. Apology accepted. We won't mention it again."

"Deal."

She took a deep, liberating breath. Amazing. "Do I still have a job?"

"Of course you do. Why wouldn't you?"

She took another deep breath, this one not quite so pleasant. "I know what happened last night, if I can trust the almighty grapevine. Was Isaac's garage really empty?"

He wouldn't meet her gaze. "I'm afraid so."

"So why haven't I been escorted off the premises? I falsely accused a director of a crime. Sounds to me like grounds for dismissal."

"Because your name never came up. I told George and Hamilton that the tip came from a reliable source, but I didn't tell them who."

"You...you protected me?"

"I couldn't just throw you to the wolves."

Jillian was so stunned, she didn't know what to feel. Even after the terrible things she'd said to him last night, after she'd *slapped* him, he'd shielded her identity.

"You trusted me with the information," Conner said, "and I told you I'd take care of it. At that point, it became my problem, not yours. From this point on, you should deny all knowledge. Isaac Cuddy isn't someone you want for an enemy."

Unfortunately, it was too late for that. Cuddy had to know who'd ratted him out.

"I don't know what to say. Do you still believe me?"

"Yeah. Of course. Why would you make that up?"

Conner stood, indicating their meeting was over, and offered her a hand up. She allowed Conner to pull her to her feet, then threw her arms around his neck and hugged him as her gratitude bubbled over.

"Thank you, Conner. Thank you for believing in me despite the evidence. I need this job. Really I do. And thank you for the flowers. They're beautiful."

"You're welcome." He slid his arms around her body, wrapping her in their warm security, and for a long time they just stood like that. He ran his palm up and down her back reassuringly.

It felt so good, Jillian never wanted to let go. He was so solid, a rock, really. He'd grown from an irresponsible kid into this…this man, standing firm for what he believed, taking care of those he perceived weaker than him—not that she was weaker, of course, but she was pretending to be.

And he smelled so good—like soap and starch and maybe a touch of wood smoke. People in Houston seldom built fires, certainly not in September, but she smelled it just the same, and it made her think of fall and football games and cuddling beneath a stadium blanket with a thermos of hot chocolate….

Another of her girlish fantasies intruding where it had no place, but she indulged in this one. Conner was here, close enough she could feel his heartbeat and every breath he took.

The embrace had gone on far too long, longer than

any friendly hug, even one borne of supreme gratitude, had a right to last. Yet she couldn't seem to let go, and he certainly wasn't making any move to release her.

With a jolt, she realized he was aroused. She could feel the evidence pushing against her abdomen and hear the change in his breathing. She wasn't sure when the reassuring rub had turned to a caress, but the feel of his hands on her body had changed, too.

She was torn. A sexual relationship with her boss sounded like the worst sort of mistake she could make. But this was Conner, someone she'd adored and fantasized about. Yes, she'd hated him, too, but he wasn't really the monster she'd made him out to be.

Oh, God, she was so utterly confused. She needed to be careful. Watch her step. Think things through—

To hell with it.

She pulled back just far enough that she could plant her mouth on his, and she put everything she had and more into that one kiss. Emboldened by so many years of keeping her yearnings bottled up—for him, for Daniel—she pressed herself even more tightly against him, relishing every inch of those defined muscles. His belt buckle dug into her stomach, but she didn't care.

She'd spent half her life paranoid that someone would know her true feelings, even as she secretly hoped they would.

The cork was out of the bottle now. No way could she pretend she wasn't feeling a boatload of pure, twenty-four-karat lust for her boss.

Lust. That was all it was, right? That, and some residual bits of a long-ago crush, which had felt a lot like love, but really it couldn't have been. What did a fourteen-year-old know of love?

Whatever it was, Conner answered it, kissing

her every bit as greedily as she kissed him, one arm clamped around her to hold her a willing captive, the other making a bird's nest of her hair.

This was gonna get messy, in more ways than one.

"Jillian," he murmured between gasps for oxygen. "What... How...?"

"I know, crazy." That was as close to a sentence as she could form. She wanted to feel more of him. Bare skin. Tongue.

Unable to control herself, she slid one hand down his back and cupped his granite-hard ass.

Suddenly he broke off the kiss, cradling her head between his large hands and forcing her to look at him.

She was afraid of what she might see there, but she looked without flinching.

She saw a crazy glint that matched the spark of insanity in her soul perfectly.

"We...have...to...stop." Each word seemed to cost him dearly.

"Uh-huh. I know."

"I don't want to."

"Me, neither."

"We have to."

"Okay. Of course. You're my boss. We can't—"

He quieted her by kissing her again with even more fervor, if that were possible. "Please tell me you're on the pill."

Whoa. The guy didn't waste time. "I'm not." His hands were all over her, exploring, seducing, claiming ownership. The zipper at the front of her shirt seemed to magically lower itself. Cool, air-conditioned air swished against her newly bared skin. Her nipples tingled and hardened. "But you have condoms in your desk."

"Why would you think that?" He cupped one of her breasts and thumbed her nipple through her bra—that lacy bra she'd dressed in especially for today simply because she'd wanted to feel good about herself. She'd had no idea…really, none at all.

"I saw them there when I was organizing your office."

His hands stopped moving. "Really."

He sounded genuinely surprised…and intrigued. Suddenly having sex right here, right now, was a real possibility.

"Conner, we can't."

He smiled at her, a sexy, to-hell-with-propriety smile, and her inside went liquid with desire. "I think we can."

She wanted him, bad. But bad enough to risk her job? Not just her Mayall Lumber job. Daniel would have her head on a platter if he found out she'd slept with someone the foundation was investigating.

"You're making things hard for me," she said as he dipped his head and licked the top of her breast, then unclasped the bra and allowed her breast to burst free. He plumped it with his hand and licked the nipple.

"So beautiful," he murmured.

Conner Blake thought she was beautiful. This was some kind of miracle. Maybe she'd gone insane, and this was a crazy delusion. If so, she didn't want it to end.

"Just let me kiss you." His voice was rough with desire. "Then we'll stop."

"Okay." She shrugged her way out of the knit top and tossed it aside.

This wasn't like her. She didn't strip out of her clothes for a man in broad daylight. In his office. She

was terrified by her own lack of common sense and
thrilled all at the same time.

She didn't feel an ounce of shyness or insecurity
about her body. There was no awkwardness between
her and Conner. Maybe all those hours of fantasy had
worked like an intellectual dress rehearsal.

"Which drawer?" he asked, and she knew immediately what he meant. If she told him, there would be
no turning back. If she left this business unfinished,
she would regret it the rest of her life.

"Bottom left. Way in the back."

CHAPTER TEN

"Do not move." Conner seated Jillian gently on the sofa, then strode to the desk and leaned down to open the bottom drawer.

He laughed softly as he dragged out a string of neon-glow condoms in clear plastic pouches. "From a bachelor party. Gag gift."

"Are they functional?" she asked, sounding a little desperate.

He straightened and grinned. "If you don't mind me looking a bit like The Incredible Hulk."

Conner had known sooner or later this might happen. Whenever they were in the same room, the air fairly sizzled with the strength of their mutual yearnings. He'd done a fairly good job keeping a lid on it. But when she'd kissed him, he'd lost any semblance of control.

These weren't Victorian times, he told himself. May-all Lumber didn't have any kind of rule against employees fraternizing.

She's your subordinate. She could charge you with sexual harassment.

He returned to Jillian, his stride purposeful, but he didn't touch her. He tossed the neon condoms onto the sofa, then studied her eyes. Such a ridiculous shade of blue, but he knew they were her own.

"What?" She placed one hand tentatively on his

chest. "You've come to your senses. I can see it plainly on your face. Well, it's good one of us still has some mental faculties in place."

Her voice was tinged with poignant regret, and her eyes, those amazing blue eyes, looked so sad. She thought he was rejecting her. In high school she'd been prepared to hand over her heart on a silver platter. He'd known it even then; her crush was obvious, and he'd thought it amusing. He hadn't let her down gently; he'd publicly humiliated her. He'd hurt her so badly that she'd carried around the injury for more than a decade while he'd danced off into the sunset, oblivious.

She was offering herself to him again. Not her heart, maybe; he suspected she guarded that particular organ a bit more fiercely than she had in the past. But she still stood here, ready to give him some part of herself, and it wasn't a decision she took lightly.

This meant something to her.

No way he would reject her. Not that he wanted to.

He reached up and smoothed a strand of hair from her face. "I don't want to make love to you because I'm too dumb to control myself. I want to do it with all my faculties in perfect order. I want to give you something so sweet it will burn away the bad memories you have about me.

"And I want you to come to me willingly. No matter what comes of this, I don't want it to become a regret. Right now, I'm not your boss. We're two equals, coming together of our own free wills."

She looked a bit bewildered by his suddenly serious mood. "Of course, Conner." She smiled. "I'm not going to sue you for harassment, if that's what you're worried about."

Was he that transparent? "I'd be an idiot if it didn't

cross my mind. It'd be one helluva way for you to get revenge on me."

"I wouldn't." She looked down at her open shirt, then back up. "You'll have to make the next move. All this talk…I'm feeling suddenly shy about the whole thing."

Jeez, she was adorable. She might give the impression of a confident woman most of the time, but right now he could see the remnants of the awkward teenager she'd been. Which just made him want her more.

With one finger on her chin, he tipped her face up. "No more talking, then." He kissed her, sweetly this time, a slow, seductive meeting of lips, teasing, tempting. But it quickly became something more.

Jillian did have a way of altering his brainwave activity. Logic gave way to pure lust roiling inside him like summer storm clouds pregnant with rain.

He ran his hand over the curve of her hip, finding the hem of her short skirt and pushing it up until he was touching her silky panties. He groaned and deepened the kiss, desperate to feel her skin.

Meanwhile her greedy hands got busy opening the buttons of his shirt, pulling the tails out from his pants until she could slide her hands over his ribs. Her hands were hot.

He grabbed a handful of silk and tugged, exposing her bare bottom. She had the most amazing ass, so firm and trim, yet sweetly rounded like some exotic, ripe fruit. He squeezed one cheek, then the other. He allowed his fingers to flirt between her legs, and she obligingly curled one leg around his, opening herself to exploration.

He tried to take it slow, but any trace of Jillian's shyness was gone. She was devouring him like he might be her last meal.

Skin. He needed more skin-to-skin contact. He yanked his shirt off, nearly strangling himself because he forgot he'd worn a tie today.

"I'll do it." She loosened the tie enough that he could pull it over his head. Somehow she turned the simple act of removing his tie into an erotic gesture, brushing her hands against his collarbone as she manipulated the silk knot and pulled the tie free, sliding it along the back of his neck.

Her bra came next. He drew her to him, pressing her breasts against his chest, teasing her nipples with his own. Those breasts were all hers. He'd thought, given how petite the rest of her figure was, that the breasts were mostly silicone, but no way. They were soft and squeezable, but also firm as plump tomatoes.

Fruits, vegetables—he wanted to consume her, become part of her until it was impossible to tell where he ended and she began.

"Jillian. I need to be inside you."

"I know." She tugged at his belt. "You're not undressing fast enough. This can't take all day."

He grinned. "Too much work to do?"

"My boss is a real brute. He'll do terrible things to me if I don't finish his budget."

"I'll speak sternly to him."

He took over the job of dropping his pants. She stooped down to untie his shoes, and he found that action erotic, too. In fact, any move she made struck him as sexual. Climbing a ladder, typing, eating…kissing. He just couldn't imagine anything more erotic than Jillian's tongue in his mouth, unless—

"Wait…wait just a damn minute." Before he'd even gotten his pants off, she'd grabbed on to his shorts and yanked them down. She took his erection in her hands, both hands, like she was grabbing onto a baseball bat and intended to swing for a home run.

"Mine," she said as she sank onto the sofa and put him in her mouth.

"Son of a… Didn't you say about two minutes ago that you were shy?"

She stopped sucking him long enough to say, "I'm over it."

"I'll say— Oh. Jillian. Wait, wait, how much control do you think I have?"

She looked up and grinned at him, her mouth shiny and moist. "A ton, I bet."

He reached down and grabbed her arms, pulling her to her feet. "Let's try something different." He sat on the sofa and pulled her onto his lap. "Let's get you naked."

He pulled off first one of her stiletto heels, then the other, caressing her feet and baby-smooth calves in the process. "What happened to your 'business casual' wardrobe?"

"I can't help it. I like pretty clothes."

"Like these?" He reached under her skirt and fingered the barely there wisp of fabric that currently did nothing to protect her femininity. Her panties were already pulled halfway down her thighs.

"It wasn't until college that I looked good in clothes. Finally I could wear short skirts and sleeveless tops and bare my stomach. I think I got a little bit high, knowing I looked good. It was a habit I never lost."

"Clearly."

"It's too much. I know. But I dress for me. As a daily reminder that I don't ever want to gain weight again."

He wished she wouldn't call up the memory of that shy, pudgy girl. He found it much easier to make love to

Jillian, his sexy assistant, without the ghost of chubby, insecure Jillybean reminding him of what a jerk he'd been.

He slid one hand along her firm thigh and along her hip, then spanned her waist with his hands.

He'd been right. Twenty-four inches. "I like the way you dress, the way you look."

She leaned in and kissed him hard. "Less talk. More action."

Normally he didn't talk during sex, other than the occasional "Move this way, please," and "Faster, harder."

But Jillian was more than an attractive body with the sole purpose of satisfying his needs. "You're pleasant to talk to."

"Fine, we'll talk later." With that she lowered the zipper on her snug, body-forming skirt and started wiggling out of it. All that wiggling was about to make him lose it. He dragged the skirt all the way off and tossed it aside. Finally, she was naked except for a dainty gold chain around her neck and a pair of bangles on her wrist that clanked together musically every time she moved.

Her pubic hair was blond, pale blond. He placed his cupped palm over her pubis, testing the texture of the springy curls.

If he had all day with her, he would crawl between her legs and kiss her most secret, sensitive parts until she screamed. He would lick her pink skin, every inch of it. Then he would take her from the front, from the back, on her hands and knees, hell, swinging from the chandelier.

But they were in his office.

She wiggled some more as he stroked her curls and her thighs, then licked his index finger and probed deftly between her legs. Heaven help him, she was drenched in moisture. His member stirred, aching to be inside her.

"Mmm, no." She forcibly moved his hand away, then maneuvered herself until she sat astride him.

"Like this?"

"Exactly like this."

He was half sitting on the string of condoms. She pulled one plastic pouch from the end of the string and opened it with her teeth.

It was hot-pink, not green. "No Incredible Hulk?"

"More like the Pink Panther." She made a great show of sheathing him, taking her time as she rolled the fluorescent latex over him, getting it just so.

"Honey, you're about to kill me."

"You'll die happy."

"There, it's perfect."

Her eyes went smoky. "It is perfect. Oh, Conner, please take me now."

She was a damn dream come true. "You want me?" He spanned her tiny waist with his hands and lifted her up. She was light as a doll.

"Yes."

"Like this?"

"Oh, yes."

"Have I ever told you how much I love hearing you say yes?" He put just his tip inside her warmth. "Even when you're just agreeing to type up a report?"

She couldn't answer him. Her eyes were closed, as if she were preparing for a great rapture.

No pressure. He slid into her, and decided *rapture* was too mild a word. She was so warm. So tight. When she squeaked in surprise at the abrupt impalement, he worried he'd hurt her. But with her next breath she let out a long, languorous sigh and spread her knees wider, taking him even more deeply.

"Oh, my."

All he had to do was rock his hips, and hers along with them, to produce the most exquisite sensations. No pumping in and out. Just a tiny friction, and with each slight movement she gave a little gasp and another squeak, which he thought meant she liked it.

"Make it last," she pleaded. "Please, don't let it be over too quickly. I waited my whole life for this."

That gave him pause. "Jillian, you're not a v—" He couldn't even say the word.

"No." Impatient, she rocked them herself, squeezing with her inner thighs like he was a horse and she was guiding him to her will. "But it's never been good before," she admitted.

"Never?"

"Forget I said anything!"

He was rapidly getting to that point where he forgot everything anyway. All of his blood had left his brain to circulate where it was more urgently needed. Now all he could do was feel—the tight, warm glove of her body surrounding him, her hands gripping his shoulders, her fingernails digging into his flesh in a way that should have hurt, but actually made him feel more alive than he'd ever felt.

He wished he could prolong this moment indefinitely, but he was too inflamed. And every time he stopped moving for a few seconds to regain better control, Jillian took up the slack. Still, he held on to every precious minute, kissing any part of her he could find with his hungry mouth, cataloging every intriguing curve and valley of her lithe body. He paid attention to the rate of her breathing, the small soft whispers into his ear, encouraging him.

"Yes," she finally said with a note of satisfaction. "Yes, yes, yesss!"

He finally cut himself loose, relaxing into the climax until it claimed his whole body. He wanted to shout in triumph, but he wasn't so far gone that he wasn't aware he was at his place of business. Not that many people wandered down to this end of the hall, but he wouldn't take a chance.

He bit his lip to staunch the shout, holding her close, burying his face in her hair as wave after wave swept over him, waves so extremely delicious he was already starting to wonder when he could manage sex with Jillian again.

As they both glided back to earth, he held her close for a long time. Their heartbeats were in sync. So was their breathing. Amazing.

"Conner." It was barely a whisper, as if she were afraid to break the magic spell.

"Jillian," he said back.

"You're due at a meeting in ten minutes."

Her statement brought reality crashing down on him in a hurry. "What happened to me not being your boss, us just being two people—"

"This is no time for jokes!" She pulled away from him abruptly, and he felt suddenly cold and lonely as she clamored off his lap and started to search madly for her clothes. "If you're late, they'll send someone looking for you. How will you explain—"

"They'll call first. Anyway, the meeting was postponed until this afternoon."

"Oh." She laughed nervously.

"Jillian, come here."

"I'd feel better if I could put my clothes on. I'm feeling really…really naked."

"You are really naked. It's nice. I wonder if we could enact a new dress code. From now on, you can show up to work clothing optional."

"Conner, please."

He made some effort to pull himself out of the pleasant daze of satisfaction. Jillian didn't seem as happy about the state of affairs as he did. "Is something wrong? Are you sorry this happened?"

"What? No. Oh, no, Conner, not at all." She sat down next to him. "But no one can know. I need this job. If anyone finds out—"

"No one's going to find out."

"Please…if I get fired—"

"You could get another job, a better job, in a heartbeat."

"No, you don't understand. I have to have *this* job."

"Sweetness, relax. You won't get fired. I'm not going to fire you, and no one else would dare, not over something like having sex in the office."

"It's so unprofessional." She all but wrung her hands together.

"I'm not going to submit it to the company newsletter, if that's what you're worried about. I have no intention of telling anyone. Because no matter how badly you feel having sex with your boss might reflect on you, it looks ten times worse on me."

She met his gaze, perhaps gauging his sincerity, then gave a little nod. "Okay. Okay, I just got crazy there for a minute."

"Sit here with me a moment, okay? Lie here beside me. There's room for two."

Looking a bit dubious, she allowed him to draw

her next to him as he lay down on the sofa. After a bit of maneuvering, he had her tucked under his arm, her head on his shoulder. He stroked her arm. "Maybe this wasn't the smartest use of our time, but I wouldn't trade it for anything."

"Really? Please don't say it if you don't mean it."

"I've spent too much of my life trying to make other people happy. It felt good, just doing something purely for myself."

"Funny, I wouldn't have guessed you grew up that way. I imagined you living life totally on your terms, beholden to no one. But that's not how you live, is it."

"No. Once, maybe, but not for a long time."

"What happened?"

"Chandra happened."

"Your ex-wife."

"Yeah. She's kind of a force of nature. Like a hurricane. Hard to run from, harder to survive. She fell in love with a dashing adventurer, then tamed him and turned him into a corner-office lapdog."

"Then you ceased to be interesting to her. Is that it?"

"Exactly." He was amazed she saw it so clearly, so quickly. He'd never talked to anyone else about the crumbling of his marriage. Most of his male friends couldn't understand why he would divorce a hot number like Chandra. "She begged her grandfather to promote me. When my boss quit, it seemed logical for me to take his place. But it was never a good fit. The marriage fell apart pretty quickly, and I spent the next year recovering from the financial wreck my life was in. I couldn't afford to give up the salary until we sold the house she insisted we buy, pay off some credit cards. But I always intended to return to timber buying."

"So why didn't you?"

"Stan. He's Chandra's grandfather, but he had a soft spot for me even after the divorce. Chandra is the apple of his eye, but he isn't blind to her faults. He never held the divorce against me. In fact, he sort of took care of me. He got Chandra to back down from some ridiculous demands. I owe him for that."

"So you stay out of loyalty?"

Conner took a deep breath. He still had a hard time talking about this. "Stan has cancer. Not many people know. He might not have long to live."

"Oh, that's terrible."

"I couldn't just abandon the job when there was no one to take my place. The company's been in chaos and Stan asked me to stay, to help Hamilton keep an eye on things. He wanted to sell the company, but I convinced him not to, that we could weather the storm.

"Now this business with Cuddy…"

"I'm sorry I ever stirred up that can of worms. I just made things worse for everyone."

"No, you did the right thing. You saw something wrong that needed to be righted, and you spoke up. That takes courage."

"So you do believe me? That I really did see all that stuff?"

"Of course. I wouldn't have protected your identity otherwise."

"Thank you. Again." She kissed his cheek. "So I take it you don't believe Stan is guilty?"

"God, no. No way. He loves this company. He wouldn't do anything to drag it down. And he's not capable of murder. He's a kind, good man." And if he didn't survive the cancer, Conner was going to miss him terribly. He'd never known either of his own grandfathers. Stan had proved a wonderful mentor.

"So what do you think happened?"

"I don't know, but I'm trying to find out. I was Greg's boss, but I really had no idea what he was up to. He was always traveling. All I know is, he used to be a good forester, and then something happened."

"I'm sure it will all get sorted out."

"Yeah. Maybe." He absently stroked Jillian's hair while he stared into space, remembering snippets of conversation he'd had with Greg, searching for some hidden meaning, some clue that would steer him in the right direction. That was when he noticed the black spot under his desk ledge.

The desk had been a gift from Stan, a gorgeous, custom-made piece of tiger maple. There shouldn't have been a mark on it.

He sat up, dislodging Jillian abruptly.

"Conner?"

Wordlessly he pulled on his boxers and pants, then went to the desk to investigate. Under the edge of the desk was a plastic disk, about the size of a quarter. It seemed to be stuck on. What the hell?

He pried the thing off with his fingernails. And when he inspected it more carefully, he found a tiny label that read The Spy Store.

Oh, God. He knew what this was.

His first instinct was to tell Jillian, to share his surprise and dismay with her. But one look at her horrified expression, and he realized he didn't have to tell her what he'd found.

"You want to tell me what this is doing here?"

CHAPTER ELEVEN

JILLIAN PANICKED. SHE COULD have played dumb, but she wasn't fast enough on her feet. Instead she just stared in dawning dread.

"I can see by your reaction that you do know something about this." His words were clipped, as if he were tightly reining his temper.

Lord help her. "I can explain." She struggled for any logical explanation for why she would know anything about a listening device planted in his office. Anything but the truth. Nothing came to her.

"Well, you better start explaining. Because I'm pretty sure this constitutes a crime. So unless you'd like to find yourself in a jail cell—"

"You could at least hear me out before you start hurling threats." How could he be so cold, so unfeeling, after what they'd just shared?

"I'm all ears."

Jillian hastily threw on her clothes while he did the same. But she could feel him watching her, and not in an appreciative way. He was deliberately making her feel self-conscious.

She should have known. He'd had a cruel streak as a boy, and he hadn't grown out of it. He still garnered some enjoyment from observing her humiliation.

Jillian had come up with a number of lies she could tell and discarded all of them. She'd been skating on thin ice with her explanation for why she'd been searching Isaac's office. Conner wasn't going to buy any more lame stories, not when his own privacy had been violated.

"I take it this has something to do with why your job is so important to you," Conner said as she slipped on her shoes. "I'd actually deluded myself into believing it was because you enjoyed working with me."

"I *do* enjoy working with you." She bit her lip. No matter how she framed this, it was going to look bad. Why had she let herself give in to her attraction? His discovery of the bug would be bad under any circumstances, but it was so much worse coming on the heels of them having sex. He would never believe the two weren't connected, somehow.

"So much so that you're setting me up. Blackmail, is that it? Were you planning to post recordings of our tryst on the internet?"

"God, no!"

He looked around the office. "I'll bet there's a video camera in here somewhere."

"No. There's not. I planted the listening device because I was hoping to learn something related to Greg Tynes's murder. But the only thing I've overheard are some distinctly unflattering comments about myself."

"Unflattering comments?"

"You and Mr. Payne. Making fun of me. You called me a pretty bit of empty-headed fluff. You said I was stupid."

At least he had the good grace to appear uncomfortable. "That was your first day. I didn't know anything about you yet."

"Exactly. You judged me on my appearance. Just like you did in high school."

"Oh, no, you're not turning this back on me. You were snooping, digging around in my life for information. And to think, I gave you access to my office. My email. I told you things about my personal life—all so you can repeat the information to…who? Who hired you?"

He narrowed his eyes and swept his gaze over her dismissively. "You're not a cop, that much I can tell."

"How do you know?"

"Because an undercover cop wouldn't have given herself away so easily. You better spill it. I will find out. Is it Chandra? Is she trying to get more money out of me? Because that ship has left port."

She could let him think his ex-wife had hired her. It would buy her more time. But like he said, he *would* find out, and then she would be simply piling one lie on top of another.

"Not Chandra."

"One of the other directors, then, trying to discredit me. Ever since Stan was arrested, there's been a major power grab. Everybody knows Hamilton is retiring, and I'm the only other one Stan trusts. If they get rid of me, the way is clear for someone else to be named CEO."

The one thing she would not do is name the client. She had to protect Mr. Payne's anonymity or Daniel would fire her for sure. As it was, her continued employment at Project Justice had certainly been called into question.

"It's not any of those things. My goal is to exonerate Stan Mayall. I was looking for any information that might explain who really killed Greg Tynes, or why he was murdered."

"And you think *I* know?"

"I never seriously considered you a suspect. But others did. And still do, I might add."

"Who are you working for? And don't say Stan, because I'll know you're lying. Stan knows I had nothing to do with Greg's death."

"I can't tell you."

"Then get your things. I'll call Security and have you escorted out of the building." He got up and went to his desk, reaching for the phone.

Jillian quickly weighed her options. Either she confided in him, or she was out on her butt and Daniel would never trust her with another assignment.

"Wait, Conner. I'll tell you who I'm working for, but only because I am one-hundred-percent sure you're not guilty of anything except trying to hold the company together. Have you heard of Project Justice?"

His hand froze halfway to the phone. "Of course I have. It's that foundation started by the oil billionaire's son, the one who went to prison for killing a guy—"

"For *not* killing a guy," she corrected him. "He was pardoned, and the conviction was overturned last year when the real murderer was caught."

"Whatever. *You're* with Project Justice?"

"Does that seem so improbable? Are you judging me again based on my appearance?"

"If Stan had gone to Project Justice, he'd have told me. Nice try."

"I'm telling the truth. We'll go talk to Daniel Logan today—this afternoon. I'll explain that I blew my cover, and I'll convince him that you should not be considered a suspect. Then we'll move forward."

"Call him. Now."

He still didn't believe her. With a shrug, she went

to his desk phone and dialed the number she knew by heart. Elena, Jillian's replacement, answered.

"Elena, it's Jillian. Is Daniel available? It's slightly urgent." *Urgent* was reserved for life-or-death situations. *Slightly urgent* was their code for an unmitigated disaster, but nothing was burning, no ambulance had been called and no one was being held hostage.

"I'll find him. Hold on."

It took two minutes. The whole time, Conner simply stared at her, accusation in every breath he took.

And he was still so damn sexy it hurt. Why was her lot in life to always fall for men who couldn't possibly return her feelings? And why did her messy emotions always get her into so much trouble?

"Jillian. What's wrong?"

She saw no alternative but to confess everything. "Daniel. I'm afraid I've—"

Conner snatched the phone receiver out of her hand. "Do you mean to tell me you're actually Daniel Logan?"

Did Conner think she'd lied about that? She pressed the speaker phone button, daring him to stop her.

"It is," Daniel replied, sounding quite fierce. "And who might you be?"

"Conner Blake, director of Timber Operations for Mayall Lumber. We need to meet. Immediately. I think you know why. Unless you'd like me to go to the police."

Jillian struggled not to bury her face in her hands. Why was he being so hateful? Didn't he understand that she'd had to keep her true reasons for being here a secret?

"I can clear my schedule for you anytime you like. Would this afternoon be soon enough?"

Conner had been prepared for a fight. He looked a little surprised to be accommodated so easily. "How about three o'clock."

"I'll tell my staff to expect you. Jillian has the address."

Conner jabbed an angry finger at the disconnect button as he redirected his attention toward Jillian. "I have a meeting to go to. I suggest you take the afternoon off. Once your boss and I sort things out, one of us will let you know if you still have a job."

She nodded, relieved that she could escape his angry presence. But he was sorely mistaken if he thought she was going to slink off to her apartment and wait there meekly until the big boys decided her fate.

Yes, she'd screwed up. And yes, acting boldly and taking initiative were exactly what had gotten her into trouble. But she wasn't going to quit now. If she was going down, she would go down swinging.

She gathered as much of her dignity as she could find and headed out of Conner's office. But she couldn't resist one parting shot. She turned and looked at him directly.

"Was it good for you? I hope so. Because hell will freeze over before you get another shot at me. Oh, and before you go to the directors' meeting, you might want to rebutton your shirt."

He looked down at his crookedly fastened shirt and she slipped out and slammed the door.

ELENA LOOKED PUZZLED by Jillian's presence at the front door of Daniel's home. "I thought the meeting wasn't until three."

"It's not. I should have warned you I was coming

early. I need to speak to Daniel before Conner gets here."

Elena gave her a sympathetic pat on the shoulder. "Come in. Jillian, no offense, but you look just awful. I mean, every time I've seen you you've always been so composed, never a hair out of place, and right now you look like you've been tumbled in a clothes dryer."

Jillian stepped inside the marble foyer with its soothing sound of running water from the fountain, and she looked down at herself self-consciously. She was a wrinkled mess. She hadn't bothered to check her appearance before fleeing Mayall Lumber.

"I guess I'm pretty upset." Not many women could outdo Jillian in the grooming department, but Elena was one of them. The statuesque brunette, with her exotic features and designer wardrobe, always looked like she'd walked out of a Calvin Klein ad. Jillian's sense of style was downright frivolous compared to Elena's understated sophistication.

"Daniel is exercising his horse, but he should be back soon," Elena said. "Have you had lunch? I can get you a sandwich or a glass of milk or something."

The thought of food turned her stomach, but Jillian knew she should eat something. She had the shakes. "Do you have any yogurt?"

"Of course. The powder room is—" Elena laughed. "How silly, you know where everything is. Why don't you freshen up and meet me on the sunporch? Meanwhile, I'll call down to the stable and let Daniel know you're here."

"Thanks, Elena." It was easy to see why Daniel had hired the woman. She had a calming effect. She was efficient and gracious without making everyone around her feel as though they were in the army—which was what everyone said about Jillian.

While working for Daniel, Jillian had never gone anywhere without her clipboard. She had viewed managing Daniel's many needs and commitments the way a general regarded a complicated military campaign. She envied Elena her easy confidence.

When Jillian looked in the mirror, she scared herself. Easy to see why Elena had been concerned. She washed her face and quickly reapplied her makeup, then combed her hair and straightened her clothes. One of her earrings was missing—where had that gone to? Probably lost between the cushions of Conner's office sofa.

When she felt reasonably put back together she made her way to the sunporch, where she found a dish of plain yogurt—served in crystal, no less—along with several dishes of fresh fruit. She had her choice of raspberries, blueberries, peaches, as well as honey and chopped walnuts.

Ah, she missed this place sometimes. She normally had to make do with a carton from the supermarket.

Elena was in the corner, on the phone, speaking softly. She finished her conversation and claimed a chair opposite Jillian, where a mug of tea sat steeping.

Another mug, a selection of gourmet teas and a pot of hot water stood by for Jillian, in case she wanted tea, too. She was impressed with Elena's attention to detail.

"Are you okay?" Elena asked. "Really?"

"Secretly I thought I couldn't be replaced," Jillian said. "But you're good."

"Make no mistake, you were a hard act to follow," Elena said with a laugh. "If I had a nickel for every time someone around here said, 'Jillian did it this way,' I could retire."

That made Jillian feel only slightly better.

"Daniel will be done with his ride in about fifteen minutes. He said you can meet him at the stable. Take one of the golf carts."

"Thanks." Jillian forced herself to eat some of the yogurt. "Mmm, this is really good."

"It's just yogurt, hardly comfort food. Sure you don't want some French silk pie? Lemon pound cake? Maybe rocky road brownies?

Jillian's mouth watered. "You have all that just sitting around?"

"When Cora gets bored, she bakes. Anyway, you know Daniel. He always likes to have plenty of choices available for guests and staff. It's a miracle we aren't all trying out for *The Biggest Loser*."

Jillian well remembered how hard she'd had to fight temptation here, though there were always healthy choices available, too.

She pushed the yogurt away. "What the hell, my life as I know it is over. Might as well have a last meal. Bring on that French silk pie."

Elena smiled. "That's the spirit. I'll even join you."

Thick slices of the pie with fresh whipped cream arrived almost instantaneously. Jillian had to force herself not to gobble it down; she savored every sinful bite and refused to think about what part of her anatomy the fat might settle on.

This was how she'd turned into a pudgy teenager to begin with; in the absence of attention from the boy she was crazy about, food was her comfort. Here she was, allowing Conner's behavior to nudge her toward sweets.

No, she wasn't going to blame him. This fiasco was

all her doing. And if the situation didn't call for an indulgence, what did?

When she'd all but licked the plate, she stood and smoothed her clothes, then quickly reapplied lipstick. "I better get this over with."

"Good luck."

A golf cart was waiting for Jillian in the driveway.

She set out for the stables, cruising across the green carpet of lawn and appreciating the beauty of Daniel's estate all over again. She missed her safe, secure existence, nestled in this cocoon of opulence. But she could never come back here.

Anyway, Jillian needed to learn how to function in the real world. So far, she'd been a spectacular failure.

When she reached the huge, climate-controlled stable, Daniel was just arriving with his favorite mount, Laramie, a lovely chestnut polo pony. Daniel loved polo and probably could have played professionally if he hadn't had so many other agendas to accomplish.

"Good workout?" Jillian asked as Daniel gracefully dismounted.

"We had a good ride, didn't we, boy?" He stroked the gelding's neck while Jillian offered him a few blueberries she'd pilfered from her lunch.

Luis, one of the grooms, stood by to take the horse, but Daniel waved him off. "I'll take care of him today, thanks." He addressed Jillian. "Walk with me while I cool him down."

They walked to an exercise ring, where Daniel led the horse around the perimeter. The gelding followed, docile as a lapdog, and Jillian picked her way daintily through the dirt in her high heels, grateful someone had recently raked up all the manure.

"So, what's the story?"

"I messed up. Big-time."

"Start from the beginning."

"I sort of planted a listening device in Conner's office."

"Jillian, really?" He didn't sound quite as mad as she thought he ought to be. More like intrigued.

"I was anxious to produce results. I wanted to do a good job."

"Where did you get a— Never mind. I know."

Great. Now she was going to get Celeste in trouble, too.

"Anyone can buy one from The Spy Store," she said, which was the truth. "Conner never should have spotted the bug, but he had a…um, an unusual vantage point."

"Meaning…"

"He was lying on the sofa in his office. With me." She had to get the whole truth out, because she didn't want Conner revealing any surprises.

"*Jillian.* Damn."

"Yes, I slept with a murder suspect. But in all honesty, Daniel, if there's one thing I know, it's that Conner isn't the murderer. Of course that doesn't excuse my behavior."

Daniel said nothing.

"Please, yell at me or something. Fire me, whatever, just get it over with." That slice of French silk pie sat heavy in her stomach now, and she wished she'd stuck with the yogurt.

"Why did you sleep with him? Was it for the sake of the investigation? Because that might be taking your work ethic a bit too seriously."

"I don't know why I had sex with him. But it wasn't because I thought it was my job. Honestly, if I'd given my responsibilities more than half a thought, I'd never have done it. But I wasn't thinking at all. I just went all adolescent-schoolgirl-crush."

There, she'd told him the worst.

"I'd be lying if I said I'm not disappointed."

"Of course you are. I did something colossally stupid."

"Yes, you did."

Wow, that stung. Daniel wasn't pulling his punches. Even the horse huffed in disapproval. The back of her throat tightened, and for one horrifying moment she thought she might start crying. But amazingly, she didn't. She held it together.

"Enough beating yourself up, okay? The important thing is, did you learn something?"

"I've learned I'm incapable of having a grown-up relationship with a man. I won't go near another one as long as I live."

Daniel had the audacity to laugh. "That's a bit extreme. How about, no more men you work with. Or for."

"That would be a start, I guess." Jillian couldn't help the bitter note that crept into her voice.

Daniel walked Laramie into the stable, where the horse found his own stall and entered. Daniel got the gelding a can of oats to munch on, then started rubbing him down.

Jillian, who had a healthy respect for horses, even friendly ones like Laramie, stood outside the stall and leaned against the top of the door, resting her chin on her folded arms.

"Are you going to fire me?" she asked. In a way, that would be the easiest thing for her. She could just walk away, never have to lay eyes on Conner Blake again.

"Not unless you insist. It took too long to get you inside the company."

"For all the good it's done."

"Give it a rest, Jillian. You made a mistake. Everybody does. It's not the end of the world."

Okay. Okay, she had to stop feeling sorry for herself. Daniel would know the best way to proceed. "It may be a moot point. I'm not sure Conner will want me working for him anymore."

"Don't go borrowing trouble. I've got a little surprise in store for Mr. Conner Blake. Let's just see what he has to say."

CHAPTER TWELVE

CONNER WAS GRATEFUL FOR the time it took to drive to River Oaks, the area of Houston where the wealthiest of the wealthy resided. He'd at least cooled off a little. If he was going to face one of the richest, most influential men in the country, he wanted to do it with calm deliberation.

As he pulled up to the scrolled iron gates, he issued a low whistle. He'd grown up privileged, to be sure, but the Bellaire home his parents owned hadn't held a candle to this pile of rocks. His family had socialized with the Baxters, and the Baxters were friends with the Logans, but that was as close as Daniel had ever gotten to the high-and-mighty oil family.

He'd heard about this place, though. When Daniel Logan had gone on trial for murder, every detail of the Logan family's existence had been up for grabs with the press—including descriptions of the lavish mansion, which looked more like an ancient English manor house than something belonging in Houston.

It definitely did not disappoint.

Conner was about to push the intercom button and announce himself, but the gates whispered open, and he found himself cruising down a cobbled drive and trying not to gawk at the vast, manicured lawn and urns as big as his car filled with fall-blooming plants. It must have taken an army of gardeners to keep this place up.

The drive ended in a circle surrounding a fountain worthy of ancient Rome; another car was already parked there. Jillian's? It irked him slightly that she'd beat him here. As he parked behind it and got out, Conner had to clench his teeth so his jaw wouldn't continually drop. He'd imagined himself coming here and giving Daniel Logan a piece of his mind for snooping into his life with his pretty little spy minion. But confronting a man with this much wealth and power shouldn't be done on the fly. Logan was personal friends with the governor. Conner had no doubt the man could bury him if he chose, though by most counts Daniel was a fair and reasonable man, if a tad eccentric.

Conner's finger was poised above the doorbell when the huge oak door opened. Obviously he was being watched.

A beautiful woman with long dark hair stood on the other side of the door, wearing an expensive tailored suit and a frown. "Come in, Mr. Blake. The others are in the library. Follow me, please. Can I get you something to drink? There's water in the library, but if you'd like juice or a soft drink—"

"Water is fine."

She led him down a hallway lined with what appeared to be museum-quality paintings, stopping at a closed door and tapping softly before opening it.

"Mr. Blake is here."

"Good, bring him in." The voice belonged to Daniel Logan. He sounded even more formidable than he had on the phone.

Conner squared his shoulders and entered the room, a pleasant, casual sort of den with a bar at one end, a huge stone fireplace in the center, and floor-to-ceiling books. An antique library table had been set up for a meeting. After taking in the room, Conner allowed his gaze to settle on the table. Burled walnut, the kind you couldn't find anymore. Daniel Logan, younger than Conner would have imagined and very fit, stood and held out his hand.

"Conner, thank you for coming."

"I believe I'm the one who insisted on this meeting."

"I'd have had my say with you one way or another," Daniel said affably.

Conner allowed his gaze to drift to the other occupants of the room. Jillian was there, looking small and pale, her ivory complexion drained of all color, her mouth stiff and her hands folded on the table in front of her.

His heart squeezed painfully. Mere hours ago, she'd been warm and wild in his arms, making love to him with crazy abandon. Now she looked terrified.

He'd done that to her. He had no reason to feel guilty—he was the wronged party here. But he felt guilty just the same.

Finally Conner let himself take in the other person seated at the table, a frail old man in a wheelchair. It took Conner several heartbeats to recognize that the man was Stan Mayall.

"Stan? What— How—"

"Why aren't I in jail? They let me out for chemo. Just so happens Daniel here arranged for my treatment to take place here." He had an IV in his arm and a bag of some clear liquid dripping into his vein.

Amazing what enough money could accomplish. Which reminded him…the Logan Charitable Trust donated significant funds to preserving rain forest habitats around the globe. He did not want to make an enemy of Daniel Logan.

Conner felt an unexpected rush of affection for the elderly man.

"How do you feel?"

"Not so bad. My doc thinks the chemo is working. So don't write me off yet. Keep an eye on Hamilton. Don't let him get too comfortable running the show." Stan's eyes gleamed with humor. No one thought Hamilton was comfortable as acting CEO. In his mind he was already fly-fishing in Montana. He couldn't wait to retire.

"Sit down, please," Daniel said, taking his own chair. He seemed eager to start the meeting.

Conner sat stiffly. "So, Stan, I take it you had something to do with my administrative assistant spying on me?"

"Oh, get off your high horse," Stan said. "If I didn't trust you, I never would have let you marry my granddaughter. I wasn't the one who contacted Project Justice. That was Payne's doing."

"Hamilton Payne?" Conner said, just to be sure. "He thinks I had something to do with the murder?"

"Simmer down, would you?" Despite his current state of debilitation, Stan still had a commanding presence. Conner shut his mouth and allowed him to explain. "You weren't the target of the investigation. It just so happened there was a vacancy near you where Jillian here could be placed without suspicion, and whose fault is that? You're the one who can't keep an assistant."

Conner nodded. Point taken.

"I selected Jillian for this assignment," Logan said, "because she had the necessary clerical skills, the business knowledge and the polish to carry off the job of assisting a busy executive. But she's new to investigating, and she did overstep her authority by placing a listening device in your office without authorization. Since she was reporting to me, I'll accept the mistake as my own, and I apologize. It won't happen again."

"No, it won't, because she's fired." And when everyone else at the table just stared at him, he felt the urge to justify his decision. "She deceived me, she invaded my privacy, and I won't have her working for me."

"Damn it, boy," Stan said in a surprisingly strong voice. Conner knew he must be on Stan's shit list for him to use the word *boy*. That was how Stan had addressed him the first six months they'd known each other—until he'd gained the older man's trust. "You act like the girl paid you a personal insult. She was just a little overzealous. She wants to find Greg's killer just like you and I do. I don't know what your beef is, unless you're being defensive because you have something to hide."

Oh, now, that was a low blow. Stan knew damn well Conner had had nothing to do with Greg's death.

"He has a right to be angry," Jillian said.

"On the contrary," Conner said, "I believe Jillian's actions *were* personal. She has an ax to grind with me. We have a previous…relationship…" Uh-oh. He'd better step very carefully or this was going to blow up in his face. Daniel and Stan were looking at him as if they believed he'd deflowered and abandoned her.

"Not *that* kind of relationship," he quickly clarified. "I knew her when we were kids. I pulled a childish prank on her and she's been mad about it ever since."

"What kind of prank?" Stan asked. "It must have been pretty serious for you to believe she would carry a grudge for so long."

"I, um, I don't want to embarrass Jillian further."

"You're concerned about embarrassing me?" Jillian

folded her arms. "That's a switch. Anyway, I already told Daniel most of it." She turned to Stan. "Conner made a paper dress from wood by-products and entered it in the science fair. He asked me to model it. Then *someone* turned the sprinklers on and the dress melted, and Conner, instead of lifting a finger to help me cover up, laughed hysterically while I fled the scene in my underwear."

"Mmm," Daniel said, and that was when Conner realized he was biting his lip to keep from laughing.

Stan faked a coughing fit.

Jillian rolled her eyes. "Come on, guys, are we all thirteen years old here? I did carry a grudge, I'll admit. But it's not like I wanted Conner arrested for murder. I never seriously believed the gossip about him."

"Fair enough," Conner said. "Jillian was playing Nancy Drew and she got carried away. But there's no reason for her to continue working undercover at Mayall Lumber. If you need someone on the inside, you've got me. I'm going to find out who killed Greg Tynes."

"Really," Daniel said. "And what have you uncovered so far?"

"Tynes was involved in something. I'm not sure what, but he'd started performing his job erratically—showing up late, not returning phone calls, disappearing for days at a time."

Daniel started taking notes. "Go on."

"Tynes had a girlfriend. They had a contentious relationship, according to his mother and some emails I read. But I don't know her name."

"What else?"

"I've tried to figure out who Greg might have connected with at the company. I've searched offices and phone logs, email accounts. Nothing."

"Would you like to know what Jillian has accomplished?"

Conner shrugged.

Daniel had a neat stack of papers in front of him. "Jillian has been filing daily reports since she began working at Mayall Lumber. Her first day, she befriended a security guard." Daniel read from the report. "'Letitia tells me everyone thinks my new boss is the murderer. I don't buy it, but I'll proceed cautiously.'"

Okay. So maybe she hadn't believed he was a murderer.

"She also cultivated a relationship with an investigative reporter who shared his opinions on who might be responsible for Greg's death, and why.

"She befriended the wife of budget director Isaac Cuddy, and though it wasn't her job, identified him as a thief."

"That was never proved," Conner said. He was feeling defensive, knew he should stop, but instead he plowed ahead. "The stolen goods were never found."

Jillian's eyes widened in shock, and he immediately regretted his words. "You said you believed me!"

"I did…do believe you. I'm just pointing out that your actions didn't produce results."

Stan glowered at Conner. "A lot you know."

"Based on information Jillian provided by searching through Cuddy's computer files and emails," Daniel continued, "our cyber investigator at Project Justice was able to accumulate proof positive that Cuddy has been stealing from the company for years. We've turned it over to the district attorney, and charges will be filed within the next week."

"Huh."

"Jillian also discovered the identity of Greg's girl-friend."

What? He'd tried every which way to discover the woman's name. He'd talked to every friend and ac-quaintance of Greg's. No one would reveal the mystery woman's name. How had Jillian done it?

"In the interest of her privacy, she'll remain name-less for now." Daniel folded the paper he'd been read-ing from and set it aside. "In short, Jillian has proved herself observant and resourceful in the execution of her first assignment. All while performing her admin-istrative assistant duties with some degree of brilliance, despite the fact that you, Conner Blake, are a pain in the ass to work for."

"Excuse me?"

Stan slapped his palm on the table. "He's trying to say you're damn lucky she's put up with your B.S. for this long."

"So, Stan, you want her to continue as my admin?" The possibility didn't bother him as much as it should have. Whether he was angry with her or making love to her, Jillian had made life at Mayall Lumber a whole lot more...stimulating.

"Provided Jillian is willing to continue with this as-signment," Daniel said, "and I wouldn't blame her if she bowed out."

Jillian actually came out of her chair. "Of course I don't want to quit."

"Then it's settled," Daniel said. "The two of you will work together. Share information. But just remember this, Conner. Jillian works for me, not you. You will treat her with the respect she deserves. And you will *keep it in your pants*. Have I made myself clear?"

Conner swallowed. He now understood why Daniel

wielded so much power. It wasn't merely the size of his bank account. "Perfectly."

JILLIAN ARRIVED EARLY at the office the next day with two Krispy Kreme doughnuts and a large coffee. She placed them enticingly on her desk and hoped Conner arrived to work hungry, as he often did.

She'd been shocked as hell that Daniel had wanted her to continue at Mayall Lumber. She'd been positive her investigative work hadn't amounted to anything, but when he'd listed her accomplishments, she'd felt a sense of pride rising in her chest. She'd clearly made some mistakes, but she'd done some things right, too.

That hadn't stopped Daniel from reading her the riot act after Conner had left. He'd told her in very specific terms that, though she had potential as an investigator, she had to leave her emotions at home. Any other boss would have fired her, but out of respect for her family, her sterling character and all of the work she'd done for him in the past, he was giving her another chance.

She was not going to reveal to Conner even a hint of her anger. Or any other emotion.

An unhappy voice mail awaited her. "Jillian." The screeching female didn't identify herself, but she didn't have to. "I thought we were friends. I knew you were too nice to be true, and now you've stabbed me in the back by casting suspicion on my husband. Well, good luck throwing the party on your own. Don't count on my help—or that of any of the other directors' wives. They won't be returning your phone calls or answering your emails." Click.

Jillian sighed as she replaced her phone's receiver into its cradle. She'd actually started to feel like Ariel was a friend. Now, due mostly to Jillian, her husband would likely go to jail. That sweet little boy, Benjamin, would be without a father, and their world as they knew it would cease to exist. Though Jillian believed people like Isaac Cuddy should be brought to justice, she couldn't feel good about what she'd done. Friends just weren't that easy to come by.

"Krispy Kreme?"

Jillian jumped. Lost in her own thoughts, she hadn't seen Conner approach. "That's right." She scooted the two doughnuts closer, picked one up and took a big bite. She felt sinful, indulging in the forbidden treat. Next to frozen Snickers bars, glazed doughnuts were her favorite.

Conner started to reach for the other one, but she snatched it out of his reach. "That's not for you."

"Who's it for?" He sounded bewildered.

"Me. I'm going to eat them both. The coffee is mine, too." She wanted to be extra sure he understood she wasn't going to wait on him anymore.

"Oh. You're pretty mad at me, I guess."

"No, not mad. We both did what we had to do, and now it's time to move forward."

"Agreed. Come into my office, and I'll tell you our strategy for how, exactly, we'll move forward." He turned and headed to his office, clearly expecting her to follow.

She just sat there, savoring her doughnut and coffee.

A few moments later he reappeared. "Jillian?"

"I'm sorry, were you speaking to me? Seems like I heard some kind of *order* hurled at me, but I'm not sure."

He cleared his throat. "Jillian, would you please accept my invitation to sit down in the privacy of my office and discuss strategy?"

"All right."

She wasn't fooled. It took longer than five minutes to break the habit of tossing orders at someone who'd been your subordinate. But she felt certain he would adjust to the new status quo.

As soon as she entered the office, memories assailed her—skin on skin, clothes flying, the sound of Conner's breathing hot and fast, the feel of him inside her, also hot and fast.

Her face flushed. She wished Conner had chosen some other location for their meeting, but Daniel's advice was foremost in her brain. She absolutely could not allow her emotions to interfere with her work.

She shoved aside the memories. Conner sat in one of the beautifully grained mission-style chairs. Jillian boldly sat on the sofa facing him, the exact spot where they'd made love.

"So," Conner began. "Who was Greg's girlfriend? She could be the murderer, you know. A femme fatale. I want to talk to her."

"You should leave her to Daniel. Really."

"We're supposed to be working together, Jillian. How can we do that if we aren't honest with each other?"

"Okay, but you're not going to like it. He was seeing Chandra."

Conner's jaw fell open. "Chandra, my ex-wife Chandra?"

Jillian nodded.

"Well, that makes sense. She fell for me when I had Greg's job. How did you find out?" He didn't seem too upset.

"Letitia, the security guard. She knows everything."

"Chandra had nothing to do with Greg's murder,"

Conner said. "Daniel is wasting time if he thinks she's capable of—"

"But she might know what Greg was involved in," Jillian pointed out. "The thing he was going to tell the reporter about."

"And you don't have any idea what that thing was?"

"None," she admitted. "Unless it was somehow related to Cuddy's theft, but that seems unlikely. From what I could tell, Cuddy and Greg never crossed paths."

"They didn't. Cuddy gave me a budget, and I administered it. Greg worked for me. There would be no reason for Greg to deal directly with Cuddy."

"So what else could Greg have discovered? He spent most of his time in the field, right?"

"Yeah. He dealt some with the mills, but I've been going over everything. Nothing jumps out. I keep going back to how Greg marked those trees at Stirrup Creek."

"Has he done a bad job marking trees at any other locations?"

"He was behaving erratically—missing deadlines, disappearing for days at a time. That's why I brought him closer to home. But I don't have any information specifically about tree marking. I've made inquiries at his last few jobs and I'm waiting to hear back."

Jillian held up one finger. "What if one of your competitors was paying him to screw things up? Make Mayall Lumber look bad?"

Conner frowned. "Why didn't I think of that? You know, you're pretty good at this investigating stuff."

She leaned back and crossed her legs. "Thank you." *Score one for the home team.*

"I'm going back to Stirrup Creek. I'll talk to everyone associated with that job. Someone must know something."

"Do you want me to go with you?" *Please, dear God, let him say no.* She didn't think she could handle spending hours with him in a car. No matter how disastrous their hookup had turned out, she couldn't stop wanting him—now more than ever.

Like Eve with her apple, she'd tasted forbidden fruit and wanted more, even if it meant eternal damnation. She forced herself to picture Stan Mayall's face. She had to be strong for that poor, sick old man. Now that she had an actual living and breathing person to attach to the name, she had stronger motivation to free him. Daniel was doing everything he could to ensure Stan received good medical care, but he was still in jail.

If he was dying, he at least deserved to die in the comfort of his own home.

"You can probably be more use here," Conner said diplomatically, and she relaxed slightly. "Don't you have a party to plan?"

"Yes. And since Ariel and the other wives have abandoned me, there's more work than ever." Lots of people to talk to, conversations to eavesdrop on, offices to snoop through. She would have to be more careful than she was when she'd searched Isaac Cuddy's office. Conner wouldn't be here to save her bacon with a steamy kiss if she got caught.

As a means of investigating, Jillian's party-planning had yielded mixed results. She had a list of who was coming to the picnic and what food they would bring, but she hadn't stumbled across any smoking guns.

The one thing she *had* discovered was that everyone was horrified at the prospect of Chandra Mayall inheriting the company. Some of the adjectives used to describe her included *scheming, grasping, lying sack of*

silicone and *man-eater*. The more Jillian learned about
Conner's ex-wife, the more strongly she believed Chandra should be considered a serious suspect. She was in
a contentious relationship with the deceased and she
had money problems, which gave her strong motive for
killing Greg and framing her grandfather.

But she certainly couldn't tell Conner of her suspicions. He'd made his feelings clear on that matter.
She reported everything to Daniel; he could decide
how to proceed.

Her "partnership" with Conner was in name only.
They were each pursuing their own agendas. Once a
day they met to compare notes. She wasn't sharing everything with him, and she suspected he wasn't being
totally open, either. She continued her admin responsibilities—Conner still had a job to perform. But she
remained cool toward him, afraid that if their relationship warmed even a few degrees, she would find herself naked in his arms again.

Keeping things on a coolly professional level was
her safest course of action.

As her third week as an investigator churned past,
she found herself stupidly excited about the company
picnic. At least this was something she knew she was
good at, and with or without Ariel and her crew, it was
going to be a success. The one thing she hadn't done
was personally visit the venue.

So on the following Thursday, almost a week since
she blew her cover, she informed Conner she would
be gone for half the day, paying a visit to Mayall Mill
Number One.

"That's fantastic," he said, which wasn't the reaction she'd been expecting. Damn, he looked good today
in a baby-blue golf shirt, fashionably wrinkled khakis

and loafers. On him, business casual looked as stunning as a thousand-dollar suit would on someone else.

It was the way he carried himself, she decided. As if he owned the whole damn world.

"You want to be rid of me that bad?"

"No, it's just that I really need to visit Mill Number One, as well. Although it's more of a tourist attraction than anything, we still mill some exotic woods there—the real fine stuff used by artists and handcrafted furniture makers. Apparently there was a problem with some bird's-eye maple from Michigan. The miller there says the wood that arrived isn't the quality that was supposedly harvested."

"Let me guess—Greg Tynes was involved."

"You got it."

"So...you want to come with me?"

"If you don't mind. We can share a car. Every little bit saved in the budget is a help. And it's ecological."

Right. How could she say no to that, just because she found her heart aching whenever she was in the same room with him? Clearly he wasn't similarly bothered. He acted like nothing had happened, that they were just two colleagues.

He was the one who'd wanted her off the case. He'd been steaming about that listening device. So why wasn't he mad anymore? Maybe he got over arguments faster than she did.

"All right," she agreed breezily. "I can leave whenever you're ready."

"Let's see what the motor pool has available."

Twenty minutes later, they were on the road once again headed to a location in the Piney Woods. Jillian made no effort to engage Conner in conversation. She was willing to cooperate for the sake of helping Stan, but that was as far as it went. She couldn't get those harsh words Conner had spoken to her out of her mind.

She let him drive, of course. Macho man probably wouldn't tolerate letting the little lady take the wheel. She sat hunched in the passenger seat of their company car, a sporty little hybrid, and focused on her phone, answering email and texting back and forth with her mother, who knew nothing about Jillian's new career. She thought Jillian was working as an admin at Project Justice, and Jillian found herself having to make up fake accounts of what her job entailed. Her mom would have thrown a fit if she knew that by day Jillian snooped around in executives' offices, and in the evenings, she practiced her shooting and learned Tae Kwon Do.

"So you're still not talking to me?" Conner asked after twenty minutes of silence.

"If there's something you want to talk about, relating to the case, I'm available."

He sighed.

She did her best to ignore that.

"I just thought we could take a step back."

"Back in time, you mean? To that brief period where we were nice to each other? Not possible."

"Can we at least be friends?"

She sent him a scathing look. "Let me think... Uh, no."

"It's going to be hard seeing each other, day in and day out, and not be friends."

"If there's one lesson I've learned over the past three weeks it's that there is no room in the workplace for emotions. Positive or negative. I intend to be responsible and efficient with you and everyone else I work with. If that's not to your liking, bring it up with Daniel."

"Daniel."

Something about the way he said the billionaire's name stuck in her craw. "What about Daniel?"

"He's really something. And he sure seems to think you hung the sun and the moon."

That made her laugh. "You have no idea what you're talking about. He came very close to firing me, and the only reason he didn't was out of respect for my family."

"He didn't give *me* the impression he wanted to fire you."

"Daniel is loyal. As long as I work for him, he has my back."

"You think a lot of him."

"I admire him a great deal."

"And there's not a little something else there?"

"Good God, Conner, Daniel is a happily married man. I would never—" She was overreacting. Because Conner had obviously spotted something—a certain intimacy she shared with Daniel from all those years of being privy to every detail of his life. It wasn't sexual. Even when she'd had a giant crush on him, he'd been more of a romantic, heroic figure to her rather than a potential lover.

"So you don't have a habit of sleeping with your bosses?"

Okay, now he was just trying to piss her off. He wanted to see her lose her temper, probably because any reaction, even anger, was better than the cold shoulder.

"No. You're the only boss I ever crossed the line with."

Did he have the gall to look pleased about that?

Her mother had sent her another text: Free for dinner Fri? I have a guy for u.

Thank heavens she had plans for Friday. She and Celeste were going to the shooting range for target practice.

Can't Fri and stop fixing me up pls. Hell, maybe she should let her mother match her to some boring, highly eligible man. She certainly wasn't doing a bang-up job finding good prospects on her own.

It took them ninety minutes to get to Mayall Mill Number One, which was in the northeast corner of Montgomery County. The mill dated from the early 1900s and much of the old buildings and equipment had been preserved. The site had been transformed into a beautiful historic park, a popular location for school field trips, parties and even weddings.

"This is really quite lovely," she said. "And if the weather stays like this, it will be perfect." It was seventy degrees, clear and sunny with a slight breeze—ideal picnic weather. The breeze teased her skirt, a rather short, flirty garment with black and white polka-dots, which she'd paired with a soft black top with puff sleeves, a wide red belt and black kitten heels.

She hoped Conner was eating his heart out.

"Want a tour?" Conner asked.

"Sure." She needed to know the layout and amenities, she figured, and Conner apparently knew this place backward and forward.

A large, open-air shed housed the main attraction, an enormous six-foot-diameter saw blade that was powered by a system of belts and gears, a steampunk dream. A tall, skinny man in overalls and an apron was applying oil to the gears with an old-fashioned oil can.

"Hey, welcome to Mayall Mill Number One. How y'all doing today? Mr. Blake, what brings you here?"

"Bookkeeping," Conner said with suitable vagueness. "Ms. Baxter here is planning the company picnic. Could you show her around?"

"Be glad to. My name's Lucas, ma'am. I'd offer my hand, but it's kind of greasy."

Jillian smiled, liking Lucas immediately. "No problem. Call me Jillian. I understand you have tables and chairs, and some way to refrigerate food?"

"Yes, ma'am. We have a lot of functions here, school picnics and such. We can put on a pretty good shindig."

"Excellent."

Lucas showed her around while Conner went to the office to find the mill's manager and sort out the problem of the bird's eye maple. Meanwhile, Jillian couldn't help but admire the beautiful boards produced by the mill's antique blade, and a huge planer.

Not all of the equipment was well cared for. Some had deteriorated. Mysterious-looking machines sat around on the grounds, reminding Jillian of great, rusty insects. Conveyor belts ran here and there, and an old steam engine sat on railroad tracks that went nowhere.

The air was redolent with the smell of freshly sawn wood. Jillian found it invigorating.

"What are these little hills all over the place?" she asked. The hills, covered with grass and some with flowers, dotted the landscape and surely weren't a natural part of the terrain, which was otherwise dead flat.

"Under those hills are big piles of sawdust. Back in the day, they would just let it collect here and there, then cover it up with dirt. Nowadays we recycle the sawdust. The cellulose is useful for a good many products—pressed wood, of course, but Mr. Blake has been experimenting with making fabric. He has this idea for cheap, disposable clothing that could be turned into fuel after it's been worn."

Jillian skidded to a halt. "You're kidding."

"No, it's true. You can see some of the prototypes in the gift shop. He's still working out all the kinks."

So, the paper dress of long ago had been more than a practical joke. He actually was interested in producing clothes from wood by-products.

"I will definitely check it out."

Lucas continued his tour. "We're headed to the drying shed. All of our wood is kiln-dried now, it's the best way. So the drying shed has mostly been converted into storage. We have a big walk-in refrigerator and freezer, the tables and chairs…well, you'll see."

"Sounds perfect."

Just as they entered the huge shed, Lucas's cell phone rang. "You can go on in and look around, I gotta take this."

"Okay."

She entered the cavernous drying shed, which stored all manner of equipment from an old tractor to bags of balloons. It didn't seem very well organized, so she just started poking around. She found a closet with at least twenty large folding tables. They looked ancient but in good repair. Another enclosure held folding chairs, all made of wood. She wondered how many parties those old chairs had seen.

She located the walk-in refrigerator, circa 1940. It was small—only a couple of people could stand in here at the same time. Part of the crowded feeling came from an old chest freezer pushed against one wall. That would work great for storing ice cream.

The fridge looked plenty big enough to store drinks

and hot dogs and whatnot, except that it already had a lot of stuff in it, stuff that apparently didn't need to be in a refrigerator—like a pile of old burlap feed bags. Good heavens, what would anyone keep those for? Horses had once been employed to haul milled lumber to waiting railroad cars, but that had to be more than seventy years ago!

She would see if Lucas would mind if she moved them temporarily. She could probably take care of that today. She grabbed the edges of several of the bags, intending to see just how big a pile she was dealing with.

And she uncovered a human hand clutching a silver chain.

Jillian screamed—what else was she supposed to do? But then she remembered herself. She was a Project Justice investigator. She had to get hold of herself.

The authorities had to be summoned, of course. But she couldn't resist a peek at the rest of the body. She needed to know who it was—and whether this murder had any connection to Greg Tynes. Her heart pounding like a jackhammer, she pulled back another wad of bags.

She knew that face.

Just then the refrigerator door opened and Conner burst in. "Jillian. What's wrong?"

"D-dead b-b-body. It's Mark Bowen."

CHAPTER THIRTEEN

"HOLY SON OF A MONKEY!" Conner's first instinct was to get the hell out of there. But then he realized Jillian was frozen in place, just staring at the man's face.

He came up beside her and put his hands on her shoulders. "Who is Mark Bowen?"

"A reporter."

Conner had heard that name recently. Wait—the email from Brazil, referring to an *Inspector* Bowen. The reporter must have been asking questions.

"Okay. Drop those bags and let's get out of here and call the police."

She couldn't seem to tear her gaze away. "Conner. Look what's in his hand."

Conner didn't want to get any closer to the body than he had to. For one thing, his self-preservation instincts dictated that he not risk dropping any miniscule particle of his DNA near the body. But he could see something silver clutched in the dead man's grip, and he took a couple of steps closer.

Oh, God. "That's my Saint Christopher medal."

"Uh-huh." Jillian was shivering violently now. The refrigerator was close to freezing and she wore only a thin top, a short skirt and bare legs.

"You don't think that I—" Oh, hell, they could sort that out later. She was either going into shock or suffering from hypothermia. He pulled the burlap bag out of her hand, dropped them on the ground, and all but dragged her out of the refrigerator.

A couple of small tables and chairs had been set up near some vending machines. He guided Jillian there and pushed her into a chair even as he tugged his cell phone out of his pocket.

The 9-1-1 operator sounded suitably impressed. "I'm sending help now," the woman said. "Are you sure he's dead?"

"Oh, he's dead." Unless live people turned that ghastly shade of green.

"Someone from the Montgomery County Sheriff's Department should be there in about twenty minutes. Please stay on the line with me until they get there. And don't touch anything."

"No, we won't." He put the phone on Speaker and laid it on the table, then took Jillian's hands between his and chafed them. They were cold as ice cubes. "Jillian? You okay?"

"I… Yeah, I think so. I just never found a dead body before."

"Me, neither. And I hope to God I never do again."

The operator was yammering at them again, trying to get as much information as possible out of them. But Conner was too freaked out by seeing his Saint Christopher medal clutched in a dead man's hand.

That reporter must have been getting too close to the truth. Someone had killed him and framed Conner—undoubtedly the same person who had clumsily framed Stan Mayall.

"Sir?" the operator said. "Are you still there?"

"Yes, I'm still here."

"Does it look like foul play was involved?"

"The body was hidden in a refrigerator under a stack of bags. I don't think he got there by accident."

"Are you in immediate danger?"

"Who the hell knows?"

"How did the man die?"

"Look, I don't know, okay? I didn't spend time studying him. I just got the hell out of there."

"He had a chest wound." Jillian broke her silence, sounding more normal than she had a couple of minutes ago. "And powder burns on his shirt, like he was shot at point-blank range."

"And who am I speaking with?" the operator asked.

"This is Jillian Baxter. I'm an investigator for Project Justice."

Conner doubted the wisdom of revealing that bit of information. These days most everyone had heard of Project Justice. The bad news was, not everyone approved of the foundation's goals. Some people—especially those in law enforcement—thought it was all about getting criminals out of jail. Project Justice, by its very nature, made law enforcement and the criminal justice system look bad for wrongly convicting innocent people.

"Well, I'm sure that qualifies you to determine cause of death," the operator said in a snooty voice.

"Excuse me for living," Jillian murmured.

They didn't have to deal with the operator any longer. Two uniformed sheriff's deputies arrived, along with a plainclothes detective.

Well, *plainclothes* was a misnomer in this case. The man who identified himself as Detective Sergeant Hudson Vale wore a pair of faded jeans and one of the loudest Hawaiian shirts Conner had ever seen—along with a tie sporting a pink flamingo.

"They let you dress like this for work?" Conner asked. "Seriously?"

"Conner, let him be," Jillian said, extending her hand to Vale. "Detective Vale, I know you by reputation. I understand you were a big help when our investigator Billy Cantu was working on the Mary-Francis Torres case. I'm Jillian Baxter."

"Pleasure's mine. So you're working a case?"

"Yes. Stan Mayall is accused of killing one of his employees. I'm supposed to passively gather information about the company, but this has gone way beyond anything I expected to find."

"Let's see what we got."

Vale and one of the two uniforms entered the refrigerator. A few minutes later, a lone crime scene investigator arrived, and he squeezed in, as well. They left the door open, but no one seemed to be paying much attention to Conner and Jillian.

"So," Jillian whispered as they both stood in front of the vending machine. "Should we tell them who the Saint Christopher medal belongs to?"

"We won't have to," he said grimly. "It's inscribed on the back. 'To Conner, come home safe to me, Chandra.' So unless you know any other Conners once married to Chandras, I think they'll figure it out."

"That's bad."

"Yeah, no kidding."

"It's best if we be completely honest with the cops," she said. "Daniel says any time you lie, even about something inconsequential, it comes back to bite you in the butt."

"This isn't exactly inconsequential. Jillian, what did you do with the medal?" Realizing it sounded like an accusation, he quickly added, "I don't think you killed the guy and framed me. But whoever did had to get hold of that medal somehow."

"It was still in the console when I drove home that Friday morning. I put it in the top drawer of your desk."

"I never saw it there."

"So someone took it on Friday or over the weekend. But I locked the office door. I'm sure of it."

"Lots of people have keys. You broke into Cuddy's office easily enough."

She pressed her fingertips to her temples. "I'm trying to think if I saw anyone loitering nearby in the past few days."

He took her hand. "You don't think I did it?"

"Conner, of course not. I'm not going to pretend you're my best friend right now, but I've said it before and I'll say it again, no way on God's green earth you're capable of murder."

He was so moved by her faith in him, he didn't know what to say. He squeezed her hand. Their gazes met. In the span of a heartbeat, they came to an understanding, and he knew she would take his side. Regardless of their quarrels and misadventures, he could think of no one who would be a fiercer champion. Even if sometimes she wanted to see him skewered and cooked slowly over an open flame, she would stand up for the truth.

He was deeply afraid he was falling in love with her.

"Excuse me, Mr. Blake?"

Conner whirled around to find Detective Vale standing just outside the refrigerator door, holding a plastic bag with his Saint Christopher medal inside.

"'To Conner, come home safe—'"

"Yes, it's mine. And no, I didn't kill him. I didn't even know him."

"You're sure? You didn't look closely enough to see the gaping chest wound, but you studied his face?"

"Actually, no. Jillian recognized him as a reporter, Mark Bowen. I've heard his name, but that's about it."

Vale focused on Jillian. "You know him, then?"

"I met him just once. He'd been talking with Greg Tynes, the victim in the case I'm working on. Greg was a potential whistle-blower. He told Bowen he knew something was going on at Mayall Lumber, something illegal that would take the company down. But Greg died before he could tell Mark what it was."

The detective looked thoughtful. "So you think the reporter might have died for the same reason—he found out about some illegal activity…here? What could be going on at a historic park?"

"There might be a connection," Conner said. "That's why I was here today, actually. The mill manager has been receiving substandard grades of wood from timber operations managed by Greg Tynes before he died. There's something going on—I haven't figured it out yet. He was either deliberately sabotaging the company, or…selling off the best wood on the side."

"I'll want to hear all about it. You won't mind coming with me to headquarters for a little chat?"

Oh, boy. This didn't feel good.

"Is that really necessary?" Jillian asked. "He didn't do it. He's been clumsily framed—just like Stan was for Greg's murder."

"If that's the case, we'll sort it out," Vale said mildly.

Jillian took out her phone and made a quick call. "Daniel. Can Raleigh come to the Montgomery County Sheriff's Department right away? Conner needs a lawyer."

Vale made a face. "Raleigh Shinn? Really? With one phone call you got enough clout to summon her?"

Conner didn't know if *clout* was the right word, but Jillian certainly had the ear of the almighty Daniel Logan. He felt a stab of jealousy even as his heart swelled. He was lucky to have Jillian in his corner.

Despite the terrible things he'd said about her yesterday.

He just hoped to hell her faith would be enough, because if not, he was in a heap of trouble. He'd been questioned in Greg Tynes's murder, mostly because the guy had worked under him. Despite the gossip mill, the cops hadn't seriously entertained him as a suspect—the Houston police had already marked Stan as their man.

But now, the fact he'd been questioned at all would look bad.

"DO YOU THINK I KILLED that man?" Jillian blurted out the moment Vale's butt hit his chair. She'd been so intent on proving Conner's innocence, it hadn't occurred to her that she might be a suspect, as well.

But as soon as she'd arrived at the sheriff's department, she'd been taken to an interrogation room. She'd waited there, alone, while Vale questioned Conner in another room, Raleigh at his side. Two hours later, Vale and Raleigh had joined her.

Vale had the nerve to look faintly amused. "You knew the deceased and you discovered the body. I would be a dunce if I didn't at least question you. So, Ms. Baxter, how did you come to find that body? What made you go into the refrigerator and start digging around in a pile of old feed bags?"

"I was planning the company picnic." She went on

to explain that she was checking out the food storage facilities.

"And why was Conner with you?"

"He hitched a ride with me. To save gas. He had business at the mill as well—as he explained earlier. He needed to talk to the manager about some bird's-eye maple."

"You've been working closely with Conner for a couple of weeks, now, is that right?"

"Yes. Project Justice arranged for me to fill the vacancy of Conner's assistant as my cover. But it became necessary to bring him into our confidence, so we were working together, trying to figure out who might have killed Greg and framed Stan."

"Did you come up with any theories about that?"

"I have several theories. Would you like to hear them?"

"I'd be delighted." Why did she get the idea that Vale was humoring her?

She went over her theories—that Greg was involved in something illegal; that someone had paid him to make his employer look bad; that Mark Bowen had learned the truth and confronted the murderer. She told him about Isaac Cuddy, the office thief, who could be involved in other nefarious activities.

"Finally," she said, "I hesitate to mention this, but… Chandra Mayall, Stan's granddaughter, was dating Greg Tynes. Isn't the significant other always a suspect?"

Vale didn't even look surprised. "I'll forward your theories to the Houston police."

Conner must have already told the detective everything.

Vale drummed his fingers on the table. "You don't

think Greg's choice of girlfriend might have infuriated Conner?"

"Made him jealous? Enough to kill Greg? No. I'm
the one who told him about Chandra and Greg. He was
surprised, but not upset or jealous. Anyway, you're investigating the reporter's death, and *he* wasn't dating
Chandra."

Vale smiled faintly. "Your logic is impeccable, Ms.
Baxter. Just one more question—Where were you last
night, between the hours of 8:00 p.m. and 6:00 a.m.?"

Raleigh interrupted. "You can't narrow down the
time of death any better than that?"

"The body was refrigerated. A lot depends on exactly when it was stashed there and what temperature
the fridge maintains. But the security guard at the mill
reported that some person turned off the security alarm
last night. Presumably someone who knew the code.
That suggests to me someone in upper management."

"For the record, I was at home alone during those
hours. And I'm a lowly secretary, last I checked."

"A secretary who is—if I guess correctly—very
close to her boss. Who *is* in upper management."

Jillian couldn't believe her ears. "Right. So you're
saying Conner and I conspired to kill Mark Bowen,
then we broke into the mill in the middle of the night,
hid the body in the fridge—"

Raleigh touched her arm. "Jillian, be careful what
you say."

Jillian ignored her. "—then came back the next day
so we could discover the body and make ourselves suspects, while carefully not bothering to pick up a clearly
visible Saint Christopher medal that would implicate
Conner? Does that make even a tiny amount of sense?"

"I don't know yet. But I have one more question.

Are you involved in a romantic relationship with Conner Blake?"

"Define romantic."

"Anything other than professional."

It was so tempting to lie. But she knew better; the truth always comes out. "We had sex. Once. It didn't work out. In fact, we're quite irritated with each other right now."

"Didn't look that way to me. You were holding hands."

"He took my hand and squeezed it as a gesture of comfort and support. It was nothing more than that."

Damn him, Vale wasn't even trying to hide his smile. "Okay, that's all for now. You can go."

"Thank God." She waited until they were in a hallway out of earshot of the detective, then turned to Raleigh. "Let's find Conner and get out of here."

"Um, yeah, that won't be possible. They took Conner into custody."

Jillian's head spun. They'd arrested Conner? "Oh, *no*. Raleigh, you have to do something."

"I will. His bail hearing is set for tomorrow, and I can argue that Conner isn't a flight risk. He has a good job and family here—"

Jillian lowered her voice. "And a plane ticket to Indonesia."

"What?"

"I saw the reservation confirmation in his email. He has a trip to Jakarta scheduled for next month. I didn't want to read too much into it—and I still don't. The company has business there, Conner has to take up some slack now that Greg is gone."

"But the cops will read something into it." Raleigh only said what Jillian was thinking. "They'll think he was planning to flee. They've also got a huge piece of physical evidence that's pretty hard to dismiss."

"The medal was stolen from his office. I mean, why would Conner leave the medal in the victim's hands? That would be really stupid."

"Criminals sometimes do stupid things. Look, Jillian, this will get sorted out. But Conner is not his own best friend right now. He lied to Detective Vale."

"He did? About what?"

"He said you and he had never been involved. Apparently he thought telling the truth was less important than protecting your virtue."

The situation was dire, but Jillian felt a warmth in her belly at the realization that Conner was trying to protect her. Stupid thing to do…but sweet.

DESPITE THE FACT A BODY was found at the picnic venue and one of the company's directors had been arrested on suspicion of murder, and another director was about to be indicted for grand theft, acting CEO Hamilton Payne declared he wanted the company party to go on as planned.

"Company morale is at an all-time low," Payne said in his office the next morning, when Jillian paid him a visit and explained the situation. "Now is the time to rally the troops. Stand up for what we believe in. Make a show of solidarity."

Could he come up with any more clichés?

"But our refrigerator is a crime scene," Jillian said.

"Everyone's looking forward to the picnic. We can't disappoint them. Our employees have been loyal and supportive during this trying time. We should be loyal and supportive back."

"You don't think we'll all look a bit…frivolous for throwing a party at the site of a recent murder?"

"I'm sure the police will release the scene before Saturday. Anyway, I understand that reporter wasn't killed at the mill. The body was simply dumped there. It might not even be related to the current unpleasantness."

"Of course it's connected. They've arrested Conner!"

"Believe me, I'm as distressed as you. I've known Conner since he worked as a college intern for the company, and of course there's no way he could be guilty. I've got our lawyers working hard to free him as we speak."

"Will you be at his bail hearing?"

"I can't. The company is in crisis. I need to be here. We all need to be calm and carry on business as usual. Our customers have to see that no matter what, the company won't fold. Stan wants to save the company— it's his most fervent wish. Now, please, do whatever you can to make the party a success. I've informed my wife that she should make herself available to you no matter what Ariel Cuddy told her. She's willing to help in any way she can."

Since hearing Ariel's angry message, Jillian hadn't even attempted to contact any of the directors' wives. But she would give Beatrice Payne a call to at least thank her for the offer—and see if she really meant it. Most of the preparations were in place, but Jillian could use some help on Saturday to set things up.

"If you think it's best."

"I do. Jillian, are you any closer to finding out who's behind all this?"

"Conner has been checking into Greg's activities in the months before he died. There's definitely something squirrely there. As to who killed him, I'm afraid we're at a loss. But please don't give up."

"I have complete faith in you. Let me know if there's anything I can do to help—anything."

"Thanks, Mr. Payne."

She really felt sorry for him. So close to retirement, and now this. If the whole company went down, would it wreck his pension?

She hurried from Payne's office to the garage and prayed traffic wouldn't be too bad. She had to make it to Conner's bail hearing by ten. But just as she was about to start her car engine, the *Mission: Impossible* theme song floated up from her purse. Celeste had been playing with Jillian's ring tones again. She fished out her phone and checked the screen; it was Elena.

"Elena. What's up?"

"Daniel wanted me to let you know you don't have to come to the bail hearing."

"Oh. But I want to come. I think it's important to let the judge know how critical his presence is at his employer's." Why didn't Daniel want her there? Was he afraid she would get too touchy-feely?

She got it, she understood. She'd let emotions get in the way of her effectiveness, and Daniel was right to doubt her. "Can I talk to him? Or is he too busy?"

"It's not that he doesn't want you there. The hearing has been delayed."

Poor Conner! Would he have to spend another night in jail? Although she'd never been arrested, she'd spent enough time around Project Justice clients to know jail wasn't a happy place. Mitch Delacroix, the foundation's cyber sleuth, had been assaulted when he'd been held overnight in a Louisiana lockup. Only his superb fighting skills had saved him from a beating.

Conner, while obviously strong and fit, didn't have a black belt in anything.

"There's some big meeting going on—Daniel, Raleigh and some people from Houston and Montgomery County law enforcement. Even a lawyer from the lumber company. I think the idea is to get all charges dropped. If everyone can compare notes, maybe they can see a pattern."

"And Daniel doesn't want me there?" Why the hell not? She knew as much about this case as anyone.

"He just told me to tell you the bail hearing was postponed."

Jillian took a deep breath. No emotions. Cool as a cucumber. "Okay, Elena. Thanks."

But after she hung up, tears sprang to her eyes. Daniel didn't trust her anymore. She'd become a liability. She'd thrown away her career for a man she'd fallen in love with—a man who couldn't love her back.

She was so angry with herself. Why did she fall for men who were so wrong for her? Making love with Conner had felt so right, like the beginning of something epic. He'd felt something, too, she was sure of it—or was she remembering things the way she wanted them to be?

She couldn't afford the luxury of tears. She had a picnic to plan and a murderer to catch.

That was the only way she would ever redeem herself, she realized. She would have to discover the identity of the murderer herself. And she was going to have to disobey Daniel's orders to do it. She would either succeed or find herself in the unemployment line. Those were the only two outcomes she could stomach, because she wasn't going back to being an intern, trusted by no one.

As she made her way through the garage from the hinterlands where they made secretaries park, she passed the row of reserved spaces where the directors and other top executives parked their luxury cars.

Both murder victims had been killed at unknown locations and the bodies transported to the places where they were found. Bodies tended to leave a trail of DNA behind. Greg Tynes, in particular, had been found wrapped in a blood-soaked blanket. Ergo, someone's car had blood in it. And even if it had been scrupulously cleaned, a spray of luminol would still show where the blood had been.

Her brain was clicking as she made her way back inside. Saturday was the perfect day. Everybody would be taking buses from this facility to the mill. The cars would be sitting here all day long with no one coming and going. It was an ideal time.

Letitia was at the security desk by the back door.

"Thought you were leaving."

"Sudden change of plans. Hey, Letitia, how would you like to help me catch a murderer?"

Letitia's eyes lit up. She leaned forward "I'm in. How?"

"Are you working tomorrow?"

"Saturday? No."

"Can you trade shifts with someone? In particular, whoever patrols the garage?"

She thought for a moment. "I probably could. Everybody likes to get Saturday off."

"If I had a friend who showed an undue amount of interest in some cars in the parking lot, could you look the other way? Maybe be real slow to respond if a car alarm goes off?"

Letitia frowned. "No way. If any of those cars goes missing on my watch, I could lose my job."

"The cars won't go anywhere. No one will be able to tell my friend was there. She's just looking for evidence." It was a long shot. But at least Jillian would be doing something. She couldn't just blow up balloons and pretend this case and her career and her *life* hadn't reached crisis state.

"I guess that doesn't sound too bad. What's in it for me?"

"I'll double your pay." Her trust fund ought to be good for something besides keeping Jillian in designer stilettos.

"You're on."

"Great." Now she just had to convince "her friend" to give up a Saturday while risking arrest and ruin.

CHAPTER FOURTEEN

"NICE WORK, GIRLFRIEND." Celeste examined the tight cluster of holes in the paper target at the public shooting range. "Your aim is really improving."

"I've been practicing."

Jillian and Celeste had met after work at the Junseo Kim School of Martial Arts for their weekly Tae Kwon Do class. Celeste was a second-degree black belt. Jillian had only been taking for six months, but she was finally starting to feel halfway coordinated. She had sparred against an aggressive red belt and had actually won, for once. After class, they'd stopped by the shooting range for some target practice.

"I'm starving," Celeste said. "Let's go scarf down some pizza."

"Good plan." One nice thing about working out: she could indulge in some of her forbidden foods, at least occasionally. They walked one block to their favorite little Italian bistro, ordered a large mushroom and green pepper thin crust and a bottle of Chianti. Jillian felt her muscles finally relaxing for the first time in days.

"You haven't said much about the case."

"I don't know much. They shut me out."

"Oh, Jillian. What I wouldn't give to smack those men's heads together. They have no idea the gem they have in you."

Jillian laughed without humor. "Yeah. A gem who slept with the client."

Celeste choked on a piece of pizza. "You did what?"

"I know, it was a huge mistake, and stupid."

Celeste removed her purple glasses and pinched the bridge of her nose. "Not stupid, don't say that. Sometimes the heart wants what it wants. We all crave connection." For a few moments, Celeste appeared to be far away as she stared past Jillian, her eyes defocused.

"You speak from experience?"

Celeste flashed a sad smile. "Shrewd girl. You didn't corner the market on self-destructive, hormonal, angsty behavior. I once made a fool of myself over a man I worked with."

"You?" Sure, Celeste flirted with every handsome man she encountered, but it was mostly for show. She'd never demonstrated the slightest bit of real interest in a man, not since Jillian had known her.

Not unless you counted the cupcakes she left for Phil the night watchman.

"I wasn't always so smart. Or so secure. You can't imagine what it was like being the first female police officer on the force. The first they actually let do more than write parking tickets, anyway. The men hated me. They were afraid of me. They did everything they could think of to trick me and make me look foolish. Their wives hated me even more—thought I was there to steal their husbands.

"The worst was, I never knew if the guys really had my back, or if they'd stand by and let me get hurt."

Jillian felt for her friend. "That must have been awful." At least she knew Daniel had her personal safety at the forefront of his concerns. Conner, too. Neither of them would ever want her physically harmed.

"Then there was Chuck. The only one who saw something in me. Who took me seriously. He believed in me. And how easy it was for me to fall in love with him."

Jillian could see that. Trying to prove herself, surrounded by hostility, then one person who believed... yes, she could see it all too well.

"It was way against the rules for us to see each other. So we did it in secret. It lasted about a month. Then the novelty wore off, and Chuck got worried we'd be discovered. He broke things off."

"Oh, Celeste, how awful. At least it was only a month. At least you didn't *marry* the guy."

"There were...other consequences."

"Did someone find out? Did you get in trouble?" At that moment, losing her job or being publicly humiliated sounded to Jillian like the worst thing that could happen.

"No, no one found out." Celeste paused, as if evaluating how much more to reveal. Finally she said, "I'm tall, and I was heavier then. I was able to hide the pregnancy up to about six months."

Jillian gasped. "Oh, my heavens." Celeste, pregnant? Celeste had a baby? She was about the most unmaternal woman Jillian had ever met.

"Even in the wild sixties, you couldn't up and have a baby out of wedlock like it was nothing. Not like today. And certainly not working for the Houston Police Department."

"What did you do?"

"I faked a knee injury. Went on disability. Had the baby." Celeste paused, her eyes misty as she traveled back in time, seeing things Jillian couldn't. "I wanted to keep her. She was the most beautiful baby you ever saw, had these huge blue eyes…but I couldn't. How would I have supported her?"

"You gave her up for adoption?" That had to be the saddest thing. Jillian knew if her ill-begotten tryst with Conner had resulted, God forbid, in a pregnancy, she would have fallen in love with the baby instantly. She never would have given it up, even if Conner wanted nothing to do with her or his child. She would find a way to keep the baby.

But Celeste hadn't had as many choices.

"My older sister adopted her. But on the condition we never tell her the truth. We thought it would be too confusing. And I preferred to be Judy's favorite Aunty Celeste than *that woman* who gave her away."

Jillian swallowed hard. She reached across the table and took her friend's hand. "That must be incredibly difficult. Even today, she doesn't know?"

"She doesn't know. My sister and brother-in-law are both passed, and I think it would be okay to tell her now, but I just can't. What if she hated me? We have a good relationship now. I don't want to ruin that."

Normally Jillian would recommend the truth—full disclosure. But she hadn't been doing a very good job with her own personal life. Not now, not ever. So she kept her counsel to herself.

"I have a grandson, too. Jason."

"The one who came to Daniel's Fourth of July party?"

Celeste nodded, radiating her fondness for the boy. "He's an amazing young man."

"You two seem to share a special bond. I believe he's the one who conspired with you about bringing a live baby javelina to the office?"

"Please, don't remind me. I'm still paying off the damage that stupid beast did to the carpets." But at least Celeste had smiled. "Yes, that's my grandson. Don't tell anyone, Jillian."

"I would never."

"I just wanted you to know. So you won't repeat my mistakes."

"Don't worry. I'm done with men."

If anything, Celeste looked more worried. "No, you're not getting it. The mistake I made was to throw away any chance of personal happiness for my career."

Now Jillian was confused. "I thought you loved being a police officer."

"I'm proud of what I achieved. I blazed a path for other women. I held my ground. I didn't let them bully and intimidate me. But was I happy?" She shrugged. "Royally pissed off, most of the time. It's no way to live. If I had it to do over again…"

"What? You'd have quit?"

"I'd have kept my baby girl. Moved to a new town, passed myself off as a widow, and started over."

"Celeste. I've spent a lot of time and energy convincing myself not to let my emotions rule me. To focus on the career I want. Working for Project Justice is important to me. Are you telling me that's wrong? I should fall in love, marry, have kids and give up being an investigator?"

Celeste drained her wineglass in two gulps. "Not at all. It's not fifty years ago. You can do whatever you want, be whoever you want. You're going to be one of the best investigators Project Justice ever had. Just don't cut yourself off from all other possibilities. There's room in your life for more than one dream."

Nothing was said for a few minutes. Jillian picked

the peppers off her last piece of pizza and ate them. *There's room in your life for more than one dream.* What a concept. She would mull that one over—right after she found out who killed Greg and Mark and saw them behind bars.

"Celeste, I need to ask you a favor. And please, feel free to say no. It's a little on the illegal side."

Celeste's eyes shined brightly. "I'm your girl. What is it?"

"Do you know anything about breaking into cars?"

"Are you kidding? I worked in Auto Theft for seven years."

"Yeah, but cars are a little trickier these days. They have all kinds of fancy computerized locks and alarms and whatnot."

Celeste waved away Jillian's concern. "Please. All you need is a code grabber or a scanner box, and you can defeat any alarm in the world. Between that and a Slim Jim I can steal you a car in under thirty seconds."

"Oh, I don't need you to steal any cars. Just get inside them. And the trunks. And check for bloodstains with luminol. Take pictures, if possible, and don't leave any evidence of the break-in behind. No broken windows or popped locks." She didn't want to get either Letitia or Celeste into trouble.

Celeste shrugged as if it were no big deal. "I have everything I need at home. Where are these cars?"

"In the lumber company garage."

"What about security?"

"I've already bribed the security guard to look the other way."

Celeste gave her an admiring look. "Nice work. Give me the address and tell me when to show up."

FOR THE REST of that evening, every time her phone rang Jillian jumped, hoping it would be some news about Conner. But no one called her, no one saw fit to keep her informed.

That was okay, she was just the hopelessly romantic intern whose only qualifications for this job was that she could type 110 words a minute. She finally had to just turn the phone off, rather than wait for it to ring like some heartsick teenager. To help herself fall asleep, she mentally went over the list of things she would have to take care of in the morning for the party. The process actually relaxed her; lists, tasks and chores were as easy as breathing to her. Whatever else happened, Mayall Lumber's company picnic was going to rock.

Hey, if she failed at Project Justice, she could always get a job as an event planner, right?

She slept surprisingly well under the circumstances, and when she powered up her phone the next morning, she discovered a voice mail from Daniel.

"Just wanted you to know we got Conner released. It's two in the morning, hope you're getting some sleep. We'll touch base tomorrow. But at least Conner will sleep in his own bed tonight."

She could read between the lines: Conner had *better* sleep in his own bed.

"Thanks for the vote of confidence, Daniel," she murmured. Had she actually once considered herself in love with him? How had she never realized how arrogant and superior he acted toward her? If she ever got involved with a man again, it would be someone who could be her equal.

As she took her shower, her thoughts drifted to Conner. During a few brief shining days, they'd worked together as a team. Yes, he'd been her boss, but her organizational and clerical skills had awarded her power in the relationship, too. They had functioned well together.

He wasn't the mythical hero she'd worshiped in her youth, nor was he the villain she'd built up in her mind. He was a wholly imperfect man.

There's room in your life for more than one dream. Once this case was solved, she would no longer have any professional connection with Conner. Daniel wouldn't have a damn thing to say about whether they slept together.

Recognizing the dangerous nature of her train of thought, she squelched it and got down to business. She had a zillion things to deal with this morning, like confirming with various people about picnic food and entertainment—the band, the bounce house, the pony rides, the brisket, the bartender. She'd called in favors from vendors she'd hired for Daniel's parties, and they'd given her their best prices, so she was still under budget.

Take that, Isaac Cuddy. She wondered if anyone would even notice her economic efficiency, now that he was gone.

She dressed with care in a retro, sleeveless summery dress with a full skirt. The bright floral print seemed appropriate for a picnic.

After searching fruitlessly for her sunglasses, she gave up and headed out the door, her phone wedged between her shoulder and chin as she made rapid-fire decisions about how many bags of ice to buy and where to locate the porta-potties.

She was supposed to meet Beatrice Payne at the Mill at nine o'clock. The first busful of guests was scheduled to arrive at 11:00 a.m.

Every time she hit a stop light, she grabbed an envelope from the pile of mail in her passenger seat and ripped it open with her teeth. Electric bill, a plea for membership from the Sierra Club...that one she set aside. Her brief stint with Conner in the woods had convinced her she needed to do more to preserve nature. His reverence for trees was a bit infectious.

She didn't look at the return address on the bulky manila envelope, just ripped it open as she waited at a light at Milam and Capitol.

A thumb drive fell out into her lap.

What the hell?

The light turned green. She whipped into a gas station parking lot and threw her car into Park. The envelope also contained a sheet torn from a reporter's notebook.

"I didn't want to chance sending this to your office email where it might be intercepted. Here's what someone you work with killed for. I think I know who, but I need your help to prove it. Please get back to me. Stan Mayall is innocent."

The hastily scrawled note wasn't signed and there was no return address on the envelope, but none of that was necessary. Jillian knew who sent this to her. It was Mark Bowen. He must have put it in the mail mere hours before he died.

He'd been murdered for what was on that thumb drive. And if anyone knew she had it, she was in danger, too.

She tucked the letter and envelope under the floor mat and dropped the thumb drive into her purse. Surely she could get hold of a computer at the mill, maybe in the office, and find out what was on the drive.

Then she would take it to Daniel. And that detective,

Hudson Vale, who was in charge of the Mark Bowen murder case.

Unless, of course, the evidence pointed to Conner. Then she didn't know what she would do.

Beatrice Payne was supposed to meet Jillian at the little gift shop, which sold a number of items made from at least a dozen varieties of exotic woods. Visitors could buy everything from a chainsaw-hewn totem pole to a carved bunny rabbit no bigger than her thumb.

And paper dresses. A mannequin took pride of place in the center of the store, wearing a low-cut halter dress in a rich royal-blue cinched with a wide belt. The styling was a vast improvement over that potato sack of a dress Conner had asked her to wear in high school. She had to look close and feel the fabric with her fingertips to notice that it wasn't normal fabric. Cellophane packages containing several sizes and colors of the dress sat in a basket near the mannequin, and a sign explaining how the dresses were made and the ecological implications.

On impulse, Jillian selected one of the dresses in hot pink and tucked the package under her arm, intending to pay for it as soon as Lucas had readied the store for business. He was there now, setting up displays and turning on lights.

Just then Beatrice Payne rushed in, out of breath. "Sorry I'm late." She looked like she ought to be on one of those *Real Housewives* shows—velour tracksuit, teased hair, long acrylic nails and enough makeup for Halloween.

Another trophy wife—what was it with the Mayall executives, anyway? Was marrying a woman twenty years younger a qualification for getting on the board of directors? Maybe Conner ought to be trolling the junior colleges.

"It's nice to finally meet you after the barrage of emails," Beatrice said. "You are quite the organized one, aren't you?"

Jillian hardly considered three emails a barrage, but she wasn't going to argue. "Nice to meet you, too. I so much appreciate your offer of help."

"As the acting CEO's wife, I really didn't have much choice." She smiled while she said this, as if it wasn't a dig. Beatrice was friends with Ariel and had made it clear she was helping under protest, solely because her husband had practically ordered her to step in.

It's just one day. I just have to get through this one day. If there really was proof on the thumb drive as to what illegal activity had been going on behind the scenes and who was responsible, Jillian had done her part. The party would be her swan song.

"So what is it that you need me to do?"

"Here's a map of the grounds." She handed Beatrice an eight-by-ten sheet of paper with a rough drawing showing where the buildings, machinery and trees were located. "I sketched in where the various attractions should go. The guys with the bounce house drove up behind me in the parking lot. You can meet with them and show them where to set up. They'll need access to electricity—they can run their cords to this building."

"Oh. Okay. Is that the, um, drying shed?"

"Yes, that's right."

"Where the body was found?"

"I'm really hoping we can not mention anything about that today. Most of the employees don't know."

"I'm just not sure I can bring myself to go inside that building. There could be a madman on the loose."

"You don't have to go inside. Just point to the door."

"Well, okay. I might have to leave a little early today. Ham and I are leaving for vacation this evening. For a cruise to the Cayman Islands."

"How nice for you. I'm sure Ham's ready for some R & R, after all that's happened." Jillian was a little surprised no one had told her of Ham's vacation, but she was happy he was getting away for a few days. She wished she could stow away in one of the Paynes' suitcases. "It's fine if you want to leave early. Once things are set up, the party will run itself."

"Great. What else needs to be done besides the bounce house?"

"I'll be supervising the Porta-Potty setup."

"Fun. See you later." Beatrice shot out of the gift shop like a lightning bolt, as Jillian had figured she would at the mention of a more unsavory task than the one she'd been assigned.

Lucas was just turning on the cash register. Despite the party, the park would still be open to visitors.

"You do a bit of everything around here, I guess," Jillian commented as she handed him the dress and her credit card.

He rang up her purchase. "Yeah, I fill in wherever. Gina, who usually runs the gift shop, is running late today. I see you decided to try one of the paper dresses. I'm gonna get one for my girlfriend."

Don't let her walk in the rain.

"Is there a computer available for me to use?" she asked. "I'm having trouble getting internet on my phone out here in the boonies, and it's crucial that I check my email."

"Sure. There's a little office through that door right

there. Computer's already on." He gestured toward a
door in the corner.

Her heart beating like a hummingbird's wings, Jillian sat down in the cramped office. What could Mark
have uncovered that not even Daniel had found? She
pulled the thumb drive from her purse and inserted it
into the USB drive. A few clicks later she had a list of
files—several document files and a half-dozen photo
files.

She opened one of the photos first. The computer
was old, with a slow processor, so the photo only gradually revealed itself. The image made Jillian's stomach turn. It was an aerial photo of acres and acres of
clear-cut forest.

There was no caption, and Jillian couldn't tell where
in the world the photo was taken. But did it matter?
Even in the short time she'd been working at Mayall
Lumber, she understood that the company would never
authorize this kind of tree harvest.

Each of the photos showed another scar on the land
where bulldozers and chainsaws had done their deadly
work. Maybe the documents would explain something.

She opened one at random. It seemed to be a Mayall
Lumber bill of sale for lumber—teak wood—to a company in China. It was signed by Greg Tynes. The client
was not anyone Jillian had ever heard of, and she'd become familiar with the company's overseas customers.

She opened another document. It was a copy of a
letter to the same client, authorizing Greg Tynes to bid
on a certain timber harvesting operation in Brazil. It
was signed by Conner Blake. Except that was not Conner's signature.

Desperate to figure it out, Jillian opened a third document, a series of ledger sheets somehow connected to

the property in Brazil and a handwritten note scrawled at the bottom of one page, indicating to someone— who?—that communication should bypass Conner Blake and come directly to—who? It was signed with initials only. H.P.

H.P. H.P. Hamilton Payne! Her elation quickly dissipated. For heaven's sake, that didn't make any sense. Mr. Payne was their client. He was the one who'd contacted Project Justice in the first place. But that looked an awful lot like Mr. Payne's handwriting.

Payne was director of sales, so maybe it made sense that he would want a client to deal directly with him. But this was a landowner, not a lumber buyer.

She could just ask Mr. Payne what this was all about. There was probably a perfectly rational explanation. But when she went back to the forged signature… there had been no attempt to make it *look* like Conner's nearly illegible scrawl. In fact, the handwriting was quite distinctive, tall and thin and strongly slanted to the right. She was not a graphologist, but Project Justice had access to one.

Hell, she couldn't wait for that.

She emailed all the files to herself and to Daniel, then closed them, made sure they weren't stored anywhere on the computer, and pocketed the thumb drive.

The door opened quickly and Jillian nearly hit the ceiling. Standing in the doorway was Conner Blake.

CHAPTER FIFTEEN

FOR A FEW MOMENTS, all Jillian could do was stare. He looked so good dressed down in jeans and a baseball jersey—apparently the company had a team called the Mayall Lumber Barons.

Finally she stirred herself. "Conner, what are you doing here? Did they drop the charges?"

"The D.A. wouldn't drop the charges, but Daniel bailed me out. Pretty civil of him, given his low opinion of me. He made it pretty clear he was doing it because you asked him to."

"You don't seem very grateful."

"Sorry. The guy just bugs me."

Because Conner saw him as a rival? Fine, a little jealousy would be good for him. "Why are you here?" If she'd spent thirty-six hours in jail, she'd be home resting and recovering from the ordeal.

"Are you kidding? I wouldn't miss this party for the world. Someone at the company framed me for murder. I want to see the look on that person's face when he sees me here, smiling and festive instead of locked up."

"You think the person will give himself away?"

"We'll find out. Why are you hiding in here? Beatrice Payne has run amok. She's hollering at the bounce-house guys to move faster, and then she stepped in pony poop and almost blew a gasket."

"Who cares about Beatrice? Close the door."

He followed her orders, smiling mischievously. "I hadn't realized you wanted to be alone with me."

"Cut the crap, Conner, this is serious. I received a packet of information from Mark Bowen in the mail. He actually found something—sent it to me as a safeguard, I think, for all the good it did."

"What are you talking about? What sort of information?"

"Pictures. Documents. Do we have clients in China?"

"No. China has its own vibrant forestry industry. They would rather sell to the U.S. than buy from us. Why?"

"Because Mark sent me documents indicating Mayall Lumber clear-cut a parcel of land in Brazil and sold the lumber to China."

"That doesn't make much sense."

"Unless it's some kind of black market deal."

"Instigated by who?"

"You, apparently. Someone made it *look* like you're behind it." She lowered her voice to a whisper. "I think it was Hamilton Payne."

Conner's expression of shock was almost comical. "Are you out of your ever-lovin' mind?"

"Well…no, I don't think so." His reaction hurt. She'd stuck up for him, professed his innocence to anyone who would listen, got Daniel involved, and this is how he repays her?

Just then the door opened and a young woman whom Jillian presumed was Gina stepped in, looking harried and out of breath. "Excuse me— Oh, Mr. Blake, it's you."

Jillian edged toward the door. "I borrowed your computer for a moment, Gina, thank you."

"You're welcome." The young, curvaceous brunette

gave Conner what could only be described as a preda-
tory smile. "Come back anytime."

On top of everything else, a wave of irrational jealousy swamped Jillian. Did he know this woman? Had
they dated, maybe shared a quickie on a slow afternoon, maybe right in this office?

No. There was no room for emotion now. For all she
cared, Conner was sleeping with every single Houston Texans cheerleader. She had to get this mess sorted
out. Maybe he would have a rational explanation for
why Hamilton's handwriting was on those documents.

As they stepped out into the parking lot, Jillian
squinted against the glaring sun. Where were her
damn sunglasses? The only ones she could find were
the video glasses from The Spy Store. Oh, well, they
would have to do. She slipped them on.

"Jillian. I thought you were going to supervise the
porta-potty placement." It was Beatrice, flapping
around like a wounded bird. "That just falls waaay
beyond my job description. As does stepping in horse
manure. I could be home packing right now, you know."

Just then a spotted Shetland pony thundered past,
chased by a man in chaps and a clown nose.

"Are you just going to let those beasts run wild
around the party befouling everything?" Beatrice continued. "It's not sanitary!"

"I'll take care of it. I have another job for you. Inside the drying shed you'll find stacks of party supplies in the corner just to the right of the door. I need
you to unwrap the plastic tablecloths and put them on
the tables those guys are setting up. There's also a bag
of clamps you can use to secure them—"

"The drying shed! I can't go in there. That's where

the body was found. It's unsanitary to store supplies where someone was decomposing—"

Conner deftly took Beatrice's arm. "I'll fetch what you need, Beatrice. You can wait outside."

"Wait, Conner," Jillian said, "we need to talk."

"I'll be back in a minute."

Oh, he was so aggravating. She'd just told him who might be behind the murders, and he'd blown her off.

Beatrice looked up at Conner and batted her eyelashes. "I still don't think that shed is sanitary." She allowed him to lead her away.

What woman wouldn't?

The escaped pony, clearly having a great time, continued to lead the clown-cowboy on a merry chase across the lush green lawn. The beast was headed straight for Jillian.

"Get him!" the cowboy yelled at her.

A lead line attached to a halter was trailing behind the spotted pony as he galloped past. Jillian grabbed for the line, and five hundred pounds of equine force yanked her right off her feet while the rope gave her a nice rope burn as it pulled free of her grasp.

Although it could have kept running, the yank apparently got the pony's attention. It slowed, then turned to look at her, then came over to investigate as Jillian just lay there on the grass, wondering where she'd left her brain today.

"You okay, miss?" The cowboy offered her a hand up, which she accepted.

"Peachy."

The cowboy reached down and calmly picked up the rope, and the pony followed along, docile as a puppy, having had his fun for the day.

There were 101 problems to solve. Jillian put the

lumber mystery out of her head temporarily while she dealt with faulty propane tanks, misplaced baseball gear and a shortage of duct tape. But things were shaping up as the first bus rolled into the parking lot. The band was getting set up on the temporary stage, the grill-masters—Joyce's husband and the guy who ran the cafeteria—were putting the first pieces of meat on the barbecue. Balloons were flying, the face painter stood by ready to turn the kids into lions and dragons.

Parties used to give Jillian a great deal of satisfaction, but now that it was here, she couldn't get too excited about this one. She just wanted to get through it, so she could get on with the important task of catching a murderer.

Conner sidled up beside her. "This is fantastic. How did you put all this together so quickly?"

She shrugged, uncomfortable with the compliment. If he thought he could distract her from exploring her theory about Mr. Payne, he was mistaken. "I can do this in my sleep. Listen, Conner, about those files—"

"You do realize, of course, that Hamilton Payne can't be a suspect. He's the one who brought the case to Project Justice in the first place."

"I know. But I need for you to review the documents Bowen sent. Maybe you can figure out what was going on."

"I will."

"Sooner, rather than later." She didn't want to belabor the point, but the Paynes were leaving the country this evening.

"The first bus is here," Conner announced. "I'm going to greet people as they leave the bus. See if I take anyone by surprise."

"I wish you'd told me this was your plan," she

groused, following him to the parking lot. "I could have arranged for Claudia Ellison to be here. She's an expert face reader and she could spot if someone is surprised, even if they successfully hide it from you and me."

"Really? You could do that?"

"Project Justice is one of the most powerful organizations of its kind. We have access to any kind of expert you could want. I wish you would confide in me instead of going maverick."

As the first employees stepped down onto the blacktop, Jillian greeted them and instructed them to place their potluck dish on a large rolling cart that waited nearby. The food would be categorized into appetizers, salads, side dishes and desserts, then placed on tables set up as the buffet line. In the memo that went out about the picnic she'd instructed everyone to put their names on their dishes, but she also had some pens and labels ready for anyone who'd forgotten.

"You think of everything," Conner commented. "Hi, Jerry, Mindy, nice to see you."

"Hey, Conner." The two males partook in a handshake thump-on-the-back male-bonding ritual. Jerry Bewick was the communications director. Mindy pointedly walked away, avoiding any sort of small talk with Jillian. She was a friend of Ariel's and one of the volunteers who'd backed out.

Other than stinging her feelings a bit to have so much animosity aimed her way, the wives' defection hadn't bothered Jillian much. She'd easily recruited more volunteers.

Once the first bus was emptied, Jillian and Conner had a breather. The rolling cart was filled to capacity with covered dishes, and she motioned for a couple of her volunteers to take it to the buffet tables, set up under the shade of some ancient live oak trees, and start organizing the dishes.

"Anybody suspicious in that group?" she asked Conner.

"No," he said glumly. "How many buses are there?"

"Three. Here comes the second one now."

"So tell me again about these files you received in the mail."

Finally. "A thumb drive. From a dead man. He said it contained evidence of illegal activity, and it pointed to the responsible party. The murderer must have realized Mark was getting too close."

"And what kind of files? Photos?"

"I only looked quickly. But someone representing themselves as Mayall Lumber has been clear-cutting forests. They made it appear as if you authorized the deal. Greg was the timber buyer involved."

"Greg couldn't have done that on his own," Conner said. "Someone would have had to front some money, hire crews and equipment, arrange for the milling, all without me finding out."

"How many people do you know with that ability?"

He sighed. "I know what you're getting at. It's not Hamilton Payne."

The second bus pulled to a stop, and passengers began unloading. A second empty cart had appeared to take the place of the first, and Jillian went into her song and dance, welcoming the guests, instructing them where to put their covered dishes and where the various festivities were taking place. Children shrieked as they spied the now fully inflated bounce house and caught sight of the ponies and a few small horses housed in a temporary corral.

"Well, well, isn't this a fine sight."

Jillian held her breath. It was Hamilton Payne, climbing down from the bus with his cane, waving off the bus driver who attempted to help.

"I can make it."

"Good morning, Mr. Payne," Jillian said with a smile she hoped didn't look too pasted on. "I'm so glad you could make it today. Mrs. Payne has been a tremendous help to me, I just couldn't have coped without her."

"Oh, I'm so glad to hear— Conner. I didn't expect to see you here. I understand you had a late night last night."

"I couldn't miss the company picnic," he said brightly. "We have to stand together, show our employees that we're weathering the crisis."

"Exactly. You see there, Jillian? It's like I told you yesterday. In a time of misfortune, we have to carry on."

"Hamilton, there you are." Beatrice had appeared, looking not quite as polished as she had two hours ago. "Come with me, I have a chair all picked out for you. And you can see what I did with the tablecloths, it was really quite challenging." She led Mr. Payne away.

"He seemed surprised to see you," Jillian commented.

"Yeah, but that doesn't count. He knew about the arrest and he knew about the release. He sent a lawyer and everything."

"Why would he do that?" she thought aloud. Why would he frame someone for murder, then do his level best to get him freed from jail?

"Because he's a stand-up guy, that's why. Come on, what motive does he have for ruining the company, and possibly destroying his pension? He was about to retire."

"Money is a good motive. His pension was a pittance compared with what he could get for black-market teak."

"And how do you know—never mind. You snooped. Look, I don't care if someone used his name," Conner said sharply. "You said my name was on one of the documents, too, but I didn't authorize any clear-cutting."

"That's true…if your signature was forged, his could be, too. Oh, I don't know what to think."

"You're not supposed to think. Just observe."

"Right." She nodded. "'Cause that's all you can expect from a piece of fluff."

"Aw, come on, Jilly. I didn't mean you're not smart. But you don't have to do this all yourself. We'll talk to Daniel. We'll figure it out together. Okay?"

She softened. "Okay." But she wished he would have just a little faith in her. Maybe Payne wasn't guilty of anything, but did Conner have to dismiss her opinions out of hand?

After the last bus had unloaded, Conner admitted he hadn't seen any overtly suspicious expressions of surprise from those who arrived for the picnic. "But Jerry Bewick's wife was looking at me funny. I'm gonna go chat her up, see if she gets nervous."

She watched him walk away, wishing so hard that things could be different.

While overseeing the last of the covered dishes labeled and loaded on the cart, she called Daniel. "Daniel. Did you get the files I sent you?"

"I did. But I haven't had a chance to look at them yet. What are they?"

"They were sent to me by Mark Bowen."

Pause. "The dead reporter?"

"Yes. Please look at them. It's important." She took

a few steps away so she couldn't be overheard. "Some-one has been clear-cutting forests and using the May-all name to do it."

"And that's significant because…"

"Clear-cutting. It goes against everything that May-all stands for—responsible forestry, sustainability, and it probably violates international laws and treaties. Whoever is doing this is probably selling on the black market. Maybe fulfilling orders for legitimate clients, then selling the excess and pocketing the money. I don't really know."

"You think this is what got those two men killed?"

"Yes. And I know this won't make any sense to you, but I suspect the guilty party is Hamilton Payne."

"That's impossible," he said flatly.

Why did no one believe her? "Look at the files. Look at the handwriting. Compare it to Payne's. It's worth checking out. You always said to keep an open mind."

"You're right. I'll check it out."

Was he merely placating her? "There's not much time. His wife said they're leaving on a cruise—flying out tonight. If we let him leave the country we might not ever see him—"

"Jillian. I'll look into it. But why would the murderer hire us in the first place? It makes—"

"I know, it makes no sense. I get it. I have to go, work to do." She hung up. She'd never in her life hung up on Daniel. But she was so frustrated. He always assumed he knew what was best. And usually he did, but maybe, just maybe, this time he didn't? Maybe Jil-lian had a brain.

"Miss? Oh, Miss?" One of the women who'd just arrived was waving frantically at her.

Jillian's pasted-on smile was getting a bit shopworn. "Yes, what can I do for you?"

"Bathrooms?"

Jillian's phone rang. "Bathrooms in that building," she said hastily, pointing to the drying shed. "There are some porta-potties, too, behind the building. Soft drinks in the coolers in the right, beer and wine in the coolers on the left." She was getting really tired of saying that. She answered the phone, hoping it was Daniel.

"It's Celeste."

Jillian gasped; she'd all but forgotten about Celeste's dastardly duties. "Are you okay?"

"Of course I'm okay. But I found your blood."

Jillian's head spun. She hadn't really expected this ploy to work; it had been a desperate measure, an intense desire to take some kind of action that might get the investigation moving in the right direction.

"Where?" Jillian asked.

"In the trunk of a new-looking Lincoln Town Car, chocolate-brown with cream interior. License plate LKY 743."

"Excellent. I owe you."

Celeste chuckled. "That trunk lit up like Times Square when I luminoled it. Somebody didn't just bleed in there, they bled *out*. There are bloody handprints on the inside of the trunk lid, shoe impressions, the whole shebang. No room for misinterpretation. I took pictures."

Jillian tried not to picture poor Mark, breathing his last in a dark car trunk. Jeez, this was huge. "Any trouble?"

"None at all. I saw no one, left no trace. I'm a ghost."

All right. She had a car. Now she needed to find out who it belonged to. She could contact Mitch at Project Justice and see if he could run the plate for her. It wasn't exactly legal, but he apparently had back doors into several police computers.

But simply asking Conner might be easier.

The band was getting tuned up, the smell of char-broiled meat and popcorn filled the air, children shrieked, adults laughed.

The party was a success, but she couldn't enjoy it.

Several party guests waylaid her with questions. She provided information about glucose intolerance and pony allergies, casting her gaze around for Conner. She finally spotted him—talking to Hamilton Payne.

She came up behind Mr. Payne and caught Conner's eye, jerking her head to indicate she needed to talk to him.

He nodded. "Be back in a minute." He got up and joined her, and she led him out of earshot. "What?"

"Can you tell me who owns a brown Lincoln Town Car?"

His expression hardened. "You already know. Right?"

"What? No. I wouldn't ask if I knew."

He pressed his lips together, as if debating whether to answer her or not. Finally he did. "Ham drives a car like that."

She'd been both anxious and terrified to hear the answer. What was she going to do now? "Conner, he's the one. You have to trust me. The trunk of his car is filled with human bloodstains."

"*What? Are the police involved in this? What have you done?*" Conner wasn't just dubious—he was angry. She took a step back. What had happened to the man who had held her so tenderly? The one who'd moved mountains to save an owl tree?

She couldn't tell him now how she knew about the blood. "The police aren't involved. You just have to trust me."

"Jillian...I simply can't accept what you're telling me."

She folded her arms and stared him down, unwilling to back down one inch. "So you think I'm lying?"

"I think...there must be a misunderstanding."

"Oh, like I was *confused* when I saw all that stolen merchandise in the Cuddys' garage."

"Yes, okay, you were right about Cuddy, but I refuse to believe Ham—"

"Fine, I get it. You don't trust me or my judgment. Just keep your eye on him. I don't care how much he looks like Kermit the Frog, he's dangerous!"

She stalked away, her eyes filling with tears. She would have to call Daniel and tell him about the car. Daniel would know what to do. Even though he had no faith in her, either. And she'd hung up on him last time they talked.

"Excuse me. Miss, are you in charge?" asked a woman who looked like the Michelin tire man. Jillian didn't recognize her, but she didn't know every employee.

Jillian dragged out that ragged smile. "What can I help you with?"

"I forgot my dental floss. Do you have any?"

Okay, she was prepared, but not that prepared. "I'm so sorry, no."

"Oh."

"How about a toothpick?" Jillian said brightly, fishing around in her purse for one of the plastic-wrapped toothpicks she kept there.

"No, it's not the same."

She'd barely made her escape when she saw another man heading for her, holding up a plastic fork like an avenging sword.

"Excuse me, excuse me, miss, do you have any *real* silverware?"

"I'll just go check." Criminy. She all but ran to the drying shed, again pushing the persistent picture of poor Mark Bowen's body out of her mind as she entered. She might have to lock herself in the bathroom to get any privacy.

No, scratch that. A line of teenage girls stretched out the door of the ladies' room.

"Ew, like I'd really use one of those camping bathrooms," one of them said with a sniff.

The only place she could find any peace was the walk-in refrigerator. In her sleeveless dress she was going to freeze to death in there, but she would make the phone call quick.

Daniel's phone rang—and rang.

What, did he suddenly develop an allergy to answering her phone calls?

She got rolled to voice mail. "Daniel, it's Jillian. I apologize for hanging up on you but this is serious. Hamilton Payne's car has bloodstains all over the trunk. If you don't want him disappearing forever to live in the Cayman Islands off his Swiss bank account, just— just call me, please."

She sighed, and idly wondered if the ice cream had been delivered. She remembered seeing the truck, but had the frozen treats actually made it into the freezer?

After slipping her phone into the side pocket of her dress, she opened the chest freezer. There was no light. It wasn't very cold. Oh, hell, the ice cream was melting. This old freezer didn't work worth a damn. She found an empty box in a corner and started loading it with the ice cream bars. She could at least pass those out quickly before they ruined.

The refrigerator door opened.

"Whoever that is, grab a box or a bag and fill it with ice cream." She looked up. It was Hamilton Payne.

"Mr. Payne!" Her voice sounded way to shrieky and cheerful.

"I came up here looking for the bathroom, but those dang girls took over the men's."

"I'll clear them out for you." She set the box of ice cream down, but Hamilton blocked her way. Oh, dear God, had he overheard her leaving that message for Daniel? Or had he seen something in her face?

"You got a problem with the freezer?"

"Oh, it's no big deal—"

"We can't have all that ice cream melting. Here, I'll help you."

"That's really not necessary—"

"Oh, it's no trouble. Jillian."

That was when she saw that he held a gun, and it was pointed at her.

CHAPTER SIXTEEN

SO THIS WAS WHAT IT FELT like when your heart stopped beating. For several moments they just stood there, staring at each other. Jillian began to shiver violently.

"M-Mr. P-P-Payne, this really isn't necessary."

"I think it is. I'll admit, I underestimated you. When I saw you prance into my office in those ridiculous high heels, all that blond hair and shiny lips and long fingernails, I figured I didn't have a thing to worry about."

That got Jillian's dander up. And if she was mad, at least she wasn't as scared. "Shouldn't judge a book by its cover. But then, you're counting on everyone to make the same mistake, right? Kindly old Mr. Payne, with his cane and his shy smile, he couldn't possibly be guilty of anything."

"That's exactly right. Apparently you're the only one who saw through me."

Small comfort that was. She couldn't enjoy any bragging rights if she was dead. What should she do? She would play for time. "How did you know?"

"Conner. He said you'd found some invoices with my name on them, and I knew that reporter must have shared what he knew before he died. But Conner doesn't suspect me of a thing. But you...you figured it out. I saw the fear in your eyes."

Damn it. She was going to have to work on her poker face. Assuming she lived long enough to ever use it.

"I already sent the evidence to Daniel Logan," she said. "If I figured it out, he will, too. Killing me won't help you."

"It will buy me some time."

"So are you going to shoot me, too?" Keep him talking. That was the only thing she could think of to do. She had nothing at hand to use as a weapon. A box of melting ice cream wasn't exactly intimidating.

"If you don't cooperate, I'll have to." His voice was tinged with regret, but Jillian didn't buy it for a minute. The man was as cold and calculating as they came.

Then she remembered something. The sunglasses, perched on top of her head. She pretended to wipe a tear from her eye and casually switched on the video recorder. She couldn't don the sunglasses in this dimly lit room, but she could tip her head down so the camera caught Payne with the gun pointed at her.

She looked down at her feet. "I'll cooperate," she said. "Just tell me what you want me to do."

"Why don't you finish emptying out that freezer?"

That didn't sound good. "Why?"

"Just do it."

"O-okay." She moved as slowly as she dared, picking up one box of ice cream sandwiches and placing it on the floor, then another box of drumsticks.

"Move it! I don't have all day. I don't want to shoot you. I had no problem killing Greg Tynes—the guy was a slimeball. He got greedy, trying to pull the same scam here in the States as we were doing in India and the Amazon. I told him he'd get caught. And when it all started crumbling around him, he suddenly found a conscience and wanted to come clean."

"So you killed him?"

"Had to. And that reporter—he was at least smart.

He's been on to the scam for a while, but when some of my customers said he was asking too many questions, checking into permits and such—well, I couldn't let that go on."

"You aren't going to get away with this. Someone will hear the shot. They'll see you."

"You have a point." He looked around. Trying to find another weapon, perhaps? "Killing you is like killing a pretty, fluffy kitten. It's hard, you know?"

She raised her head, taking him out of the range of the video camera. But that was okay. The camera had caught plenty already. She looked him square in the eye. "I understand it's hard to kill someone who's looking you right in the eye."

"Yeah?" He turned his head and looked away as his finger tightened on the trigger.

Jillian didn't think, she just acted. She lifted and swung her leg in a wide kick, knocking the gun out of his grasp just as he pulled the trigger. The bullet ricocheted off the freezer and hit a jug of orange juice on a high shelf.

But Payne wasn't going to be defeated with a little thing like having his gun taken away. He came at her with his bare hands, growling like something uncivilized. His hands went around her neck in a surprisingly strong grip. She scrabbled at his fingers and tried to scream, but she didn't have enough air. She tried kicking again, but he got too close to her, pressing her against the freezer with his body so she had no room to maneuver.

He didn't choke her to death. Instead he kept pushing until he toppled her over—right into the half-empty freezer.

"No!" she shouted just as he slammed the lid down on her and her world went dark.

"Goodbye, Jillian," came Payne's muffled voice. The key turned in the lock. "Maybe someone will find you before you freeze to death."

CONNER MADE THE ROUNDS at the picnic, chatting up everyone he could find who was in any position of power—anyone who conceivably could have been involved in the illegal harvesting Mark Bowen had revealed to Jillian.

She actually thought Hamilton could be involved. It was bad enough the police had so quickly settled on Stan as a murder suspect, but what if Project Justice convinced the cops to focus on Hamilton instead? Stan might be happy that the heat was off him, but he'd be horrified to learn suspicion had fallen on one of his oldest, dearest friends.

Speaking of which…where was Hamilton, anyway? Conner had left him sitting at a table, his wife solicitously waiting on him while simultaneously interrogating him about which pills he'd taken and which he needed.

Both of the couple's chairs were empty now.

Without mentioning Jillian, he'd asked Ham point-blank about the invoices. But Ham had sounded confused and bewildered. And hurt that someone was trying to set him up. First Stan, then Conner, now Ham. Someone was trying to wipe out the whole board of directors. Conner's money was still on Isaac Cuddy. The man was power hungry, and he'd have been the obvious one to take over Mayall Lumber—if Jillian hadn't implicated him in the theft.

Jillian. His heart sank every time he thought of her.

Of what had gone on between them…and what hadn't gone on. If things had been different—like maybe if she really was an administrative assistant—he felt certain that they could have overcome their differences. But now they were at such cross purposes…

She'd begged him to trust her. But had she really earned that trust? First she'd sent him on a wild-goose chase to Isaac Cuddy's house which had nearly gotten Conner fired…oh, wait.

He shook his head. She'd been right about Cuddy. But trust was a two-way street. He knew Ham better than she did. Couldn't she trust him to know whether a man he'd known for years was capable of murder?

"Why so glum?"

Conner's head jerked up to meet the confident, brown-eyed gaze of his ex-wife, looking picnic chic in a plunge-neck silk halter top, white shorts that showed a long expanse of tanned leg, and wedge sandals with a high enough heel that Jillian would have been proud to wear them.

"Chandra. What are you doing here?"

"Last time I checked, I was still the CEO's granddaughter. I always come to these shindigs." She looked around. "Although I must say, this one lacks a certain elegance."

"It's been a tough year. Our workers don't want to see us blowing money on champagne and caviar. They just want to have a little fun, to know that they're appreciated. Look around. Everyone's having a great time."

"Everyone except you, apparently. What are you so worried about?"

"I'm worried about Stan."

"Yeah, me, too." Chandra's guise of invincibility slipped slightly.

"Don't lose hope. Some very smart people are working on things behind the scenes. We're going to get to the bottom of this."

"If anyone can, you can."

"Chandra, darling." A Latino man, painfully handsome in an underwear-model sort of way, sidled up to Chandra. He wore a pirate's shirt open practically to his navel and wrinkled khaki shorts almost as short as Chandra's. "I wondered where you'd gotten to." He had a thick Spanish accent. "Is this him, the ex-husband?"

"Alessandro, this is Conner."

Conner wasn't in the mood for his ex's one-upmanship. Did she think he would be bothered by the fact she'd replaced him with someone much prettier and more exotic than him? All he could say was, good luck with that. It would last until she tried to domesticate him. He wished he could be a fly on the wall the first time she asked him to take out the garbage or change a lightbulb.

"Nice to meet you. Excuse me, I need to go find Hamilton." The man's prolonged absence was slightly worrisome. He hadn't seen Jillian lately, either. He hoped to God she hadn't decided to confront him in some misguided effort to coax a confession out of him and prove her case.

"Oh, I saw Hamilton and Beatrice in the parking lot when I first got here," Chandra informed him. "They seemed to be in an awful hurry."

"Huh." Maybe they had to finish packing? Beatrice had told Jillian something about a vacation, though Hamilton hadn't said anything about it.

The kernel of unease that had started in Conner's gut grew to the size of a tennis ball. Something wasn't right. He looked around for Joyce and finally found her at the dessert table, cutting a pan of brownies into small squares. She had on baggy denim shorts and a T-shirt with a hot-sauce stain down the front, her hair unsuccessfully contained in several barrettes.

"Oh, hi, Conner. Isn't this party fabulous? I told you Jillian was a gem. This was just the sort of party we needed to lift our spirits—all apple pie and family values. The kids are having a great—"

"Joyce, did Hamilton Payne have a vacation scheduled?"

"Hamilton? No. He always takes two weeks over Christmas. Is something wrong?"

The tennis ball grew to a grapefruit. "I'm not sure. Have you seen Jillian?"

"Not for a few minutes. I'm sure she's chasing down some tiny detail. I've never known anyone as organized as she is. Did you know she has a photographic memory? Here, have a brownie."

Conner stuffed the whole brownie into his mouth. At least that way he wouldn't be expected to explain himself or his quick departure.

He pulled his phone out and dialed Jillian's number. It went directly to voice mail. Maybe she was on the phone handling some emergency. "Jillian, call me back, please. Even if you're mad at me. It's important."

The second he disconnected from that call his phone rang. "Jillian?"

"Ah, no. Daniel. I guess she's not with you, then?"

"No. Why."

"She won't answer her phone. Conner, listen very carefully. Jillian sent me some files earlier. I had a chance to look at them. There's no time for detailed explanations, but she was right about Hamilton Payne.

He's definitely behind some illegal wheeling and dealing—"

"Hamilton just left. In a hurry. I think he might be about to flee the country. And I don't see Jillian anywhere."

"Find her."

JILLIAN HAD NEVER BEEN SO cold. Granted, the deep freezer was on the fritz, but she was still wedged in among boxes of ice cream bars and other frozen treats, and it couldn't be more than thirty-five degrees in here.

Plus it was dark. Completely. She couldn't see even a crack or pinprick of light anywhere, which meant she was sealed in. She remembered reading once that a child could suffocate in a locked freezer in ten minutes. How much time would an adult woman have?

Had anyone seen Payne follow her into the refrigerator? Had anyone heard that shot? Would someone come looking for her? A few minutes ago she'd been in high demand as a problem solver. But the party was in full swing now; probably no one would miss her unless the beer ran low.

"Hello?" she called out. "Can anyone hear me?"

She couldn't hear a thing. Chances were, no one could hear her either unless they were very close by.

She had no way to get herself out. Payne had locked her in—she'd heard the lock turn. She prayed he hadn't pocketed the key or it would take a hacksaw and precious minutes she didn't have to get her out.

Despair descended on her. Her life couldn't end like this, as a human Popsicle. Sure, she had all the evidence anyone could need that Hamilton Payne was a crook and a murderer. But would anyone even recognize that her sunglasses contained a video camera?

Just then the *Mission: Impossible* theme song filled the freezer interior, jarringly loud. Her phone! She'd put it in her pocket earlier. But, dear God, she couldn't reach it. She had landed on her side, and the phone was under her, her arms wedged tightly against her sides.

It stopped ringing as the phone went to voice mail.

Jillian sobbed. She had to reach it.

She could still move her left hand. Maybe she could rearrange the ice cream. Or eat her way free, she thought with a semihysterical laugh. But she was able to shift one box and give herself an extra inch of room right at hip level. If she could just twist a bit so that she was no longer lying on top of the phone…yes. Definite progress.

It rang again. She still couldn't get to it. Her right arm, pinned beneath her body, was completely numb now, which was better than cold. Unless they had to amputate. Could she still be a Project Justice investigator with one arm?

Could Conner ever love her if she couldn't type a hundred words a minute?

The cold was getting to her. Or the dwindling oxygen. Or both. Furious that her last thoughts might be about Conner, whom she'd fallen in love with all over again despite the hopelessness of it all, she elbowed a box off her hip. It fell across her legs, spilling the contents—felt like ice cream bars.

By moving them, she'd given herself another inch. She twisted again, but her dress stayed stuck. She grabbed a wad of fabric in her left hand, raised her hips and yanked. The pocket with its precious contents came free.

Her fingers were so cold, she could barely pull the

device out of her pocket. It took her three tries to punch a button, and suddenly she had light. She couldn't see the screen, couldn't bring it up to her face. How was she going to dial? Could she feel her way through 9-1-1?

She would have to unlock the keyboard first, she realized. She needed to see the screen to unlock it. Oh, God, she was never getting out of here.

Then the ringtone sounded again.

Halleluiah, she could answer without unlocking. She pushed the appropriate button. "Daniel? Daniel is that you? I'm locked in a deep f-f-freezer..." Where was she? "I'm really c-c-cold, could you just get me out, please? If you're talking I can't hear you." Her tongue felt thick, her words sounded like mush.

"Oh, yeah, in case I die before you find me, Hamilton Payne did this and my sunglasses have it all on video. And tell Conner he's a jerk. And I slashed his tires the night he graduated. And...and...and I love him and he missed out on a really good deal..." The phone slipped out of her hand. Her chest hurt.

Damn it, she should have eaten breakfast this morning. She was starving. What did a few calories matter?

One of the ice cream bars had rolled near her shoulder. She could see by the dim light of her phone that it was a frozen Snickers bar. Mmm, her favorite. By shrugging repeatedly, she got it close enough to her mouth that she could grab the wrapper with her teeth. It seemed vitally important that she eat the Snickers. Free calories, after all. They'd never show up on the bathroom scale; she'd be dead.

She shook the bar like a terrier until it tore, and then she took a bite. At least she would die with a smile on her face.

"JILLIAN? JILLIAN!" CONNER screamed into the phone even as he ran toward the drying shed, where the walk-in refrigerator and that old chest freezer were located. Thank God he'd been here the other day or he would not know where to find her.

"Jillian!" he shouted again at the phone. She'd sounded really strange, lethargic, not quite herself. But she was alive. When that bastard Hamilton Payne had fled the scene, Jillian was still alive, and that was a very good sign.

But he'd done something to her. If Conner didn't get to her in time, if he couldn't save her life or if she suffered any harm because of Payne, he'd murder the man with his bare hands and gladly take his place on death row.

When he reached the drying shed he flung open the door and sprinted across the concrete floor like a madman, still shouting Jillian's name.

"Hold on. Please just hold on, I'm almost there!"

Lucas, who'd been showing some people the drying kiln, noted Conner's crazed entrance. "Mr. Blake, is everything okay?"

"Call the police. Call for an ambulance. Jillian's injured."

Conner arrived at the door of the walk-in refrigerator. It was locked.

"Lucas, the key, where's the key?"

"Hold on." Lucas met him at the door, a phone in one hand, a wad of keys in the other. He rifled through the keys, trying to find the correct one. "Jillian said to keep it locked because she didn't want any children wandering in since it's not exactly childproof—"

"Hurry up. Jillian's locked inside."

"Dear God." Finally Lucas found the right key.

Conner opened the door and dashed inside. The freezer. It was locked, too. "How do I get it open without a key? Do you have an ax?"

"I have a spare." Lucas moved aside a jar of pickles and revealed a key hanging on a nail.

Conner grabbed it and opened the freezer. The sight that greeted him nearly made him pass out. Jillian, looking like an ice princess, with…a half-eaten Snickers bar sticking out of her mouth.

"Help me get her out."

Conner grabbed her shoulders and Lucas got her feet; between them they pulled her out of the freezer. Conner scooped her into his arms.

"Is she alive?" Lucas asked fearfully.

"I think so, but we have to get her warm." He carried her out of the refrigerator. "Did you call the police?"

"Right, right, getting to that. Take her over near the kiln, it's the warmest place in the building."

She was so light, it was no strain at all to carry her. "Jillian, wake up. Please."

This was all his fault. Why hadn't he believed her? If he'd just listened to her instead of assuming he knew best…

It was warmer near the kiln, which Lucas had recently opened. Conner laid Jillian gently on the ground, ready to perform CPR. But that turned out not to be necessary; her eyes fluttered open as she suddenly gasped for air.

Conner chafed her arms until someone located an old horse blanket and laid it over her. "You're gonna be okay, sweetheart." *Please, God, let her be okay.*

Why had he been so stupid as to ask Ham about those invoices? He should have at least done some checking first before he alerted a murderer that they were on to him. He might as well have put a gun in the old man's hands and told him it was open season on cute, blonde administrative assistants. If anything happened to Jillian—

"Conner?"

"Oh, thank God. You're okay. Just breathe for a few minutes and try to get warm."

"Conner, Hamilton Payne tried to kill me. You have to believe me—"

"I do believe you. I know it was him. I'm so sorry I didn't believe you at first."

"He had a gun. He's going to flee the country. We have to stop him!" She actually tried to sit up, as if she was going to go after Payne herself. She probably would, too, if no one stopped her. She was that brave and that determined.

She was magnificent.

"The police will catch him," Conner said soothingly, hoping that was true. Payne had a head start, but Daniel had pull. He could alert Homeland Security and they would stop Hamilton and Beatrice at the airport.

Jillian blinked up at him. "You believe me?"

"Yes. I didn't want to. I've known Hamilton since I was in college, counted him among my friends. But I should have trusted you. You wouldn't accuse someone without a good reason. How did you find blood in his car?"

"Shh. I don't want to get Celeste in trouble."

"Whatever you say. You're the investigator. You call the shots. Can you sit up?" She looked uncomfortable, lying on the hard concrete.

"I think so." He helped her to a seated position, then

sat behind her and let her lean against him. He put his arms around her, sharing his body heat.

She licked her lips. "Why do I have chocolate in my mouth?"

"You were eating a frozen Snickers bar when you passed out. There must be an easier way to sneak a snack."

"I don't even remember doing that. I remember trying to answer the phone... Oh, all the ice cream is melting! We should pass it around before it's all a liquid mess..."

"That ice cream just became evidence."

"Conner, did anyone else see Payne going into the refrigerator? Or leaving? What if no one believes me?"

"Everyone will believe you. Daniel believes you. He called me to tell me Payne is a murderer. Those files you sent him—apparently he checked them over and saw the same thing you did."

"Okay. Okay. If Daniel knows, he'll do what needs to be done."

"You really do think a lot of him." Conner couldn't help it. He was jealous of the billionaire, happily married or not. "And why wouldn't you? He put his reputation on the line for you. He's got your back."

"I admire Daniel. I know him very well. And I once thought I was in love with him. But I was in love with an idea, not with a real man. A real man isn't perfect."

"Clearly I'm not. Jillian, I'm so sorry I didn't believe you."

Her eyes filled with a heartbreaking sadness. "You really hurt my feelings. So did Daniel, come to think of it. He had to see the proof with his own eyes."

"We were both wrong. I can't speak for Daniel, but I'll spend the rest of my life making it up to you."

"The rest of your life? That's pretty extreme."

"You could have died! And it would have been my fault."

JILLIAN WAS REALLY, REALLY tired all the sudden; almost dying could do that to a girl. The police arrived, but Conner took charge of the situation like an army general. He forbade the officers from talking to Jillian until the paramedics had checked her over.

From what Jillian knew of the police—mostly what she heard from Celeste and her other Project Justice colleagues—officers didn't take too kindly to being ordered around by civilians. But Conner was so fierce in his protection of her, the cops didn't seem inclined to cross him.

She knew she should be the one taking charge. She was the one who knew what was going on—that Hamilton Payne was a murderer, that he'd killed two men and why, that he'd almost killed her. But her brain wasn't running on all cylinders. Maybe her thinking was sluggish from the cold, or maybe the lack of oxygen had damaged her brain.

But she was content to sit in the back of the ambulance with a blanket around her, answering the paramedics' questions and letting them check her over for injuries.

If she got off with only a few scrapes and bruises from toppling into the freezer, she would be thankful.

The paramedics left her in peace for a while. She could see Conner a few feet away, talking with the police, the phone to his ear simultaneously talking to Daniel.

Her heart swelled. No matter how deeply Conner had wounded her, she couldn't help herself from loving him. He was certainly showing concern for her now. Over-the-top concern.

A guilty conscience?

She let herself dwell on his adamant declaration that he would make it up to her for the rest of his life. It was a nice thought, but of course he didn't mean it. It was the sort of thing people said when they felt really, really bad about being really, really wrong.

Conner would have to do more than go all "white knight" on her before she could forgive him for his lack of faith.

The detective, Hudson Vale, arrived, and Jillian watched almost impassively as he talked first to the patrol officers, then Conner. He and Conner seemed to be having heated words. They were both posturing, puffing their chests out.

Jillian smiled. It seemed odd that she could smile when she'd been so recently almost dead, but she did.

Finally it seemed as if Conner backed down. Detective Vale turned and headed for the ambulance; the paramedics joined him, no doubt filling him in on her condition.

"We meet again," he said. "I'm just glad it's not going to be a one-sided conversation."

"Hello, Detective Vale."

"You feel like talking? Your boyfriend warned me I better not overtax you."

"My boyfriend?"

"Conner. He's guarding you like he's a Rottweiler and you're a particularly juicy bone."

She laughed at that description. "Not my boyfriend."

"Huh." Vale took out his notebook. "So what happened here?"

Jillian started out telling him calmly about her encounter with Payne in the refrigerator. But the further she got into the story, the more agitated she became. It felt as though her brain was coming back to life.

"Wait, here, it's all here." She reached atop her head for her sunglasses, but they weren't there. "What happened to my sunglasses?"

"Is that important?"

"There's a video camera in them. I got everything on video."

Vale nodded. "Oookay."

"Please believe me. I'm not crazy. You can't let Payne leave the country. He's a murderer and an international ecological…bad person."

Vale suppressed a smile. "Is that the technical term?"

"Well, I don't know what you call it. He stole trees, he raped some forestland and he sold the lumber on the black market. That makes him a pretty bad dude."

"That's a little outside my jurisdiction," Vale said, all serious. "But I can get him for the attempted murder for starters. The rest will come out. He'll pay."

"You believe me?"

He seemed to be holding something back. Finally he let loose with a shit-eating grin. "Hamilton Payne was stopped for speeding about ten miles from here. He would have simply gotten a ticket and been on his way, but the highway patrol officer who pulled him over thought he was acting very strangely—agitated, nervous. His wife started crying. Then the officer spotted a gun sitting in plain sight on the backseat.

"That was reason enough to search the car. They found a suitcase full of cash in several foreign currencies and a printout from Expedia describing plane reservations for two to the Cayman Islands."

Jillian sagged with relief. "Then you have him."

Conner had come up behind Vale. "I just talked to Daniel. He confirms Ham is in the custody of the Texas Rangers, and he's personally making sure they understand the magnitude of his crimes. I don't think you have to worry about him coming after you."

She hadn't even considered that.

Conner handed her a large cup of steaming coffee. "With half-and-half, no sugar, just the way you like it."

"This is quite a switch." She accepted his gift, surprised that he even knew how she took her coffee.

"I have a feeling you won't be bringing me coffee anymore. And I'll be looking for a new assistant."

That thought made her a little sad. She'd enjoyed some parts of working for Conner. But her heart was with Project Justice now. She'd had a taste of what it felt like to solve a mystery, and she wanted to do more of it.

If Daniel would have her. Yeah, Stan would go free and the bad guy would pay, but she'd made more than a few disastrous decisions along the way.

One of them was standing right in front of her.

Vale took a step back. "You sure he's not your boyfriend?"

"I'm not sure of anything except this coffee tastes really good."

"When you have a brush with death," Vale said, "for a while your senses might be more acute. Colors brighter, sounds louder, food tastes great."

"Maybe, but I never want to see another frozen Snickers as long as I live."

The paramedics were packing up. "We'll take you to the hospital if you want to go," one of them said. "But you're gonna be fine. You might want to follow up with your regular doctor."

"No hospitals." She gave a delicate shiver.

"I'll take care of her," Conner said, helping her out of the ambulance.

"Listen to you, all Sir Galahad all the sudden."

"You think I'm kidding?"

Vale told them they were free to go. That was when Jillian remembered that there was a company picnic going on. "The picnic—"

"The picnic will run itself without you. Everyone's having a blast. How often do people get to attend a party where there's an attempted murder?"

She raised her hand. "This is my second. The first was Daniel's Christmas party last year."

"So maybe you should stay away from parties."

"My purse, my phone—"

"Part of the crime scene," Vale cut in. "Take Mr. Blake's advice. Go home. Rest. Job well-done."

"Was it?"

"Jillian. Honey." Conner put his arm around her, and she let him. "You figured it out before anyone else. Yes, job well-done."

She gave in. She let Conner drive her home. He walked her to the front entrance, where the doorman called the on-site manager to let her into her apartment, since her keys were in her purse. He rode up in the elevator, saw her to the front door, and invited himself in.

"You can go home now, Conner," she argued. "I'm fine."

"I know you're fine. You're more than fine. You're exceptional. I don't want to leave. I just want to bask in your exceptionalness."

"Conner!" She giggled nervously.

"You think I was kidding when I said I wanted to spend the rest of my life with you."

"Uh, you didn't say it quite like that…I mean, it was

the heat of the moment. People are prone to hyperbole in times of high stress."

"I meant every word. You. Me. Eternity."

"What?"

"You heard me. I know I screwed up. I misjudged you, I underestimated you and I hurt your feelings. But don't kick me out of your life. Give me a chance to prove myself. I'm not the same self-centered jerk you knew in high school, any more than you're the same naive, infatuated girl."

"And fat, with a big nose, don't leave that out."

"I didn't say that. I would never say that."

"What *are* you trying to say here, Conner? My frozen brain can't figure it out."

"I'm trying to say I want to get past all the stupid stuff and go forward."

"Forward to…"

"I love you. That simple enough for you?"

Jillian was so stunned, she couldn't speak. In fact, she staggered to the living room and fell into the first chair she saw.

"Jillian?"

She always imagined that if Conner ever said those words to her, she would shriek for joy. But she never truly believed it would happen. Now that it had, she was terrified to respond. What if she messed it up?

"Jillian. Say something."

"When you said 'eternity,' did you mean, like—"

"Marriage. A house. Kids, dogs. Or cats, maybe you like cats better."

"Two cats in the yard?"

"Or inside. Would you prefer fish? Less care. But I'm not compromising on the kid. We have to have at least one."

Jillian moved to the sofa and crooked her finger at Conner. He sat down obediently and looked at her expectantly.

"Conner Blake, this better not be a joke. Because if it is, I'll kill you. Don't think I can't do it. Celeste has shown me seven ways to kill with my bare hands."

"It's no joke. I love you. Please say you'll give me another chance."

She sighed. "I love a man who begs." She put her arms around his neck. "What about your job?"

"What about it? I'll survive at the office without you, though it won't be pretty."

"No, I mean, you're planning to go back to being a timber buyer, right?"

"I was, but...how did you know that?"

"I know about your reservations to Jakarta. I was totally snooping all over your computer, you understand. How do you plan to make things up to me if you're jetting all over the world doing your responsible harvesting thing? I totally support you wanting to do that, you love your trees and I'm sure they love you. It's just—"

"I won't do that. I don't want that lifestyle anymore. I have something here that's more important to me. Besides, someone has to put Mayall Lumber back together. With Ham gone and Stan still doing chemo, it's up to me to run the company or there won't be anyone to buy timber for."

"But the trees—"

"There are plenty of trees in Texas. I just have to remember to get out there and visit them more often. Do you like camping?"

"I don't know. I've never been. But I'd be willing to try. I've got all the clothes and gear for it."

Conner burst out laughing. "You looked so cute in

camouflage and your jungle hat. Like you were ready for the apocalypse. I started falling in love with you that day, you know. You cared. About the trees and the owls."

"Oh, Conner." She couldn't stand it any longer. She kissed him. And when he kissed her back, she knew it was real, he wasn't teasing or overcompensating or doing anything out of guilt. He did love her.

She could feel it in his kiss.

"You haven't answered me," he murmured, pulling her into his lap.

"Make love to me. In a bed. Then I'll think about it."

"You're deliberately torturing me."

"Yes."

EPILOGUE

"DOM PÉRIGNON?" CONNER whispered in Jillian's ear. "Your boss serves the most expensive champagne in the world every time you get someone out of jail?"

"Well, for the difficult cases, anyway," she replied. To celebrate the successful conclusion of her first assignment, Daniel had thrown a party at his house. For once, she hadn't lifted a finger to plan the event.

Almost everyone from the office had turned out to congratulate her.

Conner had been invited, too, since he'd been an integral part of saving Jillian's life. But so far, no one else knew that she and Conner were an item. They'd decided they would wait a decent interval before announcing their engagement, so as to not call attention to the fact that Jillian had become involved with him during an active investigation. Daniel was still a little steamed at her for that bit of unprofessionalism.

Celeste, wearing a skintight dress of lurid purple spandex and a pair of white suede ankle boots, drained her champagne in one gulp. She held out her glass toward Daniel. "More, please."

"So this guy was harvesting twice the number of trees specified on the legitimate contract," said Griffin Benedict, who was trying to get a handle on the crimes Hamilton Payne had committed. "Clear-cutting the land instead of responsibly harvesting trees to maintain a healthy forest."

"That's right," Conner said.

"And he was selling the excess on the black market to clients who weren't too fussy about the wood being certified by…"

"The International Forest Stewardship Council," Conner supplied.

"The timber buyer was in on it," Griffin continued, "but then he got greedy. Started trying to run his own scams here in the States."

"Payne's not talking," said Detective Vale, who had also been invited to the party. "But according to what he told Jillian, Greg got cold feet and decided to blow the whistle to the reporter. Payne found out somehow—then he had to silence Greg *and* the reporter."

"But here's what I don't get," said Griffin. "Why did Hamilton frame Stan for the murder? Stan, supposedly one of his best friends."

"I can answer that."

Heads turned as Elena escorted Stan Mayall himself, leaning heavily on a walker, onto the patio.

"Stan, look at you on your own two feet!" Conner went to his ex-grandfather-in-law and gave him a hug. He didn't care if people thought he'd gone mushy.

"Oh, knock it off, I'm not dead yet," said the crusty old man. "When Ham contacted you, he made my condition sound worse than it was. In about another month, I'll be back at the office."

Conner was relieved to hear that. Though he was willing to work hard to get Mayall Lumber profitable again, he'd rather do it *with* Stan than *instead* of Stan.

"Ham and I disagreed over the terms of his retirement," Stan explained once he'd settled into a chair.

"He didn't think he was getting enough. He thought by forcing me out of the CEO position, he could just take over, give himself a raise—"

"And minimize the chance someone would catch on to his little side business," Jillian jumped in. "Excuse me, Mr. Mayall, I didn't mean to interrupt. Go on."

"What Ham didn't realize was that my arrest would send the company into a tailspin. He was about to lose everything because no one wanted to do business with a company owned by a murderer."

"That's when he called me," Daniel said, taking over the story. "He wanted to restore Stan's good name while still deflecting suspicion away from himself. He'd already selected an alternate suspect—Conner—and laid the groundwork to frame him. He even went so far as to plant some fake emails between Greg and Conner."

"The utter arrogance." Conner's hand unconsciously clenched. The revelation that his old friend was a monster had shaken him. "He must have thought he was pretty smart, if he believed he could outwit Project Justice."

"He didn't count on our Jillian." Daniel smiled approval at her.

Cora, Daniel's chef, chose that moment to bring out a cake with a candle in the middle.

"Is it someone's birthday?" Conner asked.

"This is a congratulations cake." Daniel indicated that Jillian should blow out the candle.

She did, though she was so breathless by the attention that it took three tries.

Daniel held out a small, wrapped package toward her.

"For me? Champagne was enough, really."

"This is something you've earned."

She ripped open the pretty paper like a six-year-old, filled with curiosity. What she found inside was a box of business cards. She opened it and pulled out one of the cards, and her eyes brimmed with tears:

Jillian Baxter, Investigator

"Oh, Daniel…I don't know what to say."

"You'll do the title proud."

Celeste hugged her. "Way to go, girlfriend!" Then she whispered, "You didn't tell me Conner was such a stud-muffin. I'd have slept with him, too."

Every single person there hugged her. Jillian couldn't remember a time when she felt so loved, so much a part of something larger than herself.

Last to hug her was Conner, but he didn't stop there. He kissed her, too, earning catcalls and whistles from the increasingly rowdy group.

"Sorry, baby, but when Daniel called you 'our Jillian' I realized I needed to make it clear you're *my* Jillian. I can't hide how I feel any longer."

"It's okay." She couldn't keep it secret for long, anyway; she felt as if her entire body was glowing with her love for Conner. Saying today was the first day of the rest of her life might be a cliché, but it was exactly how she felt.

She'd found where she belonged.

* * * * *

REQUEST YOUR FREE BOOKS!
2 FREE NOVELS PLUS 2 FREE GIFTS!

Harlequin®

Super Romance®

Exciting, emotional, unexpected!

YES! Please send me 2 FREE Harlequin® Superromance® novels and my 2 FREE gifts (gifts are worth about $10). After receiving them, if I don't wish to receive any more books, I can return the shipping statement marked "cancel." If I don't cancel, I will receive 6 brand-new novels every month and be billed just $4.69 per book in the U.S. or $5.24 per book in Canada. That's a saving of at least 15% off the cover price! It's quite a bargain! Shipping and handling is just 50¢ per book in the U.S. and 75¢ per book in Canada.* I understand that accepting the 2 free books and gifts places me under no obligation to buy anything. I can always return a shipment and cancel at any time. Even if I never buy another book, the two free books and gifts are mine to keep forever.

135/336 HDN FC6T

Name _____ (PLEASE PRINT)

Address _____ Apt. #

City _____ State/Prov. _____ Zip/Postal Code

Signature (if under 18, a parent or guardian must sign)

Mail to the **Reader Service:**
IN U.S.A.: P.O. Box 1867, Buffalo, NY 14240-1867
IN CANADA: P.O. Box 609, Fort Erie, Ontario L2A 5X3

Not valid for current subscribers to Harlequin Superromance books.

**Are you a current subscriber to Harlequin Superromance books
and want to receive the larger-print edition?
Call 1-800-873-8635 or visit www.ReaderService.com.**

* Terms and prices subject to change without notice. Prices do not include applicable taxes. Sales tax applicable in N.Y. Canadian residents will be charged applicable taxes. Offer not valid in Quebec. This offer is limited to one order per household. All orders subject to credit approval. Credit or debit balances in a customer's account(s) may be offset by any other outstanding balance owed by or to the customer. Please allow 4 to 6 weeks for delivery. Offer available while quantities last.

Your Privacy—The Reader Service is committed to protecting your privacy. Our Privacy Policy is available online at www.ReaderService.com or upon request from the Reader Service.

We make a portion of our mailing list available to reputable third parties that offer products we believe may interest you. If you prefer that we not exchange your name with third parties, or if you wish to clarify or modify your communication preferences, please visit us at www.ReaderService.com/consumerschoice or write to us at Reader Service Preference Service, P.O. Box 9062, Buffalo, NY 14269. Include your complete name and address.

HSR11

Harlequin *Super Romance*®

Enjoy a month of compelling, emotional stories, including a poignant new tale of love lost and found from

Sarah Mayberry

When Angela Bartlett loses her best friend to a rare heart condition, it seems only natural that she step in and help widower and friend Michael Young. The last thing she expects is to find herself falling for him....

Within Reach

Available August 7!

"I loved it. I thought the story was very believable.
The characters were endearing. The author wrote beautifully...
I will be looking for future books by Sarah Mayberry."

—Sherry, Harlequin® Superromance® reader, on *Her Best Friend*

Find more great stories this month from
Harlequin® Superromance® at

www.Harlequin.com

HSRSM71795

Angie Bartlett and Michael Robinson are friends. And following the death of his wife, Angie's best friend, their bond has grown even more. But that's all there is...right?

Read on for an exciting excerpt of WITHIN REACH by Sarah Mayberry, available August 2012 from Harlequin® Superromance®.

"HEY. RIGHT ON TIME," Michael said as he opened the door.

The first thing Angie registered was his fresh haircut and that he was clean shaven—a significant change from the last time she'd visited. Then her gaze dropped to his broad chest and the skintight black running pants molded to his muscular legs. The words died on her lips and she blinked, momentarily stunned by her acute awareness of him.

"You've cut your hair," she said stupidly.

"Yeah. Decided it was time to stop doing my caveman impersonation."

He gestured for her to enter. As she brushed past him she caught the scent of his spicy deodorant. He preceded her to the kitchen and her gaze traveled across his shoulders before dropping to his backside. Angie had always made a point of not noticing Michael's body. They were friends and she didn't want to know that kind of stuff. Now, however, she was forcibly reminded that he was a *very* attractive man.

Suddenly she didn't know where to look.

It was then that she noticed the other changes—the clean kitchen, the polished dining table and the living room free of clutter and abandoned clothes.

"Look at you go." Surely these efforts meant he was rejoining life.

He shrugged, but seemed pleased she'd noticed. "Getting there."

They maintained eye contact and the moment expanded. A connection that went beyond the boundaries of their friendship formed between them. Suddenly Angie wanted Michael in ways she'd never felt before. *Ever.*

"Okay. Let's get this show on the road," his six-year-old daughter, Eva, announced as she marched into the room.

Angie shook her head to break the spell and focused on Eva. "Great. Looking forward to a little light shopping?"

"Yes!" Eva gave a squeal of delight, then kissed her father goodbye.

Angie didn't feel 100 percent comfortable until she was sliding into the driver's seat.

Which was dumb. It was nothing. A stupid, odd bit of awareness that meant *nothing.* Michael was still Michael, even if he was gorgeous. Just because she'd tuned in to that fact for a few seconds didn't change anything.

Does Angie's new awareness mark a permanent shift in their relationship? Find out in WITHIN REACH by Sarah Mayberry, available August 2012 from Harlequin® Superromance®.

celebrating
15
YEARS

Patricia Davids

brings you a tale about unexpected surprises
and new beginnings

Yearning to find a meaningful life in the outside world, nurse
Miriam Kaufman strayed far from her Amish community.
She also needed distance from Nick Bradley, the cop who
had caused her so much pain. But when her mother falls ill
and a baby is mysteriously abandoned on her doorstep
she turns to Nick for help. Can two wounded hearts
overcome their history to do what's best?

A Home for Hannah

BRIDES OF
Amish Country

Available in August
wherever books are sold.

www.LoveInspiredBooks.com

LI87757R

Discover an enchanting duet filled with glitz,
glamour and passionate love from

Melanie Milburne

THE
Outrageous
SISTERS

*The twin sisters **everyone's** talking about!*

Separated by secrets…

Having grown up in different families, Gisele and Sienna live lives
that are worlds apart. Then a very public revelation
propels them into the world's eye.…

Drawn together by scandal!

Now the sisters have found each other—but are they at risk of losing
their hearts to the two men who are determined to peel back
the layers of their glittering facades?

Find out in

DESERVING OF HIS DIAMONDS?
Available July 24

ENEMIES AT THE ALTAR
Available August 21